DEATHBLOW

by
John A. McCormack

First Edition

Library of Congress Catalog No. 87-91069

Copyright © 1988 by John A. McCormack

Libra Publishers, Inc.
3089C Clairemont Drive Suite 383
San Diego, California 92117

Manufactured in the United States of America

ISBN 0-87212-207-7

Sammy, finally and forever

PREFACE

"Aspen Control! Aspen Control!" The pilot's voice was strained, near hysteria.

"Aspen Control, here," came the even reply, the traffic controller's voice in sharp contrast to that of the pilot.

"I'm heading straight for a mountainside! The controls . . . they're not responding!"

"Repeat! Repeat!" The voice of the controller now carried a tension of its own.

The last words of the pilot were lost as the Lear Jet slammed into the side of the snow-covered mountain. Immediately, metal pierced the fuel tanks, causing an ear-splitting explosion. But there was no one in the high mountains to hear the deafening roar.

The pilot had been watching the fast-approaching mountainside, knowing his death was inevitable. The passengers sat relaxed, talking, unaware there was reason for concern. Death came swiftly. No one aboard experienced the usual sensations connected with the loss of life. There were no remembered regrets; no feelings of missed opportunities; no sense of loss. There were no cries of anguish or pain. Only searing heat and death.

A small, irregularly shaped patch of snow at the center of the explosion melted instantly from the intense heat. The bare ground lay blackened, stark against the surrounding snow and wreckage. Beyond it lay additional wreckage and a ground cover that, from a distance, took on the appearance of a grotesque flower garden. The light amber of unexploded fuel, the black of engine oil, and the greenish tint of hydraulic fluid mingled with the whiteness of the snow. There was no blood. The searing explosion had erased all traces.

What was left of the bodies remained close to the center of the crash.

CHAPTER 1

A gentle rain had been falling for most of the day. He regretted having to stand exposed to it while waiting for the man to emerge. There wasn't a dry spot on his body. Each time he moved, the cold water in his shoes squished. If he ever got back to his apartment, he would pour the water down the drain, a seemingly trivial act. But how many times had he been forced to do just that? Five, ten. No, more. It had been a wet spring.

Movement at the door caught his eye. Maybe the wait was finally over. Security people were making those tell-tale movements that meant something was about to happen. Instead of standing around talking in small groups, they began to separate, heading for their assigned positions—their thoughts turning from the mundane to the safety of the man about to emerge. He knew those sunglassed eyes were darting to every location an assassin might choose to hide. They scanned the crowd of onlookers for some sign—a nervous reaction—before it could be translated into an assault. For a moment the eyes of one of the guards fixed directly on his face. Was there recognition? Had the guard been shown a picture of him? It was possible, but not likely. These men were a combination of local police and Secret Service. It was not likely that a picture could have been circulated to any of them, if one even existed.

The final protection was his disguise. Should he choose to walk up to the guard, tap him on the shoulder and start a conversation, there would be no recognition. He had to count on this. Without such anonymity it would be impossible for him to function. Disguise was a way of life.

He smiled at the security guard, a broad friendly smile that drew a bare flicker of a smile in return. The face of stone

1

instantly turned back to a deadpan, inquiring expression. The eyes moved on to others in the crowd.

As he did so, the wet man knew he had several seconds to do some searching of his own. If the schedule was being maintained, his prey would emerge from the small door, only sixty feet away, in thirty seconds. He was intent on memorizing the position of each person; their exact assignments when the celebrity emerged from the building.

There were only four full-time Secret Service personnel—one positioned on either side of the door, two others inside, glued to every movement of their charge. This time the remainder of the security force, six men, were local police, enlisted for this single occasion. Their number usually varied with the function being covered. The locals were habitually assigned positions near the crowd and alongside the waiting car, positions of lesser importance.

As the rain-soaked man watched, it became obvious that none of the guards commanded a position with a strategic view. All eight outside personnel were on street level. If this had been his home country, guards would have been assigned to roof tops and windows, with a clear view of the street, and they would have conspicuously displayed automatic weapons, leaving no doubt as to their intent.

In America, a pretense of nonviolence was maintained, a charade that was shattered as soon as one opened a newspaper and read of the numerous killings that occurred daily. Instead of openly displaying weapons, they were concealed under coats or in nearby police cars. They ranged from handguns to automatic weapons, able to destroy a good portion of the human body on impact. Only the uniformed police officers displayed their sidearms, passively holstered.

In any action the wet man undertook, he sought to avoid provoking the use of these weapons. He knew that if he made the slightest mistake, he would draw fire instantly. Without warning, movement at the main door increased; people began filing out. The second man to exit was the one he wanted, and the wet man went into immediate action. He adjusted his movements to the reactions of the crowd, carefully concealing his

2

rising arm. The prey was now in clear view. Sighting the cross hairs along the center of the man's forehead, he steadied his arms and took the shot, repeating the action until the man disappeared into the back seat of the waiting limousine.

The wet man had been oblivious to the cheering crowd, many of whom idolized the man he stalked. As his attention shifted from the man to the crowd, he realized that the roar was deafening. If everyone felt this way, he could almost understand and condone the lack of security. But that was not his concern. He was grateful that Americans were so overconfident; it made his assignment easier.

As the limousine sped away, the wet man carefully placed the camera back inside its case. For the time being his work was done.

SUPPORT LINES UP

WASHINGTON: Today, the White House announced that support is lining up behind the president's proposed placement of strategic nuclear weapons in the Sinai. The placement around Ras Banas, a military base operated jointly by Egypt, Israel, and the United States, has been applauded by most major western powers. A high-placed source in the French government stated, "It is time decisive action is taken in that part of the world to insure peace." Since Israel's independence, in 1948, the Middle East has been repeatedly engaged in war. The last war, between the Soviet-supported armies of Syria and Jordan and the American-backed Israelis, in 1983, threatened to destroy the delicate balance of power in the area. However, that war found more nations remaining neutral than during any prior military engagement.

Several Arab nations and the USSR have condemned this proposal. Russian Foreign Minister Fydor Ashkenazy was quoted as saying "such aggressive, militaristic action by the United States only confirms what we have been saying. This American president has set out on a course

3

designed to enhance the American position at the expense of independent nations around the globe."

In a related incident, President Askins stated that the recent death of Vice President Carlson would have no effect on support for his proposal. Vice President Carlson had been the major force behind the weapons proposal. There had been much speculation, prior to his death, that Carlson was the chosen successor to President Askins.

"Your speech was excellent, Mr. President. You really gave it to 'em. Now, if the media will just carry what you said, instead of taking everything out of context."

The voice was that of Peter Fitzsimmons, the president's chief of staff. On his authority, only a limited number of persons were allowed to speak directly with the president. All others were required to clear appointments through him. It was his responsibility to screen each bit of information, both oral and written, to ensure that the president was not inundated with superfluous material.

President Robert T. Askins had decided early in his first term that his multitude of responsibilities necessitated the delegation of this function. After discussing the idea with several past and present employees of the executive branch, he chose to utilize what was termed the Halderman-Nixon system. In that capacity, it was often said that Robert Halderman served as Nixon's son of a bitch. Everyone had to have one. Peter Fitzsimmons was the latest.

Fitzsimmons's responsibilities as chief of staff went beyond filtering information. If it was necessary for someone on the president's immediate staff to be fired, Fitzsimmons called him in and broke the news. He was also responsible for notifying cabinet members or high ranking assistants that their ideas were being discarded. He often participated in some of the tougher decisions that faced the chief executive; his input was deemed essential. The president counted on Fitzsimmons to weigh all facts and present all sides of an issue.

"Some of those newscasters are really killing us. I can't understand what they've got against this administration. In the beginning, they seemed to be willing to bend over backwards to help. What happened?" President Askins said, staring down at his massive desk, not really expecting an answer.

"Have you spoken with Senator Thomas?" Fitzsimmons inquired.

"No. He has an appointment in fifteen minutes. I decided not to call him."

"I'm not sure it's a good idea to ignore his calls. He's a powerful man. You'll need his support if you want to get your nuclear arms legislation through congress. After all, he's supposed to be on your side."

"I know. I know. But sometimes I just get tired of his pressure to nominate him for vice president. He brings it up almost everytime I see him. If Carlson hadn't died, I wouldn't have to put up with Thomas."

"You were close to the vice president. I know his death was a shock."

"He was like a son to me. With my support and his charisma, I'm positive he would have been elected in November." Askins hesitated for a moment. "Now, look at the mess we have. At last count there were four announced candidates—two Democrats and two Republicans. If Carlson were alive, he would have been the *only* serious candidate. But he's gone, and we don't want to do anything to help the Democrats get control of the White House.

Sensing the irritation in the president's voice, Fitzsimmons changed the subject. "About your speech, Mr. President. . . . "

Just then the secretary buzzed, announcing the arrival of Senator Thomas of South Carolina. Askins looked up at Fitzsimmons. "Wish me luck, Peter. I need to keep his support—without offering him the job."

President Muammar el-Qaddafi sat alone in his spacious office, pondering the events of the last forty-eight hours. Things moved rapidly in his part of the world, but the news he had just learned had been a shock. The question was, how could he best make use of it? The Russians would pay handsomely for the information he now possessed. But there were major draw-

5

backs to letting the Russians have the information. Control was essential. The one who controlled the situation was the one who had the power, and power—political, economic or military—was what it was all about. It was what he had sought when he organized the coup d' etat that had overthrown King Idris I. And since coming to power, his nation was feared around the world. Even those top-level American business executives, who thought so highly of themselves with their precious contracts were only seeking power. All America was corrupt. Those precious contracts which were so important to Americans, the negotiating ability they bragged about, it was all a facade. They were after the money all right, but what did the money mean? Power. They threw money around like it was grains of sand, and Libya had more sand than money. The American businessmen thought they could buy their way into control of the country. And why not? King Idris had allowed them to do so.

Qaddafi had nothing but contempt for Idris's sellout to American business. When he became president at Idris's death, he broke those contracts; he broke them with the same disregard shown by the Americans when they felt a better deal could be made elsewhere. Qaddafi had thrown out the leeches and the exploiters, leaving only those who would benefit his people. Eventually his people would learn the skills required to run the machinery that was the life blood of his nation. They would master the technical aspects of the vast oil industry. They would master the use of the highly sophisticated military machinery. Then, he would throw out all the foreigners. Libya would be for the Libyans. His nation would be free of outside influence.

In the interim, while his nation was working toward its freedom, he would continue his quest to promote international instability. Terrorism, assassination, and political manipulation was the way to power—the key to bringing his nation into the ranks of the world leaders.

A knock on the door broke his concentration.

"Enter."

"Mr. President, I have a cable from the United States . . . Miss

6

Anderson," advised the aide as he entered the room. He remained standing by the door until bidden to come further into the room.

"When did it arrive?"

"Within the hour. I thought it might be of importance so I brought it personally. I told no one of the contents."

"That was very good of you. I shall remember your loyalty," Qaddafi replied, sincerely. "Leave the cable on the table beside the door."

When the aide had gone, Qaddafi crossed the room to the table. The envelope had been sealed. Quick hands tore the message from its container.

WILL BE ARRIVING TRIPOLI APPROXIMATELY 8 P.M. TOMORROW EVENING YOUR TIME. AM HOPING FOR A CHANCE TO COMPLETE OUR INTERVIEW.

SHANNON ANDERSON

CHAPTER 2

Unknown to the man standing in the New York rain, camera ready at every outing, a fellow countryman stood broiling in the California sun. Both his situation and assignment were identical to that of his New York counterpart. He, too, felt the uncomfortable trickle of water down his back. But for him, it was sweat. Although an unexpected heat wave had caused the temperature to soar above the 100 degree mark, and an unrelenting sun and high humidity compounded his discomfort, he waited patiently for a second celebrity to emerge from a side door.

He also had positioned himself among the waiting crowd. For three hours he had been standing there, wearing a suit from J.C. Penny's. It blended with the attire of the nearby office workers, many of whom had taken part of the day off to catch a glimpse of a celebrity, maybe even take a few pictures. He had arrived early to assure himself a position near the front of the crowd. It was essential to be standing where he would have the optimum opportunity.

Utilizing a different system, one which left nothing to chance or memory, he took pictures of everything. Two days earlier, he had spent hours roaming the area, dressed like a tourist, taking pictures which would reflect any changes. The major change was the presence of the security personnel. Although he had nothing with which to compare the security precautions, he felt they were inadequate. Within his immediate view were eleven security guards, eight of them "volunteers" from the county and city police force. The remaining three were a permanent part of the security detail assigned from Secret Service personnel. Inside were two additional Secret Service personnel,

8

always near the man he sought. They never allowed him to stray from their sight; even at the most secure meetings or parties, they were never more than a few feet away. With their nearness came their readiness.

The man they guarded was controversial. He stirred strong emotions among his listeners, and that was why he required greater protection. He evoked the classical love-hate pattern. His close followers and a peripheral fringe hung on his every word, willing to follow him into the abyss, if necessary. Another group, thought his policies and principles were twenty years behind the times. The age of Camelot had passed. A third— a small lunatic fringe—wished him dead.

As the man waited he thought about these things. His research on the man inside had been thorough, consuming almost a year. Still, these matters were not his concern. His only concern was to gather all possible data on the man's security system, and he had almost completed the research phase of his assignment. A last look at the surrounding area satisfied him that the security on this occasion, like those previously, was insufficient. There were no observers on rooftops or windows which would afford a strategic view.

Peter Fitzsimmons sat alone in his White House office. He had just left the president. The meeting with Senator Thomas had been a private affair between the president and the senator. Later, the president would tell him what the senator had said. Fitzsimmons sincerely hoped Thomas had not been offered the vice presidency.

He began to reminisce. According to the polls, Askins was a popular president. Most of the people were happy with the way he was handling both foreign and domestic affairs, and they had a right to be. When Askins took the oath of office, a little over seven years ago, the nation had been suffering its worst economic decline since the great depression. Slightly over ten percent of the nation's workers were unemployed, and the economy had been experiencing a ten-year inflationary spiral. Disastrous programs undertaken by previous presidents had caused the United States to lose much of its prestige in the world community. The era of brinkmanship and power politics had receded with the loss of face accompanying the Vietnam War.

President Carter, with his intense concern for human rights, had allowed the Soviets to invade Afghanistan and set up other demi-satellites. Instead of using the military might of the United States to prevent the invasion or to force the Soviets to retreat, Carter had instituted a grain embargo; an embargo that had proved to be more harmful to the farmers of the United States than to the Russian economy.

International terrorism had increased to an alarming degree. All nations had been compelled to take extra precautions to protect their overseas personnel. Although few acts of terrorism had been directed against individuals while within the confines of their own country, everyone believed that as the terrorism continued it was only a matter of time.

Askins had restored respect to the nation. His economic policies, at first received with scepticism, began to take effect, and inflation was brought under control. Price increases in general were drastically curtailed, and in housing and the auto industry prices were actually reduced. Even food prices eased.

In international affairs the nation had again become strong. Increases in defense spending had brought the military back to its post-World War II peacetime level of readiness. There was no longer concern that assault or rescue equipment would break down as it had under the Carter administration during the aborted rescue mission of the hostages in Iran.

Pressure had been placed on allies to stand behind western positions in the areas of economic growth, the money supply, and interest rates. The president was willing to admit that the United States should not always come out on top, but should work in concert with its allies. He realized that there were situations where the short-term interests of the United States should take a back seat to those of its allies. In the long run, this form of give and take would provide greater benefits. The position of the West was stressed, not just U.S. interests.

President Askins also had declared himself a staunch foe of international terrorism, introducing and supporting sanctions

10

against nations that involved themselves in such activities. Libya was one of those nations. During the 1970s, the United States had purchased twenty-five percent of Libya's oil exports. With the Askins's embargo, the United States no longer purchased Libyan crude. In addition, Askins began high level discussions to remove all U. S. civilian personnel from Libyan employment. This action, alone, could cripple that nation. Without the technical expertise of the American workers, the Libyans would be unable to run the highly sophisticated oil industry machinery. Askins had even gone to the extent of calling Libyan President Qaddafi a barbarian, stating that he would not negotiate with him because Qaddafi could not comprehend the workings of a civilized world. The constant pressure had had its effect on reducing terrorism.

All of this progress, which Fitzsimmons considered to be extraordinary, had been made over the past seven years. But it was about to come to an end. The president was in his second term, and he was seventy-seven years old. With the untimely death of Vice President Carlson, there was no one who could step into his shoes. From the beginning, Askins had decided to include Carlson in the decision-making process. Every president in modern times had said he would utilize his vice president to the fullest. Askins had actually done so.

Being the oldest man in the history of the nation to assume the office of the presidency, Askins thought the presence of a younger man might help his image. He also saw how the responsibilities of the office had aged such men as Roosevelt, Johnson, and Carter. These considerations, coupled with Tecumseh's brother's curse, made Carlson look even more attractive. The president was not superstitious, but every president elected in a year ending in zero had died in office, beginning with William Henry Harrison, in 1840. Many people had worried about a man of such advanced age being able to win the office, but with a younger man on the ticket, the possibility was increased.

Allen Crosby sat in deep concentration, giving his full attention to the papers spread before him. It seemed that everything was there, down to the finest detail, and fit perfectly into place. But his years of training and experience told him something was amiss. The buzzer on his intercom sounded, breaking his concentration. He reached over and depressed the intercom button.

"Crosby!" he said.

"Allen, do you have that final report on Carlson? My meeting with the president is in fifteen minutes, and he's going to want to see it."

Before answering Fitzsimmons's question, Crosby glanced back to the file. Of course, the final report was complete. When the report was turned over to the president, it would come to an official end, and after a while, Carlson would be all but forgotten. A man destined for greatness, but, like so many men Crosby had kown, he had died before reaching his full potential.

"Allen, are you there?" came an impatient Peter Fitzsimmons.

What was he going to say? He couldn't just keep ignoring the voice. But he was certain more answers were needed. He just didn't know the questions.

"May I come down and speak with you about this report?" Crosby finally said.

"It *is* complete, isn't it?"

"Of course, it's complete. I just want to talk to you about it before you take it to the president!" Crosby almost yelled into the intercom.

There was silence. He was taking out his uneasiness on the wrong man. There was no reason to raise his voice to Fitzsimmons. Peter was the one who had helped him get into the White House, away from the intelligence service.

"I'm sorry Peter. There's just something about this whole thing that bothers me."

"What is it, Allen?"

"I don't know."

Crosby sat across the desk listening to Fitzsimmons explain to an irate congressman why the president would not be able to see him until the following week. After several attempts at calming the man, Fitzsimmons finally told him he had already mentioned the congressman's problem to the president, and he had not seemed disposed to help—that the appointment the following week was a courtesy extended by the president, not an invitation for complaints. He went on to explain that he understood the congressman's position, but there was nothing further he could do.

Placing the receiver back in its cradle, Fitzsimmons turned to Special Assistant Crosby.

"It's a terrible job, but someone has to keep those people from bringing every petty complaint to the president. Some of those freshmen congressmen are actually naive enough to believe the president runs the daily operation of the government."

Seeing that his comments were lost on the man sitting before him, Fitzsimmons came to the point.

"Well, Allen, what do you want to discuss about Carlson? I thought everything had been said. The only thing that remains is for you to tie together any loose ends."

"To put your mind at ease, the report *is* finished. I have it right here," Crosby replied, waving the folder containing the Carlson report.

"So, what's the problem?"

"I just feel there's something wrong—something missing about his death. People make mistakes . . . when an investigation begins . . . mistakes are uncovered. They may be unimportant mistakes, unrelated to the investigation, but they're there. Nowhere in this report . . . not in one single area . . . is there the slightest hint that anyone made an error. Everyone involved performed to perfection."

"Don't you believe in perfection, Allen?"

"No."

"Are you sure you're not letting your past experience influence your judgment? You're no longer with the CIA. There isn't a conspiracy or a hidden motive behind every death."

"No, there isn't an ulterior motive behind *everything* that happens, but we *are* investigating a death. Deaths have causes, and they're not always what they appear. I have a gut feeling that this one isn't what it appears."

"Is that all? A gut feeling?" Fitzsimmons exclaimed, showing his irritation. "You're implying that I should go to the president of the United States and tell him one of my assistants has a gut feeling that the vice president was murdered. I won't go to anyone, especially the president, with only a gut feeling.

Movement began the moment word was received over the hand-held radios that *he* was on his way out. He came out quickly, his trim and athletic body evident in the mere act of waving to the crowd. Picture after picture was taken by the sweat-drenched photographer, his Japanese camera with its automatic accessories, maintaining a steady whirr. A small boy, standing on an old crate, cheering wildly, caught the photographer's eye. The man came closer, reached out and touched the head of the boy.

Automatically, the photographer lifted his arm, brushing the chest of his prey, exactly at his heart. The movement had been quick and natural, unnoticed by security. After the man had turned from the crowd and sped away in the limousine, the photographer started back to his rented room. Along with his pictures, he had information that was essential to the success of his mission. He would not forget his chance position next to the small boy.

CHAPTER 3

"I thought you already had all the material you needed to air your interview. You've been working on it for over two months!" Clark Welch said, betraying his irritation.

"Clark, you know I want the interview to be just right. There's no reason to run it if it's not up-to-date. Since I last talked to Qaddafi, President Askins announced his intention to place nuclear weapons in the Sinai. My God, he called Qaddafi a barbarian in front of the cameras! My interview is old news," Shannon Anderson replied.

Shannon Anderson was used to getting her way, and this was to be no exception. Using a combination of her beauty and ability to persuade, she was able to change people's opinions, often without their realizing it had happened.

"Look, Shannon, if we don't get something on the air soon, they're going to have my ass. And, if they get mine, I'm going to get yours." It had slipped out again. Clark had been in the business for a long time, but he could never get used to talking to women. In the old days, there were no women in the business—except for secretaries. Secretaries were different; he was not quite sure how, but they *were* different. Welch was thankful Shannon had learned to ignore his comments, even though they always sent a pang of guilt through him.

"Just let me finish my story . . . get some updated tape. I'll have the finished product on your desk by the middle of next week. I know that's not too late. The producer hasn't even scheduled me yet."

Welch knew he had lost the argument. She was right. Without the updated interview, anything they put on the air would be old news; the viewers would want to know what Qaddafi thought about Askins's nuclear proposals. And, Qaddafi was sure to comment on Askins's most recent accusations. That would make good tape. If the network intended to steal the thunder from Barbara Walters, they couldn't go into the show half way; it was all or nothing.

The twelve-passenger Lear began its rapid descent to the private airport of Libya's President, Muammar el-Qaddafi. The airport was strategically located only two miles from his personal residence, and designed to accommodate planes as large as a Boeing 727, the size most often used by world leaders. Although leaders of the United States and the Soviet Union utilized 707s as their official government transportation, high officials of the Middle Eastern countries had more extravagant tastes. Without exception, the various princes, presidents, and kings felt it necessary to spend a portion of their oil revenue for what some westerners called "traveling palaces." They furnished the interiors of their planes in the same luxurious manner as their fathers had decorated their tents in the not too distant past.

Qaddafi was not concerned about the ability of Russian or American jets to land at his private airport. Nor was he concerned with the extravagances of his fellow leaders—only with their ability to reach him easily. He was striving to pick up the fallen legacy of Abdulla Gamal Nassar in uniting the Arab countries behind one leader. And, he had chosen himself as that leader. Having appropriate facilities for his allies was a plus.

He wanted them to feel they could come to him—that they should come to him. He wanted to provide a place where they would feel at home, indulge in their extravagances, and at the same time be awed by his display. In the rear of the descending Lear sat Shannon Anderson. Following the landing of her commercial flight from New York by way of Geneva, she had been picked up by one of Qaddafi's private planes at Tripoli International Airport. Qaddafi had given specific orders that further interviews would be conducted in private. The waiting Lear

16

Jet would take her and only her to his summer residence outside Bengazini.

After informing her camera crew that they would not be continuing the trip, and being given last minute instructions on the operation of a handheld camera, Shannon was ready to embark. Porters quickly placed her luggage and equipment aboard the plane. Her confused companions were left standing on the tarmac disappointed, but a little relieved that they would be leaving Libya.

Once aboard the plane, Shannon discovered that two attendants had been assigned to see to her every wish. She was told that the plane contained a well-stocked bar, including many American brands, and a small kitchen from which she could select from a number of entrees. Shannon turned down the offer of food but asked for a drink—scotch. When the attendant returned with the drink, Shannon could not resist inquiring how he had learned to speak such fluent English. His diction was almost flawless. She was surprised by his answer.

"Like many of the people around President Qaddafi, I was educated in an American university," he said, matter-of-factly.

"I hope I don't offend you," she responded, flashing her most winning smile, "but it seems a waste of your education for you to be working as an attendant."

Again, she was surprised as the man broke into a hearty laugh.

"I'm sorry, Miss Anderson, but I guess I failed to introduce myself when you came on board. I was concerned only with your comfort. My name is Jadallah 'Abd al-Ati. I am one of President Qaddafi's special assistants."

"I don't remember seeing you on any of my previous visits. Are you new to his staff?"

"No, Miss Anderson. I have been with the president since he came to power. On your previous visits, I was away on trips to our allied nations."

"Are you going to the summer house to see the president, or have you been assigned to brief me on what not to bring up when I conduct my interview?"

With his own winning smile, perfect white teeth glistening

against his olive skin, he ignored the question and spoke generally of his just completed diplomatic mission to Iran; that his plane had touched down only moments before hers, and knowing the Lear was headed to Qaddafi's residence, he had decided to hitch a ride.

"That still doesn't explain why you're fixing drinks for me and offering to serve me dinner."

"Regarding dinner, I was only inquiring. Mudar would have taken care of that. He is the regular attendant for this particular plane. As to the drinks . . . what can I say? Any time I am to be favored by the company of such a beautiful woman, I can, at least, make an attempt to see that she enjoys herself."

Shannon suddenly realized she should have asked him to sit down and join her in a drink since proper etiquette dictated that he be asked before he would do so. Now, it was her turn to resort to flattery in an attempt to cover her gaffe.

"Please join me in a drink, Jadallah. I'm sure you could use a little relaxation after such an important diplomatic mission." Again, the winning smile.

"Did I say an important mission?" he replied, smiling in return. "It was rather routine, in fact. I'm sure there is nothing that would be of interest to you or to the people who watch your program."

With that, he started toward the rear of the cabin to mix himself a drink.

She did not want to irritate this man with her questions. She sensed that he would know she was probing for a story. She knew she had to guard against being too obvious, but it was difficult. The habit of ten years as an investigative reporter was not easily controlled. When he returned, she tried to explain.

"Jadallah, I'm sorry for the questions. Its just second nature. In my business, if I don't ask questions, I don't get stories, and if I don't get stories, I don't get paid."

"There is no need to apologize, Miss Anderson. I knew you were on this plane before I decided to board. I expected your questions. I am the one who must apologize for not answering. It is not my nature to deny anything to a beautiful lady."

"Please call me Shannon," she said, trying to hide her embarrassment.

A gusty wind blew thick clouds of brown dust into his face. It swirled around the group with whom he was standing. He had difficulty breathing, and the dust left an unpleasant taste in his mouth—a taste as foreign to him as he was to the land from which it came. Inside his valise, which remained on the yellow-orange school bus, were his official traveling papers. They established his credentials as a political correspondent for the *London Daily News*, on assignment in the United States to cover the increasingly complicated presidential campaign. Within the past two weeks, he had sent dispatches to London about the tragic death of the Republican front-runner, Vice President Henry R. Carlson, who had been killed in a plane crash near Aspen, Colorado. He had also reported on the sporadic announcements for that high office, spawned by his death. He described the heightening rhetoric resulting from the increasing number of primaries—the views expressed by the candidates and the effect those views would have on the British Empire and the world if they became policy. Almost daily he wired a comprehensive article to London. From all outward appearances, he was no more than the international journalist he portrayed. His manners and speech were proper, upper crust English. He even had the title of "Lord." Everyone aboard the press planes and buses thought he was a "regular guy," at times a little too proper, but one of the boys. He did indeed enjoy himself. It was part of the job. He was a professional, and professionals executed with precision. But his profession wasn't journalism. For three years he had been working as a correspondent for the *London Daily News*—his file said twenty.

Although it had been only three years, and he liked most of the work, he had lost his taste for certain things. The constant travel was beginning to take its toll on his body. Getting up at 5 a.m. and never going to sleep before 1 a.m. was not really his cup of tea. And now, being whisked from a small, rundown airport aboard a ridiculous looking bus to an rural football field left much to be desired.

19

From where he stood, he could see the gathering crowd, perhaps a thousand people. He had a clear view of the local dignitaries seated on a makeshift stage near a goal post. What he would give for a tall, cold beer, he thought.

The cheers of the crowd focused his attention on the man—his assignment for the last two years—who was standing upon the makeshift stage, before the podium, starting to address the crowd. The man spoke of ideas *he claimed* were truths, principles *he claimed* were essential to a democratic nation, and policies *he claimed* were necessary for a nation that was a world power.

" . . . the course of history has placed the United States in a strategic position. A position that is unparalleled. We are a nation that neither wishes to suppress the rights of other nations, nor to repress ideas that can develop in free societies around the globe. These beliefs are not shared by the present ruling class in the Soviet Union. Instead, the Soviets are engaged in an active process of exportation. Through their constant aggressive behavior, they are attempting to export their brand of government to other nations. The Russian elite wish to bring their form of repressive dictatorship to the western hemisphere. They wish to export it to the Middle East. You and I stand at the gate of freedom. By our actions alone, the fate of many nations will be determined. It is our choice, the choice of the United States, as to whether the gate will be open to these nations, or whether it will be permanently closed, causing them to fall prey to the communist aggressor. However, it will not be an easy task to maintain an open gate. There will be sacrifices. This great nation must remain strong. Those who ask you to support defense cuts and to adopt a neoisolationist attitude are to be ignored. They are the false prophets . . . ."

As the "Lord" took his pictures, the speaker continued to explain the United States' duty as watchdog of the world. On this occasion, however, the pictures were less important; security was almost nonexistent. The local personnel, consisting of the county sheriff, his deputies, and a few highway patrolmen—five or six in all—were assigned to traffic control. On the platform sat the sheriff, old and fat. If anyone were to make a move to harm the speaker, the sheriff would still be sitting on his large rump after it had happened.

In front of the platform stood the real security force—two men—totally inadequate for any occasion. They were typical—dark sunglasses, dark suits. Anyone could spot them. They were far from secret Secret Service men. These two men were assigned to provide the ultimate protection. If necessary, they were to sacrifice their lives. If bullets were fired at their man, they were to use their own bodies as shields. They must have some kind of death wish, the "Lord" thought to himself. Courage was not the word for such behavior, no matter how much the books tried to glorify it.

When Shannon Anderson felt the tarmac under her feet, she sighed with relief. Ever since she was a child, heights had frightened her, but the decision not to allow this fear to dominate her life had come easily. There were things she wanted in life, places she wanted to see, and she was not about to let anything so trivial stand in her way. Born in the mid-1950s, Shannon grew up as television was coming of age. Her memories were filled with the brief, early black and white newscasts. As she reached her teens, the newscasts lengthened with Chet Huntley and David Brinkley becoming the most celebrated. The burgeoning industry brought in new names— Chancellor, Utley, Brokaw. And then came the women. In 1968, when she saw Katherine Mackin on the floor of the Democratic convention, doing the same job that formerly had been reserved for men, her hopes soared. And, when Barbara Walters began in-depth interviews with political figures, Shannon knew there was a camera in her future as well.

By the age of nineteen, she was a woman—a beautiful woman. She had the face and figure Americans wanted to see on their television sets. The sparkle of her green eyes, her fine-featured, well-tanned face, framed by her shining auburn hair, captured new viewers, young and old. Her long, slender legs and narrow waist had caught the eye of many suitors, but all were rebuffed. Intelligence and charm, inherent in the breeding of the deep South, assured her a prosperous future, and she did not wish marriage to stand in her way.

Her career soared from local stations to national television as wise producers saw in her the opportunity to increase their ratings. After years of hard work, she had gone to Libya for the first time just three years ago. She had been sent there to investigate corrupt practices in international contracts, specifically oil. What she had uncovered had brought her immediate fame, not to mention a sizable bonus and the freedom to pursue her own stories. Since then, there had been several interviews with world leaders and an occasional "big" story, but nothing of really major import. Sometimes when she was alone, she would worry about her freedom to pursue international issues being taken away. For all her confidence, at the age of thirty-one, she was concerned about being a "has been."

"Here is our limousine, Shannon." Jadallah brought her thoughts back to the present. "It is only a short distance to the president's home."

"I know. I've been here before. . . . on previous visits. President Qaddafi's home is very lovely."

"Pardon me. I was not aware any of your interviews had been conducted at the private residence. I understood they had been conducted in the Presidential Palace."

Jadallah 'Abd al-Ati gazed at her, awaiting a reply. He thought it unusual that he had not been informed of the interviews at the private residence.

"Twice before, President Qaddafi flew me and others of my crew here to see the beautiful setting. It is just lovely. There is nothing in America to compare with it." Jadallah eyed her closely. Nothing in her expression told him what he wanted to know. There was only that haunting way her eyes seemed to smile when she talked. It distracted him.

Shannon continued. "I think he was trying to demonstrate his softer side. Here in his own country, in his own home, there is no reason to display the tough guy exterior he shows to the world."

Maybe there was something . . . Jadallah thought. He could not tell for sure. But one thing was certain, this young woman

22

understood his president far better than any other American, including the so-called experts whose job it was to anticipate his actions. There was no further conversation as the limousine sped through the night along the private, well-guarded road to the president's summer home.

CHAPTER 4

"Mr. President, I have the final report on Vice President Carlson," Peter Fitzsimmons declared, walking into the Oval Office, making a concentrated effort to hide his reluctance.

Looking up from the papers on his desk, the president spoke angrily, "I just spent over two hours with Senator Thomas. Sometimes that man can be very irritating!"

"You knew the meeting was going to be tough," Peter rejoined, soothingly. "What did he say about not returning his phone calls?"

"Can you imagine . . . that son of a bitch had the nerve to tell *me* that it was not *polite* to ignore phone messages of friends. Friends. Damn, *southern* bullshit."

Fitzsimmons sat silently as the presidential tirade continued. If Fitzsimmons saw himself as a Halderman type, it was highly likely that he saw Askins as Nixonesque. If the future brought other Alexander Butterfields to testify about the existence of an electronic taping system, there would be a public equally shocked at the language the tapes would contain. There would even be speculation as to whether some people's suggestions were rational.

" . . . damn people think they can do any damn thing they please. . . . "

On many occasions, Askins made some pretty derogatory references to both high and low government officials—references the public should not hear. His vituperations, however, were not limited to government employees. When he felt he was being crossed by people from business or labor, he was more than willing to expound on their heritage or sexual habits.

" . . . won't continue to put up with his attitude. . . . "

Just as with Nixon, most outsiders would misunderstand both the language and the comments. It was like those jokes—where you had to be there to see the humor. Taken out of context or simply read from a cold page, the emotional content is lost. Newspaper editorials and radio and television commentators would condemn him for his comments because they would not know the whole story. As it always happened, no one would mention the good things.

Suddenly, the tirade was over. The president was now quietly reviewing the papers on his desk. That was the way it usually happened. They had been together for several years, and both knew when to speak and when to remain silent. Their relationship was more than president and subordinate; Fitzsimmons felt they stood as equals.

"Are you ready to go over the report on Henry's death?" the president asked. His voice was now calm and controlled.

"I've brought the complete file with me. Where do you want to start? I know you want to know more than what is written on these few pages."

"Yes, I do. Henry was too close to just let him pass on with a few words on paper. I've probably heard it all before, but let's start from the top. Start with the departure from Washington."

"Well, as you know, he left Washington on a Monday on a commercial flight to Denver where he met with local officials to discuss their future water problems. We know the meeting took place, but he didn't file any notes on what was said. From conversations our investigators had with others at the meeting, nothing of major consequence was resolved. It seems he used the meeting, more or less, as a briefing for the broader conference the next day. After the meeting, he ate dinner alone in his suite. The Secret Service men on duty outside his door saw no one enter, and Henry did not leave. According to telephone records, he made only one call. At a little after 9 p.m. he called his wife, here in Washington. She stated that the call was their routine communication when either was away from home. However, Mrs. Carlson told us that he seemed charged up, ready to take to the campaign trail as soon as he returned."

A wave of guilt washed over the president. If he hadn't sent

Carlson to that conference, he would be alive today. Unaware of the president's feelings, Fitzsimmons continued.

"The next morning, after a routine breakfast with two of his aides, he was driven to the airport. On inspection the previous evening, an equipment failure had been discovered aboard the plane that was to transport him from Denver to his meeting in Aspen. Another plane was substituted. The new plane was fueled and ready when he arrived at the airport. Take off was on schedule, the weather perfect—right up to the moment of the crash. Records from the flight recorder indicate that the pilot was having only routine communication. There was no indication that anything was amiss until just seconds before the crash. The pilot radioed that he could not get the plane to climb. His exact words were: 'The controls are not responding. I can't get her to climb.' A couple of seconds later he yelled, 'We're going to fly right into a mountain.' "

Fitzsimmons looked up from the file to determine the president's reaction. None was evident.

"A search was begun after the plane was reported missing. Planes followed the flight plan and found the wreckage. Just as the pilot had radioed, they apparently flew straight into the side of a mountain. The wreckage was scattered over the mountainside."

"Was the plane off course? Was the pilot familiar with the area? What the hell happened?" The president interrupted angrily.

Fitzsimmons had nothing in his file to relieve Askins's frustrations.

"Our investigators calculate that the plane was as close to its course as would be expected. Visibility was exceptionally good; the pilot should have been able to see for miles. As he radioed, he saw that he was headed into the mountain but he could not get the controls to respond. The pilot had been flying in the area for several years. His knowledge of the terrain was beyond question."

"A damn equipment malfunction—and Henry is dead!"

Fitzsimmons wanted to say something to alleviate the pain—the anger. The President had counted on Henry Carlson to take over at the end of his second term—to be his successor, to carry on in the direction he felt was essential to maintain international peace. Progress had been made, but there was still much to be done.

"Is that all?" Askins asked suddenly.

Fitzsimmons hesitated a moment. Should he tell him about Crosby's suspicions? Could he burden this man with another problem—something based on nothing more than a gut feeling? Yet even if there was a slim possibility that the death of the vice president was actually a murder, the president should be told. It would then be up to the president to decide if further investigation was warranted.

Fitzsimmons cleared his throat uneasily. It was not going to be easy. He hoped Crosby was not putting him out on a limb out of some paranoia he had developed while working at the CIA.

"There *is* one more thing, Mr. President."

"Well, what is it, Peter? About Carlson?"

"Yes, Mr. President. You remember my assistant Allen Crosby, the man I got from the CIA?"

"Of course I remember him. And I remember questioning your judgment. Long-time field agents aren't usually brought in like that . . . especially into the White House."

"Allen doesn't believe the vice president's death was an accident." There. It was out. Let the president react as he wished; let him make the decision.

A look of shock spread across Askins's face. A moment earlier, he had been angry at the waste of a human life. Now, he was concerned with the stability of the government. Fitzsimmons had never seen that look before. To his surprise, Askins responded in a calm voice.

"On what does Crosby base his suspicion?" Fitzsommons marvelled at the recovery of his composure. Askins was always best in times of crisis.

"I think you should talk directly with him."

Like his counterparts, Barry Nelson, was unaware that there *were* counterparts. As far as he was concerned, he was alone.

All of his assignments for the past ten years had been as a lone wolf; he shunned the idea of being part of a team. If the project was big enough to require a team of professionals, that was probably a good reason not to do it. Too much risk. Nelson felt the same about partners. Although he'd had one once, he had declared that to be the last time. On a backstreet in Paris, the fool had almost gotten him killed. They had become separated just after completing an assignment, and instead of leaving the area and returning to a predesignated safe house, his partner had stayed. Why he had done so was never determined. Nelson maintained that the man panicked, but dead men don't explain and, therefore, he would never know. The Sûreté, a branch of the French police dealing with terrorist organizations, had captured his partner within minutes of completing the assignment. He was whisked away to a remote village where "proper" questioning could take place. Contrary to common belief, torture was no longer the accepted method of civilized nations for extracting information. The simple use of chemicals was much more reliable, and far less bloody.

Since the captured partner had information his employers did not want disclosed to the French government, it was essential that he be "recovered" before chemicals were administered. That meant there was no time for development of a plan. Nelson knew he would have to shoot his way in; and that is what he did. Twenty minutes after the shooting began, he walked away from a quiet farm house, leaving four dead bodies, three of them Frenchmen, the fourth, his former partner. The pain in his shoulder and hand reinforced his belief that accidents were the result of the errors of others. When a man performed alone, he was responsible only for his own life and the completion of the assignment; fewer mistakes would be made.

Six months ago he had walked off the street into a Washington, D. C., campaign headquarters. No one had asked any questions about his past or his future plans. Their only concern was with how hard he wished to work and how long he would stay. His first assignment was to make phone calls to select county chairmen, seeking their support in the primaries the following year. After demonstrating his persuasive abilities at this level, he was moved to the state level. Again, success brought increased responsibilities. Finally, he was introduced to the candidate. First impressions were always the best, he felt, and he immediately decided that the man was intelligent and sincere. But, like his counterparts, this was not his concern.

Within six months, Nelson was moved to second in command of the national campaign, a position he had not sought and had not wanted. It was highly visible; anonymity was the modus operandi for his profession. From reading background information, he knew that the people Nixon's reelection committee had planted in the various Democratic camps had worked their way up to top posts. Nelson understood the risk of this happening and had tried to avoid it. On the other hand, it was important that he obtain a position that would give him access to essential information.

His access to the candidate was absolute; he could see him any time he desired, including one-on-one, private conversations that got him past the security guards. He could walk in and just "take out" the candidate, practically under the noses of the security detail. With proper timing and the right amount of advance planning, he could be back in his home country before the body was discovered. The only drawback was that the security people would know who had pulled the trigger. Though his name would not be traceable, they would know what he looked like.

CHAPTER 5

The room was perfectly quiet. It had taken several minutes for Fitzsimmons to locate Allen Crosby, and it had taken several more minutes for Crosby to make his way to the Oval Office. During the wait, the president had stepped out, leaving Fitzsimmons to his own thoughts. Askins's grandchildren had arrived earlier in the day and he wished to see them before their afternoon nap. He tried to see them as much as possible, but it was not easy. He often complained of the problem.

Sitting beside Crosby, waiting for the President to return, Fitzsimmons couldn't help wondering what the President would do when he heard what Crosby had to say. Without a doubt, Allen Crosby was good. He seemed to have insight, an inner sense of things not being quite right. Crosby had such a feeling now, a "gut" feeling he had called it.

Fitzsimmons knew Crosby had spent fifteen years in the field developing that sixth sense one needed to survive. Survival in the field meant knowing something was going to go wrong before it happened. Swift action was often necessary to remain alive; not just any action, but the correct one. But it had finally been too much for him; he had simply burned out, as they called it over in Central Intelligence. It was a stage reached by field agents who had heard too much, seen too many people die and assumed too many roles. It was common for an agent to begin to believe he was the person he was portraying. When that stage was reached, the man became dangerous, not only to himself, but to his government.

Crosby had not quite reached the final stage, but the psychologist at Langley had diagnosed him as potential. He had seen more people die than he was willing to admit, and had directly participated in the deaths of some of them. He had saved lives and his life had been saved. Although caught up in several roles, he had never slipped over that fine edge—believing he was one of his own characters. The few times he had come close were at night, in his dreams. Terrible dreams. The horrors of those nights had kept him awake for days at a time.

Crosby's personal life was also a mess. Why these men ever got married was beyond Fitzsimmons's comprehension. The life they led had contributed to the ruin of two marriages for Crosby; neither woman had been willing to wait while he traveled around the world playing spy.

It was all there in his file. At first, when Jerry Combs, an old friend at the Company, had brought him to Fitzsimmons's attention, Fitzsimmons had been unsure. If the man was burned out, would he be able to function in the high pressure atmosphere of the White House? He would be forced to deal with important issues, foreign and domestic. Issues requiring immediate attention. The White House was not a place for retired employees from other departments.

Combs had pressed Crosby's case, using his best methods of persuasion—stressing Crosby's long service record, the many sacrifices he had made for his country.

Fitzsimmons assumed such tactics were an attempt to invoke sympathy over Crosby's broken marriages, and it wasn't going to work. But Combs had calmly explained that Crosby had many good years of government service left if given the opportunity. In the end, Fitzsimmons had relented, but he had imposed conditions. For one, it was understood that Combs would owe him a big favor, regardless of whether Crosby proved to be good or bad. It was also understood that Crosby would be employed on a temporary basis until he proved his value. If he did not work out, Combs was to accept the responsibility.

That had been three years ago, and since then Crosby had proven himself many times. Fitzsimmons had no regrets; he could not have hoped for a better, more thorough and innovative an employee. The ideas and insights came consistently, and his performance was always excellent. Jerry Combs had been right about Crosby having many good years left. But in spite of his feelings for Crosby and the man's uncanny instincts, Fitzsimmons prayed he was wrong. Why would anyone want to kill Carlson?

Sitting beside Fitzsimmons, Crosby's thoughts weren't far removed from those of his superior. During his three years at the White House, he could count on one hand the number of times he had been in the Oval Office. At times, he would envision it being off limits to him, a place built on hallowed ground that lesser men were not permitted to defile. Only those of exalted status were allowed through the sacred doors, to walk upon the Great Seal of the United States sewn into the carpet.

Deep down, he was not convinced that these men, men responsible for the safety of the western world, were exalted or, for that matter, really knew what they were doing. None of them had experienced the hell of working in the field. They were totally unaware of what it took to keep the United States strong—the spying and counterspying, the insurgence and counterinsurgence, sponsored coup d'etats, kidnappings, and murders. Their knowledge was limited to what came to them in the form of written reports.

It didn't seem too farfetched to require anyone who was to assume the responsibilities of high office to undergo at least some field experience. Only then, would they realize the effect their decisions had on the lives of those in the field, to say nothing of the effect on their families at home. If he had told the head shrinkers over at Langley of this belief, they probably would have locked him away, stamped his file "beyond salvage" and arranged for a fatal accident.

The leadership of America felt it necessary to maintain a facade of innocence. Without having seen the things he had seen, they were left with no choice but to believe in a pristine world. Their lives were so far removed from the real world that their decisions, made in a vacuum, were often unrealistic.

Both men's thoughts were brought back to the present when they heard a muffled noise to their right, near the rear of the room. The president was emerging from a door concealed in

32

the wall. He often used it to leave the office when he needed a few minutes alone or, like this afternoon, to catch a few moments with his grandchildren. But it had been designed for a much more vital function. In case assassins stormed the White House and broke through security, the president could be secretly whisked away to a prearranged location in the basement.

"I'm sorry for the delay gentlemen, but I had to steal a few minutes with my grandchildren," the president said, taking his seat behind his desk. Looking straight at Crosby, Askins came directly to the point. "Peter tells me you have some sort of idea that the vice president's death was caused by something other than an accident."

It was funny, Crosby thought, how these people always had a way of talking about things like a murder without actually saying it.

"You could put it that way, Mr. President," Crosby replied, looking straight into his eyes. "I believe that Vice President Carlson was murdered."

Askins seemed taken aback. In spite of his own outbursts, and more than occasional bluntness with subordinates, he was not used to being on the receiving end. Before proceeding, Askins looked Crosby over carefully, attempting to measure the man who sat before him. Could he trust this man? he asked himself. Physically, Crosby was impressive. Women probably found him attractive. He was about six feet tall, with light hair, and a smooth face that showed few signs of age. His body was slender and athletic looking. But what was his mental condition? Only time would supply that answer.

"Henry Carlson was more than a vice president, Mr. Crosby!" the president said, displaying some irritation. "He was a friend. A very good friend!"

More concerned with getting his point across than with selecting the proper form of expression, Crosby decided to play the game. When in Rome, he thought.

Fitzsimmons shifted nervously in his chair, not knowing exactly what Crosby would say next.

"To rephrase my comment, I would say the vice president

died as the result of sabotage to his airplane or pilot, if indeed he was killed in a plane crash."

His expression changing to puzzlement, Askins replied, "Of course he was killed in a plane crash. That was in the report you filed . . . . It was plastered all over the television."

"I agree that a plane crash occurring a few miles outside Aspen was widely reported by all the news services . . . right down to the one-man operation. But the news services did not confirm the presence of the vice president. That information came through this office. And from the information I was able to obtain, that confirmation was based on the fact that Carlson was scheduled to be on that plane. . . . "

"At least half a dozen people saw him board at Stapleton Airport," the president interrupted.

"That's correct, Mr. President. However, that by itself is no indication the the real vice president boarded the plane. There could have been a substitute. We both know of several occasions in the past where look-alikes have been used. You utilized one yourself about eighteen months ago when that liver flare-up prevented you from traveling. As for my report stating the vice president was on the plane, that also is not proof. I was only told to make a report which was a compilation of investigative work done by others. The report you speak of is not my original work, nor do I agree with its contents. My orders were to compile the report. I did that. I also felt it necessary to convey my doubts to Peter. Evidently, Peter has conveyed those doubts to you."

Crosby fell silent. Askins's hand was suspended in midair, his index finger extended. He was about to speak, but paused for a few moments. Then he began, more subdued, "I'll admit there is the possibility of an impersonator being substituted for Henry before he boarded the plane. But for what purpose? And who would knowingly get on a plane that was going to crash? I just don't see it," the president said.

"The purpose could be one of many. Probably the most remote possibility is that Henry Carlson was disillusioned with his life or with his position in the government and simply decided to disappear. Over at the Company we call it burnout. . . . "

"I can't believe that," Fitzsimmons interrupted. "Henry Carlson was going to be elected president in November."

The president remained silent, but nodded his head in agreement.

"As I said, that's the most remote possibility." Crosby continued. "More plausible is the scenerio that would have the vice president a victim of a kidnapping by either internal dissidents or international terrorists. If this were true, there should have been some form of ransom demand, and there hasn't been . . . at least, I haven't been informed of any."

Askins shook his head indicating there had been none.

"The absence of a ransom demand places doubt on that view, but does not rule it out. For reasons of their own, the kidnappers could be awaiting further developments, such as the appointment of a new vice president. At that point, Carlson would be trotted out, placing the government in turmoil in an election year. A lot of congressional and administrative time would be consumed debating who was the legal vice president. Political alliances would be shuffled and reshuffled. The result would be chaos, possibly affecting the upcoming election and certainly affecting any legislation you wished passed. Congressional time would be diverted."

"I'd never have dreamt anything like that," Askins declared, obviously impressed.

Crosby went on. "On the other hand, if there are kidnappers, they may have no intention of seeking ransom or releasing him. It is generally known that the vice president was in on every major decision you made. He was not only consulted, but he received the same background briefing and updates you were given. Whoever snatched him may want that information. And let me assure you, they have ways to get it, no matter how determined he may be to withhold it. Again, if this is true, we will probably never see Carlson again. The information he possesses will be used against the government in ways that will best achieve the goals of the possessors." Crosby stopped for a moment. Neither man seemed to have any questions.

He continued, "Well, what I have gone over, thus far, is based on the assumption that Carlson was not aboard the plane.

There is another side of the coin, however, and I believe that is what originally prompted this meeting. The vice president may have been murdered."

As Askins and Peter Fitzsimmons listened, the former CIA agent outlined an equally undesirable set of alternatives surrounding a potential murder.

The meeting, which lasted almost four hours, with Crosby dominating the conversation, was finally ended by the president.

"Mr. Crosby, I believe I understand your position and your reasoning, and I must admit you are very convincing."

"I agree, Mr. President," Fitzsimmons responded. "At first, I must admit I was very skeptical, but this meeting has opened my eyes. Of course, there is nothing certain here, but I believe we should pursue the matter to make sure that none of the scenerios Allen has presented are true."

His position declared, he sat back. He had performed his function of advising the president prior to the making of a decision. On most occasions he was able to work it in naturally without the other man in the room aware it was happening. He was proud of this ability, especially when he could pull it off in the presence of a former intelligence agent.

"What would you advise me to do about this situation, Mr. Crosby?" the president asked, his tone grave.

Without hesitation, Crosby replied, "I would like to put on my old cloak, clean the rust off my dagger, and investigate this one myself. It may be better for everyone if we keep this matter contained until we have something specific."

Askins looked over at his chief of staff, and catching a nod of agreement, he turned back to Crosby. "I tend to agree about the need for confidentiality. The fewer who know about this, until we have some concrete data, the better it will be. Any leaks to the press could create the turmoil you spoke of earlier. I can't stress the sensitivity of this matter enough."

"I understand, Mr. President. You must be aware of my background."

Rising, the president acknowledged both the comment and his newfound respect for the man who made it.

"Maybe every president should be required to have a former field agent on his staff. You do give a unique view to certain situations."

Crosby left the room thinking he might be able to get along with this president. However, he remained uneasy about one thing. Peter Fitzsimmons had a bad habit of slipping in his advice just before the President made a decision. Maybe he was old-fashioned, but Allen Crosby wanted his president to make his own decisions.

CHAPTER 6

The sparkle of the moonlight on the ocean gave her a sense of tranquility that was difficult to describe. All at once, she felt overwhelmed by the grandeur of her surroundings and at home with the splendor. Sitting in the rear of the chauffeur-driven limousine with the quiet Libyan diplomat beside her, Shannon felt truly alive. Regardless of how many times such things happened, she would never get over the feeling. Baird, Mississippi was a long way from Libya—7,000 miles and several light years of hard work and cultural contrast. Still, it was difficult to think of herself as a celebrity. Up ahead, framed in the moonlight, like a doll house from her childhood, was the Libyan President's summer house. The view was absolutely breathtaking. How anyone could refer to what she saw before her as a house was beyond comprehension. There was no other word for it than "palace." Even the great plantation homes of Mississippi, which were part of her childhood, weren't as large.

The summer house had seventy-five rooms, with over twenty bedrooms, each the size of a tenant house. From previous visits, she fondly remembered the enormous bathrooms, especially the sunken bathtubs. They were more like small swimming pools than bathtubs. How she had luxuriated in the huge pool of water, piled high with fragrant bubbles. The two attendants had been there for her every need, pouring champagne into expensive crystal, her glass never empty. The only thing she lacked was a partner.

In addition to the large staff, the elaborate security precautions dictated the need for an actual army stationed just outside the grounds with its own armaments. They were independent of other Libyan forces—loyal only to Qaddafi. Within the army compound were Soviet-made tanks, armored personnel carriers, numerous combat-ready jeeps, and other military equipment, most of which were unfamiliar to her. Everything was on such a grand scale, yet it was all so contradictory. The poverty, the wealth; the kindness, the hatred. Looking back on her just-completed flight from Tripoli, Shannon saw even more contrast. Following the overthrow of King Idris I, Qaddafi had outlawed the use and manufacture of liquor within the country. He had even banned its importation. Yet, there was a well-stocked bar aboard the plane. Jadallah had even shared a drink with her.

She realized that it was simple courtesy to have a choice of liquors available to guests. This was especially important in the international setting where such amenities were often given exaggerated importance. The absence of someone's favorite brand or unsatisfactory accomodations might be interpreted as a rebuke. Such action or its perception could have serious repercussions. In spite of that rationalization, it still seemed contradictory. The use of liquor had been outlawed!

President Qaddafi had also chosen to reinstate age-old practices of the Koran—amputation as the penalty for theft, stoning for adultery. But other Moslem countries did not follow his lead. Even in the face of Qaddafi's insistence, they had held firm. Qaddafi had been upset, insisting that all Arab nations stand together against the outside world. The doctrine of Pan-Arabism dictated that support be uniform. But even Qaddafi did not always support his fellow Arabs. His stand on oil prices, his avowed determination to export terrorism throughout the world, and his practice of provoking the United States were positions he alone chose to support. Qaddafi had taken this lack of support as a rebuke. Attempting to rationalize the contradictions, Shannon concluded that they existed in all systems —even her own. At home, Ann Askins, the wife of the president, on a recent talk show had described her concern and that of the president about the worsening drug problem in the United States. During the same interview, she tried to justify budget cuts initiated by the president, which reduced the amount of federal funding to drug rehabilitation centers. Possibly, she could get Qaddafi to comment on the subject, but it was unlikely. He would declare the subject off limits.

The limousine eased to a stop in a courtyard ablaze with dozens of glaring searchlights. The beautiful moonlight and silky blackness of the night were gone, the brightness making it seem like day. Several people were standing in the courtyard awaiting their arrival. Was the reception for her or Jadallah? Peering anxiously from face to face, she discovered, to her great disappointment, that Qaddafi was not among those waiting to greet them. He probably felt it beneath him to be standing outside, waiting for a reporter—especially a woman reporter. The thought irritated her.

The door of the limousine was opened by a very erect servant, while others went immediately to the rear to collect her luggage.

"Be careful with that camera," she directed, exiting the vehicle. "My whole trip will be wasted if anything happens to it."

"No need to worry, Miss Anderson," Jadallah advised. "I am sure the president has made arrangements for taping facilities."

Shannon felt her face turn red. Why hadn't she thought it through? There had been no need to delay the flight from Tripoli or get instructions on the use of the camera. Of course, arrangements had been made. What had she been thinking of? Jadallah had known this from the beginning, but had been too polite to say anything; Shannon decided she liked him.

The walk through the courtyard, flanked on both sides by contingents from the resident army, sent a slight shiver down her spine. In addition to the soldiers with their threatening weapons—she had never liked guns—she felt unnerved by the staring eyes. Few women in their world dressed as she was— Arabs insisted that their women wear long robes and cover their faces. Unconsciously, Shannon increased her pace, hurrying to the huge doors in front of her.

Inside the main hall, armed guards were stationed everywhere. Had there been so many on her previous visits? She tried to remember, but she did not think so. To her surprise, both she *and* Jadallah were required to walk through an electronic metal detector, similar to the ones used in airports. Before going through, Jadallah turned to her and informed her that it was several times more sensitive. Why had he told her that? she wondered. What difference would it make to her? She had nothing to fear.

Jadallah was the first to pass through the electronic eye, and as expected, there were no alarms. A guard, apparently in charge of the detector, waved for her to proceed. By her third step buzzers began to sound, alarms tearing at the silent night air, lights both inside and out flashing in unison. At first, Shannon did not understand what was happening, but looking around she saw rifles aimed at her from every direction. She was terrified! A man was approaching her, sidearm drawn and leveled straight at her forehead. She could picture him squeezing the trigger, the bullet entering her brain, splattering it on the wall behind her.

A man spoke in Arabic, his voice sounding far away. Shannon thought she recognized the voice but was not sure. The man with the pistol continued toward her, his gun still pointed at her forehead. She screamed. Adrenalin was pumping through her body, sending tiny spurts of lightning up and down her nerve canals. She wanted to run, to get away from those staring, hateful eyes—human and electronic. But most of all, she wanted to get away from the terrifying guns, all aimed at her. They wanted her dead. Something deep inside told her to stand and not move.

Nothing happened for several minutes. The only movement was from the man with the pistol. He continued slowly toward her. But then there was another movement; he was raising his arm, pointing. Shannon turned her head slowly in the direction of the outstretched arm, careful not to make any quick movements. It seemed the man wanted her to look at the wall behind her. There was nothing on the wall that could affect the situation, nothing that could help save her life. She didn't understand.

Again, the voice came, distant. It was Jadallah. His voice was calm, but he was still speaking in Arabic. If only she knew what he was saying, she might understand what the man with the gun wanted her to do. She was paralyzed.

Suddenly, the gun was being lowered. Shannon could not take her eyes off the barrel as it made its slow descent. It was no longer pointed at her head. She sensed that some of the tension had left the room. It was still a mystery to her, but whatever Jadallah was saying was helping her. Out of the corner of her eye, she saw Jadallah turning toward her; he was smiling.

"I'm sure you know by now that something on your person has set off the alarm system. Colonel Ahmed Hassan Badron and his men assume you are carrying a weapon." He hesitated. "You're not, are you?"

Immediately, Shannon's fear changed to anger.

"A weapon . . . . Do I look like I'm carrying a weapon?" she screamed. "I don't even own a gun! Why would I want a gun? Do you know who I am?" she went on, her voice rising in anger.

What was she saying? Of course he knew who she was. "I want to see the president."

One-by-one the menacing soldiers began to smile. Her display of anger—although the words had not been understood—was more amusing than threatening. It was obvious the sensitive metal detector had picked up something metallic, but not a weapon. Even the frightening Colonel had begun to smile.

"Please, Miss Anderson . . . we cannot disturb the president until morning. He has important business this evening," Jadallah said calmly. "I assure you that you may see the president first thing in the morning, and if you wish, you may tell him everything that has happened to you."

Shannon's eyes opened slowly as the heavy veil of sleep began to recede. The room was cloaked in semidarkness by heavy curtains on the windows. The darkness made her want to slip back into the comfort of sleep, but her senses were being tweaked by a familiar smell. Bacon. No, maybe it was eggs.

She reached for her watch on the bedside table. No watch, but a covered tray. Turning, she lifted the cover and was greeted by the smell of bacon and eggs. How considerate, she thought. Someone was probably trying to make up for the scare they had given her the previous evening. But Shannon was not satisfied. Her anger returned when she recalled the terror she had felt, dousing her desire for further sleep. Now, where was that watch? Struggling to sit up, her body sore from the long hours in the cramped aircraft seat, she found her watch behind the tray. It was ten in the morning; she had slept nine hours. That always happened to her after flying—if she had the chance. Sleeping late was one of her weaknesses. Suddenly, a sharp ringing ruptured the quiet of her bedroom. Her first thought was that she had again activated that hateful alarm system. Her heart began to pound wildly.

A second ring.

The rushing of adrenalin having fully awakened her, she realized the ringing must be a telephone. She hadn't noticed one the previous evening, but there it was on the nightstand. Near her watch. It suddenly occurred to her that the staff made a habit of coming uninvited into the guests' rooms. Someone had delivered a phone, plugged it in, and brought breakfast. The more she thought about it, the more uneasy it made her. What else had they done? Shannon shook off the thought; she was being too suspicious.

The phone.

Picking up the receiver, she said hesitantly, "Hello."

"Miss Anderson, this is President Qaddafi." Shannon recognized the voice immediately, though he sounded so formal.

"I thought I might inquire as to how you are feeling this morning. I was informed of the unfortunate incident last evening. I hope you are all right."

"Quite fine, Mr. President," she lied. The thought of the guns—the danger—still left her shaken. "I'm afraid it was my fault . . . . Those airport detectors aren't sensitive enough to pick up my usual collection of pens. I carry them everywhere. There are four of them; they're solid gold—a gift from my father."

"A writing pen set off the alarm system!" he exclaimed.

She could hear the laughter of others in the background. For reasons she did not really understand, it irritated her that someone else was there. He might be president of the country, but, still, she did not like anyone listening in on her conversations, even if they could hear only one side.

"Mr. President, I would like to complete our interview . . . at your earliest convenience. This afternoon if possible." Her voice was not altogether friendly.

"That is satisfactory to me, Miss Anderson. I will meet you in the library at three this afternoon." The phone went dead. That, too, irritated her. No goodby—no nothing.

CHAPTER 7

"Mrs. Carlson?"

"Yes."

"This is Allen Crosby . . . a member of the White House staff. I was wondering if I might drop by for a few minutes and speak to you about your husband."

"I've already spoken with several people at the White House, including the president. What more could you possibly want to know?"

He could hear the sadness in her voice; it had been less than a month since the vice president's death. There had been just enough time for the shock to wear off and reality to set in. He felt sorry for her and regretted having to call, but if he was going to find out what really happened to her husband, he had to speak with her.

"I just left a meeting with the president, and I can assure you that I am speaking for him when I say that we all regret your loss. I am truly sorry to have to bother you, but there are certain questions he feels remain unanswered."

Crosby knew he was stretching any authority the president may have intended to confer upon him. But without invoking the office of the presidency, he was afraid she would not co-operate. What could stretching the truth hurt? He had done it many times in the past to get information. Besides, he was certain she would not check. One did not just call the president of the United States to chit-chat, not even the wife of a recently deceased vice president.

"Well . . . ," she hesitated for a moment, sadness still in her voice, but her resistance waivering. "If the questions are that important . . . I could arrange to see you tomorrow afternoon."

"I'm sorry, Mrs. Carlson. I guess I didn't make myself very clear. I really need to come by today." There was silence on the line. "If it would make you feel better, I could ask the president to give you a call to confirm my instructions," he lied.

"Oh, that won't be necessary. I'm sure if the president requested that you contact me, he has his reasons. I don't want to bother him with my problems. I can see you in an hour."

That was the phone conversation he'd had with Mrs. Carlson almost an hour earlier. Now, he was being shown to a small sitting room just off what had apparently been the vice president's study. As he waited, he noticed the early American decor. Crosby liked it. The heavy chairs and dark wood reflected his mood. He had always liked this type of furniture, but had never used it himself. He guessed the reason was that his wives had not cared much for the heavy look. He understood. They were small women, and small women were prone to more petite furnishings. But he liked the atmosphere of the room. It was warm and inviting—a place to hole-up on a rainy day, a place to sort out problems. It reminded him of his library at home.

Crosby heard heavy footsteps approaching. He half expected Betsy Ross to come into the room, and the thought amused him.

"Mr. . . . ?"

"Crosby, Mrs. Carlson. Allen Crosby. As I said on the phone, I am a member of the White House Staff."

"Yes," she replied, her tone matter-of-fact. "What is it that brings you here so urgently?" She eased into a seat across from him.

Sarah Carlson was not a young woman, a fact that surprised Crosby. He had not known the vice president well, except that he had been a young, active man, always on the go. His widow was obviously several years older and appeared to be suffering from arthritis. In contrast to the vice president, Mrs. Carlson was short, a little over five feet, and it was obvious that her weight had been a problem for some time. She had the appearance of a woman who had fought the weight battle for many years and finally given up. Possibly, it was too much for her to fight both her weight and the pain of arthritis. And from her tone, it was evident that she did not wish to mince words. Either her grief or his having pushed for the appointment so soon after her loss had brought her to the brink of rudeness.

Crosby began cautiously. "I have a few questions regarding the vice president's behavior prior to his departure for Aspen."

"His behavior!" she exclaimed, rising slightly from her chair. "Of what significance is his behavior?" she bristled.

"What I need to know is whether he seemed preoccupied. Was he overly concerned with anything?" Crosby asked, ignoring her tone.

"I don't understand . . . my husband was committed to the welfare of this government. He would never do anything that might jeopardize its future." There was steel in her voice.

Suddenly, Crosby realized the problem. "Mrs. Carlson, I am not implying that your husband did anything against the security of the United States. Although I personally didn't agree with everything he stood for, I have no doubt he was an honest man."

"That is reassuring, Mr. Crosby. If it is true, maybe I owe you an apology. It just seems that after all the questions that have been asked . . . . Now, you want to know about his attitude. Something is going on."

"Have others questioned your husband's loyalty?"

The reply was not immediate.

"No, Mr. Crosby, they have not. The loyalty of some people in this government *should* be brought into question, but my husband is not one of them."

"Do you have anyone particular in mind?"

"No. But my husband had his suspicions. However, he refused to discuss them with me."

"What makes you think that?" Crosby replied, shifting in his chair. Maybe he had found something.

"All I know is that he was secretly gathering information on someone."

Allen decided to level with her. "The president asked me to investigate the circumstances surrounding your husband's death. We . . . I'm not sure it was an accident."

"What exactly are you saying?"

"I believe your husband may have been murdered. However, the reason behind the murder is unclear." He stopped for a moment to let the statement sink in. To his surprise, Sarah Carlson showed no visible reaction. "I'm on my way to Aspen right now to ask some questions and investigate the crash site. First, I need to prove he was murdered, then I need to find out why."

Mrs. Carlson looked into his eyes and saw something she could believe in. This man was telling her the truth; it was not just some ploy to get her to speak. She was glad she had told him that her husband had been gathering information; maybe it would help. When she had phoned the White House right after her husband's death, Peter Fitzsimmons had told her not to tell anyone. He said he would check into the matter, and get back to her. He never did. She only wished she knew more.

Back in his car, Crosby looked at his watch; there was just enough time to go home, pack a suitcase, and make a phone call. He thought about the information Mrs. Carlson had given him. Did it have anything to do with Carlson's death? Did whoever he was gathering information on discover it and have him murdered?

But was Sarah Carlson's information correct? He had been so caught up in getting the woman to talk, he had ignored one of the basic tenets of the intelligence world. Always inquire into the plausibility of the information; never take anything for granted, no matter how truthful the source. Three years away from the life had made him rusty, and that was sufficient reason to be careful. False moves—mistakes—could be fatal.

Before he realized it, he was home. Everything looked peaceful and quiet as he pulled his car into the driveway. The house, located at the end of a long, dead-end street, was surrounded by two acres of partially wooded ground. He had spent most weekends and almost every day he wasn't working for the past three years working in the yard. Because it was already dark, he could not see the neatly manicured lawn and the flower beds, awaiting their spring yield. He thought of them fondly. When he had bought the house, the psychologist at the Company had said the gardening would be good therapy. At the time, he hadn't needed therapy, he'd needed normalcy. After fifteen years of living in rundown hotel rooms, in so many countries he'd lost count, and two marriages, he needed to slip into a comfortable American routine.

But that had been three years ago. Now, he was about to embark on a new assignment. He was elated to be able to use his mind again. He knew he was ready; three years had been too long. He had stagnated. He was confident again.

The inside of the house was always so immaculate, it was difficult to tell anyone really lived there. Crosby spent all of his time in the library and bedroom, the remainder of the rambling three bedroom home going unused. Standing in the library, in the soft night-stand light, which he always kept on, he glanced at the partially completed manuscript on his desk. Off and on since leaving the Company he had been working on an exposé—one of those things one reads about in newspapers—written by a disgruntled employee. Tonight he felt strange about the manuscript, as if he shouldn't be in the same room with it. If he was a religious man and the manuscript a religious tract, he might be committing a sacrilege, he thought. He had never felt this way before, and it was a good feeling.

His gun case was hidden in the library wall. To a visitor—he'd had four in three years—it was a combination of book shelves and a built-in stereo. The books and book shelves were exactly what they appeared to be, but the stereo cabinet was not. It had been specially designed in a CIA laboratory. Instead of filling the cabinet as most stereos did, it had been transistorized and compacted into a little over two inches of space. The remainder of the cabinet had room for several guns. From this secret hiding place, Crosby extracted a .38 caliber Smith & Wesson. Although the make was the same, it was different from the one he had used in his last years with the Company. That gun had been turned in with his I.D. card, his secrets, his paranoia—all conveniently forgotten until tonight. Though the pistol was different it was just as good. As he lifted it, he felt the electricity surge between his fingers. The weapon generated a warmth that spread throughout his body. He might be rusty in obtaining information, but not in his marksmanship. At least twice a week—sometimes three or four times—he went to the shooting range and fired one hundred rounds.

A glance at the digital clock on his desk told Crosby there was just enough time to call an old friend at the Company and pack some clothes before leaving for the airport. After three years, he was going on the road again. He could only hope this new experience would be better than his last.

Even the usually bland motel food tasted good this morning. He was ravenous, a fact he was sure explained the taste. Crosby attacked the meal, his first in over eighteen hours. The flight from Washington had arrived too late for him to get anything from the motel restaurant, which had closed at 10 p.m. Room service had reluctantly promised to send up a sandwich and a couple of beers, and he hadn't even been forced to offer anyone additional money. But, it never arrived. He couldn't help wondering why motel restaurants always closed early. Travelers often were not able to eat until ten or eleven, or even later, but they were unable to get decent food without going out.

He had waited an hour before deciding they had forgotten about him. In disgust, he picked up the phone and dialed, but before anyone could answer, he replaced the receiver and undressed for bed. His appetite had vanished as his fatigue increased. At first, sleep came easily; long plane flights always took something out of him. It seeemed that the older he got, the longer it took for him to recover. But tonight was different, instead of sleeping soundly for several hours, he was wide awake by four in the morning, and remained that way until he decided to go down to breakfast.

As he was mopping up the last of the eggs with a half-eaten slice of toast, he caught movement in the corner of the restaurant. He turned his head slowly, inconspicuously. His years of service in the field had taught him that quick moves were usually unnecessary. It was a general rule that more could be perceived by acting slowly, methodically. Before translating thought into action, all consequences of those actions should be ascertained.

What he saw was a man about his own age, with thick, black hair and nondescript face, but there was something about the man; Crosby was certain he had seen him before. But where? Surely, no one was following him. He had no reason to believe anyone would be. No one knew what he was doing. He had spoken only with the president and Peter Fitzsimmons. Of course, there had been Mrs. Carlson, but she was as secure as the White House. She had given him the only real information he possessed. As far as anyone else was concerned, he was just an everyday tourist or businessman. Up to that point, he had spoken to no one. He continued to watch the man as unobtrusively as possible. He could find nothing unusual about him until he noticed the man's breakfast. His scrambled eggs were covered with ketchup.

As he got up to leave, Crosby turned, hoping to get a full view of the man's face. The man looked up, but there was not the slightest hint of recognition in his eyes. Either the man was very good or Crosby had made a mistake. They had never met before. He tried to put the thought out of his mind as he walked out. There were more important things to consider.

At the front entrance to the motel, he declined the offer of a taxi, having decided to walk the short distance to the airport. He had chosen the same motel Carlson had used the night before the fatal crash. It was located among a row of motels across a long greenbelt from the main airport terminal. They were all similar in design; only the names were different.

It took only twenty minutes for Crosby to locate the offices of the charter plane companies. The girl sitting behind the information desk on his left as he entered the small, cluttered office, proved to be very helpful. She was young, about eighteen, and obviously enjoying the attention that had been brought about by the death of the vice president. Excitedly, she told Crosby that she had been interviewed by the FBI, and the Secret Service, and had even been on television for a couple of seconds. After answering a few questions, she directed him to the charter companies' communal office where he might obtain information on the dead pilot.

51

At first, the personnel supervisor was reluctant to speak with him, but after Crosby showed his White House identification, there were no further problems. The supervisor, like the young receptionist, was so cooperative, it was unnecessary for Crosby to explain why he wanted the information. In addition to answering all questions put to him, the man gave Crosby the names of two maintenance personnel who were present when Carlson boarded the plane.

After ten minutes, he emerged from the office carrying two sheets of paper containing background information on the dead pilot, Tim Ranes, and directions to the charter hangars. Apparently, someone had prepared a resume for the FBI agents investigating the crash and had left a couple of copies in Ranes's file. With this information in hand, Crosby headed for the hangars in search of Joe Johnson and Jack Peters.

"Joe Johnson?" Crosby said. "The personnel department told me you would be down here. If you've got a couple of minutes, I'd like to ask you a few questions about the plane crash the other day."

Johnson had a look of surprise on his pockmarked face.

"What kind of questions do ya' have? I don't know anything about that crash."

"Well, I guess what I really wanted to ask about is what happened a few hours prior to the crash," Crosby replied, assuming a more friendly tone.

"Who are you?" Johnson retorted, his voice defensive.

"Oh, I'm sorry," Crosby answered, displaying his identification. "I just need to confirm some of the findings of the FBI. I assume you have already given them the whole story."

Johnson nodded, appearing more at ease.

"I guess I can tell you," he mumbled, "being from Washington and all. I was standing here waiting . . . helping fuel the plane when they arrived."

Crosby interrupted, "Was anyone else here?"

"Well, there was me an' Jack . . . and, of course, Tim . . . the pilot."

"By Jack, do you mean Jack Peters?"

"Ya, that's right. How'd you know?"

There it was—in the eyes. Johnson was getting nervous; he was lying. But about what? He hadn't said anything worth lying about—or had he.

"Personnel department told me. You sure the only people here were the ones you mentioned? No one else?"

"Sure mister, I just told you."

There it was again, the eyes, the change in the pupils. Was this the mistake he was looking for—the discrepancy that would give him what he needed? Crosby kept the questions coming, not allowing Johnson time to think about his answers. "Did you see the vice president yourself?"

"You bet. I watched him board the plane," Johnson replied proudly.

The lying eyes changed to truth, the issue isolated.

"The FBI men told me the vice president got on the plane without talking to anyone; didn't look around the hangar, greet anyone . . . nothing." Crosby stopped, hoping Johnson would take the cue; he did.

"Ya. Got straight outta that big limousine and got on the plane. He kinda gave us a little wave . . . then went up the steps. I never saw him after that. I read about what happened in the papers." Johnson looked down at his shoes.

"A-a-a-h-h, you didn't see . . . ah, anything else happen? No one else was there except you and the pilot and . . . Jack Peters?"

"Sure. I already said that," came the easy response.

There it was again. Johnson was hiding something about one of the people present. Maybe it was inconsequential, but there was a discrepancy. Or, was he involved?

Crosby tried a different tack. "Could you tell me about the pilot?"

"You mean Tim Ranes?"

Crosby nodded.

"I didn't know him too well, but there were rumors that he was a strange type of guy. I heard he drank a lot. But, I don't think it had anything to do with the crash . . . drinking I mean. He looked sober to me when he came in. I talked to him for a while, and he seemed like the same guy as always. Always cheerful . . . joking. In fact, he told us a couple of jokes before getting on the plane."

Neither man spoke for several moments, Crosby planning his next line of questioning, Johnson wondering what the man from Washington really wanted. The seconds passed slowly.

"Were you one of the mechanics who found the defect in the plane?"

"Nope. Night crew . . . don't know anything about it . . . have to ask them. They had the planes already swapped by the time I came in."

"There's nothing more you can tell me?" Crosby said, hoping the desperation did not show in his voice.

"I sure can't think of anything," Johnson said, shaking his head.

"If something comes to you, give me a call." Crosby handed him a card with his Washington number. "If I'm not at that number, leave a message and I'll get back to you as soon as I can. Can you tell me where I might find Jack Peters? I have to ask him a couple of questions."

"He can't tell you any more than I've already told you," Johnson volunteered quickly, but he looked at Crosby suspiciously.

"I'd still like to talk with him," Crosby persisted.

Johnson shrugged, pointing. "He's over there . . . at the back of the hangar."

Without further comment, Crosby headed toward the rear of the hangar. He was still uncertain of what Johnson had left unsaid, but he was willing to bet it involved Jack Peters, and *that* was more than a gut feeling. Crosby wound his way threw the assortment of airplane parts and equipment spread out along the hangar floor. There appeared to be no system. He wondered how anyone could find what they needed without spending hours hunting around.

At the rear of the hangar, he could see Peters sitting on a low stool, his feet stretched out in front of him, head resting against the wall. He looked like he might be sleeping. Efficient crew, Crosby thought.

"Mr. Peters?" Crosby inquired softly.

Peters started, his eyes opening wide, blinking. "Oh! You

54

scared me!" he exclaimed. "I thought it might 'ave been my boss. Boy he'd 'ave my hide if he caught me sleepin'.""

"Don't worry about it. I just have a few questions to ask . . . if it's all right with you. I just talked to your partner Joe Johnson, and he told me you were back here."

"Well, if Joe sent you, I guess you're Ok . . . 'cause he wouldn't a told the boss I was here." Peters smiled broadly, showing silver-rimmed teeth.

"Wha' da ya got?"

"Nothing real important. I just have a few follow-up questions about the day the vice president's plane crashed. I know you've already talked to the FBI, so I assure you I'll be brief."

"Go ahead. But I'm afraid there's not much I can tell ya."

"That's exactly what Joe told me . . . you wouldn't be able to tell me much. Exactly where were you when the vice president arrived?"

"Wha'd Joe tell ya?" Peters asked, hesitating.

"He told me you weren't on the job that day" Crosby lied, sensing he was on the right track.

"No . . . I wasn't," Peters stated matter-of-factly.

He had found what Johnson had been hiding. Crosby went on. "You were not at work at all that day." He was sure he had been able to conceal his surprise. "Where were you?"

"I was sick."

"The people in personnel aren't aware you missed work that day. They seem to be under the impression you were on the job. I was just over talking to them. . . . "

"You didn't tell them I wasn't here, did ya?"

"No, no. I only got the names of those they thought were on the shift that day." Relief spread across Peters's face; his body relaxed.

"Well, we do it that way around here . . . me and Joe," Peters said. "I was at a party the night before . . . guess I got a little sick. Damnedest thing; never happened before. My wife swears somebody put something in my drink, but I don't think so. Who'd do something like that?"

"Why would your wife think so?" Crosby continued, sure he

was on the right track, and even more sure that Peters could lead him further down that track.

"Ya know women. Just overreacted."

Crosby pressed on. "Did you get another employee to take your place? It seems to me that with the vice president coming, you might have been missed."

For a full minute Peters stood staring at Crosby. Finally he spoke. "Ya sure ya wouldn't turn us in?"

"No, I don't think so," Crosby reassured, laughing. "The information I'm looking for is for me, not for your employer. It wouldn't benefit me if you lost your job."

With a strange smile Peters replied, "Joe punched me in. . . . You can ask him who was here. He got another guy to cover for me. I do it for him; he does it for me. You'll have to ask him who was here."

"I'll do that. Thank you. Thank you, very much."

Crosby made his way back across the interior of the hangar. The short walk gave him time to think. Possibly, he had discovered what Johnson was hiding—maybe something big; maybe nothing. One thing for sure, it was one of those inconsistencies he was looking for. When he reached the front of the hangar, Johnson was standing where he had left him, still cleaning a piece of equipment Crosby did not recognize.

Crosby hesitated a moment before speaking. What would be the best way to get the name of the replacement? Johnson probably wouldn't be willing to admit to covering for his partner, but what choice did he have? Peters had just spilled the beans. The direct route would save time and eliminate confusion—and it just might work.

"Mr. Johnson."

Johnson turned, it was there in his eyes; he knew that what he had been trying to cover up was no longer a secret. This man from Washington had discovered in one hour what his superiors had not been able to figure out in ten years, and what the FBI investigators didn't uncover in hours of questioning.

"Ya find Peters?" Johnson asked, pretending to smile.

"Yes, I found him. We talked for a while, and he had some strange information for me."

56

"What information was that?" Johnson asked, uneasily, the smile vanishing.

"He told me he wasn't here the day the vice president arrived. He told me you covered for him."

Johnson was silent. For several seconds he looked down at the tarmac, then he looked to the sky. Neither would help him. "Why'd ya need to know?"

"To be honest with you, Joe, I am conducting an investigation for the White House. That is all I can tell you." Crosby hoped his statement would impress Johnson, make him lose his fear of getting into trouble.

The words came tumbling out. "Well, anything the president is behind is good enough for me. I've voted for him twice. He's a good man. He knows where this country should go and he's taking us there. It's too bad his term is up . . . too bad he can't be reelected . . . it's a damn shame. Get a good man in there . . . we oughta keep 'im."

"I agree with you, Joe," Crosby replied, not sure he did.

"Could you tell me about the man who was here to replace Peters?"

"Ya see, Jack called me early that morning," Johnson began, "told me he was sick. Thought somebody put something in his drink at a party he'd been to. I don't believe it. I think he just wanted the day off. In fact, it made me a little mad—he had no reason to lie to me . . . I would 'a done it for him regardless. Anyway, he asked me if I'd punch him in. Ah . . . we . . . do it all the time. I said sure I'd punch him in, and get somebody to cover for him."

"Was the other person someone who works around here—on another shift?"

"Usually I get this friend of mine, over in baggage, to cover. He has the night shift, and for half the pay he'll come in any-time I call. But the day the vice president was coming, I called and he was sick. Couldn't come in.

"Well, I didn't want Jack to get in trouble for missin' work, but I didn't know what to do. Then, I remembered this kid who came by the week before and told me he was available for work if I ever needed any help. He couldn't have been over twenty. Said to give him a call, anytime."

"Did he come in?"

"Sure, he said he'd be glad to. Only I ain't callin' him no more."

"Why's that?"

"Do you know he had the nerve to walk out on me," Joe replied, indignantly.

"You mean he left before the shift was over?"

"Shift hell! That little so-and-so left not fifteen minutes after the vice president's plane took off!"

"Are you sure!" Crosby blurted out excitedly, his words more a statement than a question.

"Of course I'm sure . . . and you can't reach him."

Crosby looked puzzled so Johnson continued.

"After he ran out on me, I threw his name and number away. To tell you the truth, the more I think about it the less I think he really worked here. He didn't know how to do nothin'. I asked some friends on the night shift about him. No one ever heard of him. . . . Didn't even recognize his description."

One person being sick could have been a coincidence, two people were highly unlikely. Couple this with an unknown person coming to fill-in, then disappearing as suddenly as he appeared. It was the ultimate inconsistency, it was a *planned* inconsistency.

Before leaving the hangar area, Crosby toyed with the idea of trying to locate the young substitute worker, but with the little information he possessed, he figured it would only be a waste of time. By now the guy was probably long gone.

CHAPTER 8

"A decision must be made about the office of the vice president, Mr. President," Peter Fitzsimmons repeated loudly for the second time, hoping his voice would penetrate Askins's thoughts. Although not completely sure he had been heard, he continued. "We must put the Carlson incident out of our mind. There isn't anything we can do until Crosby completes his investigation. He's a good man. If there is anything amiss he *will* find it. I have complete confidence in him."

Askins continued to stare into space, seemingly oblivious to time or sound. Watching the immobile figure sitting before him, Fitzsimmons became even more unsure he had been heard. Finally, the president shook his head from side to side and looked up, his face void of expression.

"I know," the president began slowly, "but I can't help thinking about it. Carlson was a good man and he would have made a damn good president. I kept him abreast of every decision —everything that was going on. His input was invaluable. And Henry was behind this Mideast strategy . . . I was counting on him to carry it forward after I left. We're going to have to get the legislation passed before the end of my term, and Congress is going to want to get out of here by late summer because of the elections. Some of them aren't on the Hill much now. We don't have much time."

"What about Senator Thomas? Can we count on his support? You haven't told me what was said at your meeting yesterday."

"That man wants to be president so badly he can taste it," Askins replied, a look of disgust settling on his face. "He has been running for this office in every election for the past twenty years. I guess I've been on the opposite side in too many political battles. I just don't like him."

"Yes, you and he always seemed to clash," Fitzsimmons agreed. "That's why I was surprised when he came out in support of your Mideast strategy. Several times over the past few years, it seemed as if he opposed you just for the sake of going against you. Your ideological differences are not that great. After all, you're members of the same party."

Askins shrugged. "Thomas's position is not that hard to explain. You've got to understand, Peter, I've known him a lot longer than you have," Askins replied obviously making reference to their almost forty-year age difference.

"As long as I can remember, Thomas has supported a strong military. His position on the Middle East has always been pro-Israel, even when that position wasn't popular. I am sure he can see how my proposal has a good chance of ending the wars in the Middle East."

"Do you really think that's why he is supporting you?"

"Sure. I may not like Senator Thomas, but I do know that he believes the United States should remain strong. And one way to remain strong is by protecting your allies, and preventing the constant flare-up of crises that can easily escalate into a nuclear confrontation. The placing of strategic nuclear weapons at Ras Banas will bring about a balance of power that is not possible today. The surrounding Arab nations have a combined population of over fifty million people, while Israel has less than five million. Even if you throw in Egypt as an ally, that won't make enough of a difference.

"So far Israel has been lucky; they've never lost a war. But if you look closely at their positions in 1973 and 1983, you have to realize that each time it has been more difficult for them to come out on top. On the other hand, with the introduction of nuclear weapons, the superiority of population and equipment held by the Arabs no longer matters. Any surprise attack on Israel, or for that matter, Egypt, could provoke a nuclear response. Actually, it is doubtful we would be willing to go along with such a strategy. I am sure the situation would have to be extremely critical before the command to launch was actually

60

given. However, the missiles would be there, and deterrence is the name of the game. Most of the strategists on both sides of the ocean agree that the only thing that has prevented Russia from throwing nuclear weapons at us, and vice versa, is the fact that it would be a no-win confrontation. Both sides have the same capabilities. It might not be the best form of deterrence, but it sure as hell has worked for us—and them." The president smiled broadly, obviously enjoying his explanation. Then he continued, "All I am trying to do is set the stage in the Middle East. If the damn French had not given Iraq nuclear capability, this probably wouldn't be necessary. . . . "

"Do you really think the French knew Iraq would be able to steal enough material to build a bomb when they decided to help them build that reactor?" Fitzsimmons interjected.

"Don't be so innocent," the president replied harshly. "They knew what was going to happen. The French position toward Israel has been shaky all along. They never could make up their mind whether they wanted to kiss them or condemn them. If I had been in Begin's shoes a couple of years ago when he knocked out that first reactor, I probably would have bombed France too. . . . "

"Mr. President!" Fitzsimmons exclaimed, pretending to be shocked.

"I know, Peter, I'm getting carried away, but you know what I'm saying. This is an important issue. In the past, some nations, including ours, have followed courses and instituted policies that *created* crisis situations. Much of my administration has been devoted to correcting that mistake. We have come a long way, both at home and in the world over the last seven years. This Mideast thing is going to be my grand finale."

Fitzsimmons sat in silence, knowing the president was correct. An acceptable balance of power in the world was what Askins stood for, and it was up to him to help the president fulfill his dream of making the world a safer place to live before his term came to an end.

"From what you have outlined, Mr. President, I can't help believing the strategy we use in nominating a vice president can help us. Since we are required to nominate someone, we might as well get as much political capital out of it as possible."

As Fitzsimmons spoke, Askins was thinking of how valuable the man was to him. That was why he had selected him as chief of staff. It was an awesome responsibility to filter the material that was passed on to a president. It was important to know what to let through and equally important what to turn away—as well as *how* it was done. You had to make enemies; it was an impossible job. Although everyone wanted access, only those with legitimate issues, those actually requiring the president's attention could be allowed to reach his desk. One of Fitzsimmons's many talents was his ability to cut to the heart of an issue. He was able to pinpoint ways that certain manuevers—some called them manipulations—would help achieve a particular goal. Relying on Fitzsimmons's insights, the president had obtained congressional approval for actions that others had believed impossible.

Finally, responding to Fitzsimmons's statement, Askins asked, "In what way, Peter?"

"At this point, we have several options. Nothing we have done thus far has committed us to any one of them."

For the next few hours, the president and his assistant discussed the options surrounding the nomination of a vice president. Finally, Fitzsimmons threw his support behind the one that he believed would allow them maximum flexibility. The option was based on the nomination of an interim vice president, a strategy which would provide all the same benefits of nominating an aged member of Congress and none of the hazards of confirmation.

What made the option even more viable was the existence of a loyal cabinet member who fit the description exactly.

CHAPTER 9

The four phone calls were received approximately five minutes apart, each coming to the same private number. It was a number known only to a handful of people, none of whom knew the location of the phone where the calls were received. To preserve the safety of the intended recipient, the phone connection had been routed through North Carolina. However, the actual location was many miles away. Each time a call came through, the phone was allowed to ring only once. The sequence of calls was not unexpected, the recipient was there waiting, he said only one word: "Deathblow." If everything was satisfactory, the answer was given: "Contact maintained. Assignment conclusion pending confirmation."

No confirmation order was given by the recipient; contact was to be maintained.

Her New York office was a mess—it was always a mess. Not only did the description, "It looked like an unmade bed" apply, but a bed that hadn't been made in years. Three years to be exact. Shannon sat among the clutter, much like a small child sitting on a kitchen floor playing with pots and pans. Shannon was not playing. At least, *she* would not have described it as playing. Lounging in her office, if lounging could be done in such a small cubicle, among piles of books and papers, waiting for her show to air, Shannon was experiencing the euphoria of professional satisfaction. Striving to get the best ratings was a war, not a game, as those on the outside or those in the newspapers described it. High ratings meant the continuation of her show, the continuation of her paycheck, her lifestyle.

63

Low ratings meant the death of everything she was doing, everything she had worked so hard to achieve.

The segment that was about to air had been the most difficult of her life, and getting it had resulted in her undergoing the most terrifying experience of her career—the Libyan palace guards holding her at gunpoint. Those people were paranoid, she thought. She understood that security was necessary for a man as controversial as Qaddafi, but it could be taken too far. And as far as she was concerned, anytime a respectable newsperson was assaulted, as she had been, security had gone way too far. Stopping an assassin was the goal, not harrassing innocent people, especially those who were there to help espouse their cause. Though her help to Qaddafi was indirect, she knew she was helping. They could—they should—respect that. She hadn't really felt any particular way about him philosophically, then. Now, she felt trapped in the middle, trapped between his government and hers.

There he was, almost as if he had come out of her memory to haunt her. The television camera closed in on him seated in a high-backed wicker chair—he had said it was his favorite, and he wanted to be photographed in it.

Shannon Anderson sat on the edge of her small desk, staring at the television monitor across from her. She could not take her eyes off the screen. Contained within the confines of the electronic square, Qaddafi looked almost Rooseveltian with that famous gray cape drawn around his arms and legs. Roosevelt had used a cape to help provide warmth for his paralyzed legs; Qaddafi used it for effect. This man was no Franklin Roosevelt—by any stretch of the imagination.

In the beginning, Shannon had believed the people she had spoken with at the State Department had exaggerated Qaddafi's quirky personality, his ruthlessness. After conducting three separate interviews with him, she came to realize they had been right. He was little more than a murderer. The realization had not come easily—changes in her beliefs never did. It had taken a combination of events, but she now was certain the view most recently expressed by President Askins was probably accurate—even though it upset her to agree with Askins. Qaddafi was one of the driving forces behind international acts of terrorism.

Shannon wondered if the rumors that he was providing sanctuary for the international assassin Carlos were true. All her attempts to get him to discuss the subject had failed; he simply ignored the questions. Any time she touched on an area he didn't wish to discuss, he simply looked past her—always over her right shoulder. The habit was so pronounced that once she actually turned to see if something of particular interest was behind her. What she saw was a blank wall.

He refused to discuss Carlos or terrorism, but what she had overheard was practically confirmation. But what was she going to do about it? What could she say? Who could she say it to? If she called some low-level flunky at the CIA, they would probably release it to the media. It would make great propaganda. The people she had talked to in the past—those with the CIA—were more concerned with the propaganda war than with concrete results or useful information. That attitude wouldn't help her; all it would accomplish would be to make the other side aware of the information she possessed. If that was all she wished to accomplish, she could go on her own show and tell what she had overheard. But the thought of all those guns aimed at her kept recurring. That was impossible. She had never pretended to be brave. Leave the bravery to others; she would just report on it. Shannon turned back to the monitor and saw herself on the screen. Each time it was like seeing herself for the very first time, even after three years with her own nationally televised show. She would never get used to it. She sat silently watching herself interview Qaddafi.

Anderson: Is it true, Mr. President, that you have said the president of the United States is no more than a terrorist, and that he should be killed?

Qaddafi: Yes, I believe he is promoting international terrorism. He blames me for such acts—he blames the Soviet Union. It is the United States who is promoting revolutions and internal killings. People in your own country who disagree with the direction of your government prove my point. Some of these people have written books exposing how the United States has attempted to overthrow certain governments. My own is an example; Chile another, Cuba, Cambodia. These are all good examples of unnecessary intervention by your government. The people who wrote these books have spoken out regarding the errors of your government; I am trying to do no more.

Anderson: Don't you think calling for the assassination of President Askins was a little dramatic?

Qaddafi: No, I do not think it was too harsh. Anyone who promotes the death of the leaders of other countries should be dealt with harshly. . . .

Anderson: If you are calling for the assassination of the president, aren't you doing the same thing you are accusing him of doing?

Qaddafi: Miss Anderson, I am just trying to prevent the unnecessary destruction of several legitimate governments. Any time the leader of a nation is murdered, the people of that nation are the ones to suffer. When your president or your CIA assist in the overthrow of another government, thousands of people are killed. The unconstitutional change of government is always a bloody act. I wish to bring these bloody acts to an end. Your president has set out on a course that can only lead to war. The people I have spoken with in the Soviet Union will not condone such action; *I* cannot condone such action. I am a leader in this area of the world. Many of the other Moslem countries agree with my views. They believe in the same causes in which I believe, and they also agree that your president has gone too far. It would not surprise me, in view of this, if some nation chose to eliminate your president.

With a suddenness that could only be accomplished through electronics, a bra commercial interrupted the steady flow of accusations.

That should catch the people's attention, Shannon thought to herself, her thoughts returning to the interview. After hours of discussion with Clark Welch and the producers, she had Ok'd using that clip as the opener. They were all convinced it was the most explosive portion, and seeing it again, Shannon was even more convinced. A number of viewers were known to watch only the first few minutes of any interview to determine if they were interested. The faithful were never too faithful. Therefore, the program had been designed to reach out and grab the viewer, riveting their attention to the screen. In her opinion, Qaddafi had just reached out and grabbed all America, especially their president, and thrown them right in the mud. But what would America say if she got on there next week and told them what that animal was attempting to do at this very moment? She was half tempted, in spite of the obvious danger of such an act.

The commercial ended. There he was again; there she was again. When those questions had been asked, she had been so innocent, her complete world consisting of obtaining access to important people and placing their views in front of an interested public. It had never occurred to her to apply her Mississippi system of values to their morals, their beliefs. News. Her goal was to ask simple questions, questions that were often prerecorded. Sometimes she even submitted the questions in advance, giving the celebrity time to formulate answers before taping. Once, when a European leader had refused to see her, but wanted to be on her show, she had taped her questions in New York. He, in turn, had taped his answers at the studio in Paris, and the technical people spliced the tapes together so that it looked as though they were made at the same time. Anyone who did not know about the process could not tell they weren't in the same room.

But the events of the past seventy-two hours had changed all this. She did not quite understand how, but she was positive that she would never let anyone do that again. It was essential that she take a more definite stance as to how her interviews were conducted; it was now more important to her than ever before.

67

Suddenly, Shannon heard herself speaking.

Anderson: I know you are aware that this interview is being taped for showing in the United States. Would you like to tell the American people your opinion of the president's proposed nuclear strategy for the Mideast?

Qaddafi: I would enjoy an opportunity to speak directly with the American people because their president is making a drastic mistake. The Moslem countries will not sit still while the United States places nuclear weapons within a few hundred miles of our borders. Neither will our friends, the Soviet Union, remain silent. They are against such an action. The idea of introducing nuclear weapons into the Mideast is most distressing. However, I do not believe the American Congress favors such a proposal. And, as I understand your system of government, the Congress must pass legislation to enable your president to place missiles outside the United States. Even Saudi Arabia, which has been friendly with your country in recent years, is opposed to this action. They feel it greatly jeopardizes their security. It greatly jeopardizes all our security.

Anderson: How do you reply to Egypt's being a part of the proposal?

Qaddafi: I have little to say about the Egyptians. They are traitors to their countrymen—they do not deserve my comments. The Egyptians are no better than the Israelis.

Anderson: Isn't it true that the United States will maintain ultimate control of the weapons? A launch would not be possible without authorization from the president.

Qaddafi: That is only for the newpapers. The Israelis have a great deal of influence with your government. And because of that influence, the United States is pursuing a policy of control in the Middle East. Your government is after the oil which our country possesses, and we do not intend to give it up without a fight.

Anderson: Well, President Qaddafi, I thank you for talking with us. I believe I can say, for the American people, that they appreciate your candid comments.

Shannon sat quietly at her desk, having moved around behind and seated herself in the soft, leather chair, listening to the interview conclude. She had actually thanked that contemptible animal when all he had done was downgrade the United States. Reluctantly, her mind floated back to her last day at the summer house in Libya. She had met Qaddafi in the middle of the afternoon, and they had spent the remainder of the day together. Most of their time had been spent walking through his expansive flower gardens, gardens he had carved from the desert. Such a nice man, she had thought. At their previous meetings there had been little opportunity to speak with him except during the taping sessions. And, on each of those occasions he seemed like an intelligent, caring man. But before that last day had come to a close, her opinion was drastically altered.

"Miss Anderson, you are a beautiful lady," he had said, catching her totally off guard. "I did not remember you were so beautiful."

They were standing in the garden, next to a brilliantly spreading palm tree. She could not help being awed by the splendor of the garden, its vastness. A garden in the middle of the desert. Shannon did not believe things could be made to grow—flourish—under such conditions. The absence of water was alien to her. In Mississippi water was everywhere, and it was constantly supplemented by generous rains. And, if the rains did not come, the crops were not good. It was that simple.

"You flatter me. . . . It embarrasses me," Shannon had replied shyly. "I have never had a president tell me I was beautiful."

"Oh, but you are . . . you should not be embarrassed."

The garden made his comments seem all the more romantic. At first, although she hadn't realized it, Shannon felt herself being drawn to him, both physically and intellectually. There was a certain irresistible mystery about him; it pressed her uncontrollably closer. She fought within herself, rebelling

69

against all those people who told her he was a murderer on an international scale. It was a difficult battle.

" . . . I'd like to show you something," he had continued. Shannon had not heard the first of what he said.

"What!" she'd replied, startled from her thoughts.

"This way." He'd pointed, his voice soft. He had directed her toward a portion of the garden which they had not yet explored. *It* was very beautiful, and she felt paled by comparison. How could he say *she* was beautiful, when he had all this?

They had walked down a winding path, lined with blossoming flowers of all varieties, the most beautiful she had ever seen in her life. They were of a multitude of colors; greens, browns, grays, several blues and whites ánd yellows. Many were of a strange blend, of indescribable color.

"Do you take care of all these?" Shannon had asked, her gaze taking in all before her.

With a sad look, he'd replied, "I get out here much too seldom. There is much business to be taken care of at the capitol. I am afraid the gardeners must take care of the flowers, and they do a very good job."

"Oh, they do!" She had agreed, somewhat disappointed that he did not show more concern for their care.

For several minutes they had walked in silence. Finally, they came to a small stream. Shannon had not noticed it earlier. It exuded peace and serenity, the water running along smoothly and silently. Occasionally, a few leaves would float by, lazily. The banks of the small stream gradually sloped toward the water and were covered with bushes and flowers, making it almost impossible to determine where the bank began and the garden ended. She could see little fish darting to and fro in the clear water, chasing one another among the rocks. In and out; in and out, under the rocks, through the little caves.

"I had this stream built," he'd noted. "This house and the gardens are in the middle of a desert. It is very difficult to·get anything to grow here, but the water from the stream helps provide irrigation. Because of it everything grows better."

Shannon had watched Qaddafi's eyes flicker as he spoke, a softness emerging; it had not been there previously. Although

70

he was unable to work in the garden, it was obvious he cared. Possibly, she had been wrong about his lack of concern. In an attempt to show her understanding of the need for irrigation, she'd used a local example. It was the wrong example.

"I read about how some areas of the desert were turned into garden places in Israel through. . . . " She stopped. What was she saying? How could she be so stupid to mention Israel? This man had been at the forefront of the movement to destroy Israel since before he came to power. It was an unforgiveable mistake.

He did not say anything, but she saw that the softness had vanished from his eyes. He was staring, coldly, not at her, but off into the distance. Shannon hoped her one unthinking comment had not ruined everything. She had promised Welch she would complete the interview. All thoughts of closeness to him had fled. The interview was so important. Finally, he spoke, the calmness of his voice surprising her. The softness had returned to his eyes.

"What are you thinking?" he'd asked. It was evident he already knew the answer, but did he know she was thinking about him too, about being with him.

"Nothing," she lied, a little self-consciously.

And then, without a word, he directed her back to the house. The cameramen he had arranged for were summoned, and the remainder of the interview was taped without complications.

Shannon was inside the house when it happened. She was leisurely strolling down a huge hallway, fascinated by the enormous wealth. Her thoughts were caught up in the happenings of the day, the way in which she had seen such a hard man soften into such a likeable person, the beauty of everything around her. Dinner had been superb. Although Qaddafi had not been present, Jadallah had joined her. The meal reminded her of an expensive New York restaurant, right down to the servant cutting her steak into bite-size portions. Shannon was returning to her room, where she planned to lounge in the large bed and enjoy a book she had brought along. She had been trying to get started on it for weeks, but her busy schedule had prevented her from reading even the introduction. There

71

was nothing left to do until tomorrow morning when she departed, and she wanted to make the most of her time. Suddenly she heard voices. She was surprised because it had seemed that the whole house had been soundproofed. When people spoke inside a room, it was impossible to hear them in the hallway. Shannon looked around, curious as to where the voices were coming from. She saw no one in the hall. She stopped to listen. At first, she was unable to distinguish what the voices were saying or who was doing the talking. After all, it was none of her business. But, the voices were definitely coming from in front of her, *and* she *was* headed in that direction. As she closed the distance between herself and the muffled sounds, she was able to distinguish their owners. It was definitely Qaddafi and Jadallah, but the words were still unclear.

Shannon had wondered where Jadallah had disappeared when he was abruptly called away from dinner. But she had thought the President had left the grounds. A twinge of anger ran through her body. If he was still here, why hadn't he come to dinner? Knowing she should ignore the voices and continue down the hall made her quicken her pace. If Qaddafi had wanted to see her, he would have been at dinner—that did not really matter. But Jadallah had been called away. Something was up, and she wanted to know what it was.

Directly in front of her was the room from which the voices were coming. Immediately, she saw the reason she was able to hear the conversation. Someone had inadvertently left the door ajar. The newsperson in her took control. She eased closer to the open door, at the same time assuring herself that no one had entered the long hall. It would not be wise to be seen sneaking around this house. She remembered the guns. The thought made her press even harder against the door, concealing herself against the jutting doorway.

Inside, through the partial opening, she could see Qaddafi and Jadallah seated across from each other at a small table. From the tone of their voices, she could tell the conversation was important. Still, she could not catch all the words. Shannon eased the door open a bit more. Her heart raced. If the hinges squeaked she was caught, and there was no telling what they would do to her.

The door moved silently. Shannon's heart slowed. The two men were speaking French, thank God for her interest in foreign languages, she thought.

"He must be shot! Everyone around him should be shot!" Now Qaddafi was almost screaming. "Their actions could ruin everything we've planned. . . . "

"But, Mr. President . . . ," Jadallah attempted to interrupt.

Qaddafi cut him short. "You, yourself said the Iranians would help us! They hate him just as much as we do."

Again, Jadallah interrupted. "But what will be the reaction of the new American president?"

"Who cares what his reactions will be! The Soviet Union will support our actions. We do not care what the Americans think—they will be too weak. The Americans will never know who did it."

Shannon drew back in shock and horror. They were discussing the assassination of the president of the United States. And, from the sound of it, they were intending to include other top officials. Fear gripped her; she began to shake. She wanted to run, to get as far away from that room, that house, as possible. Someone might see her. They would surely kill her if they found out she had overheard. Anyone who would plot the murder of the president of the United States wouldn't think twice about having *her* killed.

Sitting alone in her New York office, she still didn't know what to do, and she was still afraid. Even though she was now safe, her body still trembled. She was in America. They would not touch her here. Or would they? Regardless, she had to do something.

At least she had succeeded in getting out of Libya alive.

CHAPTER 10

Crosby knew it might be difficult to locate the crash site without involving some branch of the state or federal government, but President Askins had made it clear that the investigation remain secret. If he had strolled into any agency flashing his White House I.D. and asked to be flown to the crash site, all of Colorado and half of Washington would have known that a presidential investigation was underway. Besides, the publicity would make his job more difficult, to say nothing of Askins's reaction. Although he had never experienced it directly, Crosby was aware of what had become known as "the presidential temper."

By doing it his way, which was to rely on the greed and curiosity of other men, no one would discover an investigation was in progress. People might conclude he was a little crazy—another nutty tourist with a lot of money and few brains, but that was all.

After questioning Johnson and Peters, Crosby had booked a commercial flight from Denver to Aspen. His plane had left early that afternoon, and shortly after arriving in Aspen, he'd contacted a helicopter service, one of those local outfits that take tourists for a close-up look at the snow on the mountains. He had to admit it was an unusual sight. Most people went a lifetime without experiencing that kind of sensation. Looking down, he realized he had never taken the time to notice the scenery below, although he had been on hundreds of helicopter flights. He could not take his eyes off the snow; a sensation of floating came over him. The snow-covered mountains all seemed new to him. Always before, he had been caught up in the intensity of the moment, his mind locked on the completion of his assignment, oblivious to his surroundings. Today it was different, he noticed the earth, the snow, the sky. The early afternoon sun glistened off the snow, an endless white blanket intermittently specked by stark, jutting rocks.

The scene provoked thoughts of his first wife. They had spent their honeymoon in Switzerland—what there was of a honeymoon. On the morning of the fourth day, a call had come forcing him to leave for Geneva where a most urgent assignment awaited. Nancy had been upset—and she had told him so. But those first days had been wonderful for both of them. They were so young and in love; anyway they thought they were in love. Later, he wondered.

The first day neither of them left the bedroom of their suite. Damn she was good, he thought—he remembered the feel of her. They became so involved in their lovemaking that meals were totally forgotten. They lay in each other's arms as the sun crossed the horizon; by evening both were exhausted. Sleep finally overcame them. On the second day, they decided to go down to the restaurant for breakfast; they needed refueling. After eggs, bacon and toast, they returned to their room, undressing each other along the way. Long before they reached the room she had removed his shirt, and he had completely unbuttoned her blouse, exposing her breasts. As he fumbled with the keys to their suite, an elderly couple strolled past. The woman whispered something to her husband and both shook their heads in disgust. Crosby had noticed their reaction. "You'll have to excuse us," he said, smiling broadly, "my wife and I are allergic to clothing." The elderly couple stared in disbelief. Undaunted, the young lovers stumbled into their room, falling onto the bed laughing. They tore off the remaining clothing, scattering it in all directions, the older couple forgotten in their passion.

The remainder of that day and all of the next were spent in bed, their only interruption was to call room service for meals, which were usually left on the tray, untouched. Finally, they decided they would again venture out among the other guests. Late on the evening of the third day, they agreed to devote the next morning to skiing. Prior to arriving, Crosby had assured

Nancy he would teach her to ski, and she was looking forward to her first outing. Crosby could see the excitement in her eyes.

The following morning, while they were in the process of dressing—for the first time in two days—the phone rang. Nancy looked at her husband. As far as she knew, neither of them knew anyone living in Switzerland. Nancy picked up the phone, hesitantly. Just as she feared, it was an international operator, asking for her husband. She was aware that Allen worked for the CIA, but did not understand the scope of his involvement. Nevertheless, a feeling of apprehension flowed through her body as she silently handed Crosby the receiver. Her apprehension increased as he spoke. She did not understand the language so his words were lost, but the expression on his face delivered the message.

After several minutes, he replaced the receiver and walked over to her. Nancy knew she wasn't going to like what he had to say. His face had changed, it was harder; the warmth had drained from his eyes. They were cold steel, something she had never seen before. He spoke quickly, his voice harsh. He told her there had been a development on one of his projects, and it was imperative that he leave Geneva within the hour. A man had been killed. No, there wouldn't be time for skiing lessons before he left. No, she should not wait for him. It would be better if she left for America and waited for him at her parents' home. He would call as soon as possible.

From that point on, there was nothing left to their marriage. He had to admit, she had tried. Over and over she had begged him not to go, not to leave her at a time like that. If he did have to go, she would wait—whatever he had to do couldn't take more than a few days. He'd repeated that he would call her as soon as it was feasible, but she must go back to America to wait. Reluctantly, she gave in. True to his word, he did call. Only, it was six months later. There had been complications, complications he was not at liberty to discuss.

They were divorced three months later.

That was then, and it was over; this was now, and unless he wanted to raise unnecessary suspicions, he had better start taking pictures—which was one of the reasons he had given for wanting to be flown to the site of the crash. It was essential that he look the part—typical sightseer. Sightseers could get away with anything; they were expected to do the unexpected. Anything was okay as long as they were willing to pay for the service, and Crosby had been willing to pay well.

The people at Paul's Snow Tours, where he leased the helicopter time, advised him not to go onto the mountain alone, it was too dangerous—like swimming after eating. For only a little extra, they told him he could arrange for a guide. But he knew it was no more than an attempt to extort more money from him when they started telling him stories about being stranded on snow-covered mountains, alone and cold, the darkness closing in. Crosby quickly declined, informing the man behind the rental counter that he'd had considerable mountain climbing experience. Luckily, the man did not inquire further because Crosby had run out of answers.

Although it was obvious that the clerk did not totally believe him, he wished him a safe trip. Crosby left the office, heading straight for the parked helicopter. Now, dressed in his newly purchased, combination mountain climbing and camping gear, he was standing on a slight incline about a hundred yards from pieces of what was once an airplane. The bodies had been removed by a special contingent, composed of volunteers from the FBI and Secret Service. No one else had been allowed near the area. The government had not wanted anyone to be given the opportunity to remove or destroy pertinent information. Reports on his desk back in Washington had told him the cleanup process had been completed, not an easy undertaking considering the terrain and weather. Still, it had not taken them long. Within three days the area had been opened to sightseers, those who wished to see where a vice president had died. Regardless of the difficulties in doing so, hundreds of people had gone there. But it did not last long; after two weeks no one came. The location and the incident were forgotten.

As he stood in the shin-deep snow, surveying the scene, Crosby remembered reading that the army had flown in a specially designed cargo helicopter to extract the larger pieces of the plane. The helicopter had originally been designed for use in the jungles of Vietnam, where it was often difficult to get large cargoes in and out of small clearings. The pieces of wreckage had been flown directly to Washington aboard an Air Force cargo plane provided by Lowry Air Force Base outside Denver. After landing at Andrews Air Force Base, they were discreetly taken, under heavy guard, to an FBI laboratory outside Washington for careful examination. Working around the clock, FBI experts had determined that a mechanical failure, one that could have happened to anyone of a thousand aircraft, had been the cause of the crash. Hence, no foul play. That was naive, he thought.

Crosby intended to get a closer look at the crash site. He wanted to examine the smaller pieces of the plane, those left behind by the cleanup crew. He hoped he might be lucky enough to find some small clue that had been overlooked or ignored. If he succeeded, it would be worth the time; if not, he would try elsewhere. The original investigators had not been concerned with foul play. They had been sent, more or less, to retrieve the bodies and the plane. Like most people in those positions, they were not paid to look past their noses, to discover clues, think. Besides, at the time of the cleanup there had been a consensus that the crash was the result of either pilot or mechanical error. From the reports, he knew that the FAA had not been allowed access to the crash site, nor had they been allowed their usual investigation of the blackbox. The FBI had handled all details of the investigation under the close supervision of the White House.

From the beginning, Crosby had not been able to buy the crash story. And what better place to look for a contradiction than at the site of the crash. In spite of his feelings, he could not be certain that the site would provide anything that would confirm his suspicions. But the existence of a last-minute substitute employee, and his subsequent disappearance, coupled with the very timely illness of the regular employee seemed to confirm those suspicions. Although nothing was concrete, the circumstantial evidence was strong.

Surveying the site, Crosby realized that the snow was not as deep as he had expected. Until two hours ago, he had been unaware that Colorado was experiencing a snow drought. The fact had meant nothing to him when the helicopter rental clerk mentioned it; he thought it was simply idle conversation. But looking down at the spot where the plane had crashed, he understood the significance. The lack of new snow would make it easier to locate anything of use. He descended the rough slope slowly, aware that the force of the crash was sure to have caused debris to be thrown for some distance. He didn't want to take the chance of missing anything important on his way down. He was not sure what he was looking for, but he hoped he would recognize it when he saw it.

As he searched, he decided that the people in Aspen had known what they were talking about when they warned him about the weather; it was cold. The appearance of the helicopter would be a welcomed sight, but that would not be for another two hours. The wind whipping along the mountain ridge and the falling temperature were far worse than he had anticipated. He was thankful for the warm clothes he'd had the foresight to purchase in Denver.

The first hour of the search proved fruitless; nothing turned up that could be remotely tied to the cause of the crash. What was he expecting, he wondered, the evidence to jump up and bite him? It was going to take work. He knelt to examine several pieces of wreckage, but each looked as expected. As time passed, only one thing became apparent, though it was of little significance to the investigation. He discovered he was not in the same physical condition he had been in three years ago. The continuous bracing required to maintain his balance on the steep grade had taken a toll on his legs. He made a mental note to get back into shape when he returned to Washington.

Along with the pain in his straining muscles, he noticed that the temperature had continued to fall and the wind had begun to howl through the valley below. He hoped the weather would not become severe enough to hamper the return of his ride; he didn't enjoy the prospect of hanging by a cable ladder under such conditions. But he had to accept conditions as they were; the rental service had made it clear that there was no place for the helicopter pilot to set down. A ladder drop was the only possible means of getting to the location. That didn't bother him, and the drop *had* been easy; he wasn't so positive about the pickup.

Frustration began to set in, and Crosby was about to give up. He had searched practically the whole area. It appeared that he had gambled and lost. There was nothing left that would be of any help. The weather was closing in, his time was running out, and he was not going to find anything. Suddenly, his eye caught the reflection of a metal object, half buried in the snow. He made his way to it, and knelt to get a closer look. The object resembled a piece of broken wing. That was probably why it had not been picked up by the team of investigators. But, on closer inspection, he found that it was not a piece of wing.

It took a full minute and a great deal of tugging to dislodge the shiny object from its prison of frozen snow and earth. Finally, a thin metal case, no larger than the page of a notebook and about a half inch thick, emerged. On the outside edge was a tiny metal lock, a small tumbler device similar to those found on attache cases. Turning the notebook face up, Crosby saw the initials, HRC. Henry Randloph Carlson.

Suddenly he was distracted by a sound nearby. It surprised him that anything could be heard above the howling wind. But he immediately recognized the sound; it was one he had heard many times. The noise was repeated. Again. In the frozen snow, within inches of where he knelt, were three little round holes. Bullet holes. He was certain they had been meant for him, but the fierce wind had thrown them off their deadly course. Someone farther up the slope was shooting at him.

Quickly, he tucked the metal folder into a pouch of his parka, rolling to his left as he did so. He continued rolling until he reached the safety of a boulder. Once out of the line of fire, he lay in the snow, not moving. He could feel the furious pounding of his heart. He needed time to think.

It had been four years since he'd been fired upon. In spite of the danger, he always experienced the same emotions. To be hunted by another human being was both frightening and exhilarating. He was again treading on that special ground, reserved for only a few, those who lived on the razor's edge.

Careful not to expose any more of his body than absolutely necessary, Crosby peered around the edge of the boulder. He saw no reason to give the killer another free shot. With trained eyes, he scanned the ground in front and to both sides of his position. The only boulder of sufficient size to provide cover was the one he had chosen. There was nowhere for a sniper to hide, except on the other side of the ridge above him. The rim, its ragged edges stark against the gray sky, was no more than seventy feet in front of him, a distance that had been just sufficient to account for the wind diverting the bullet from its course. Crosby almost regretted having cursed the wind only moments before. If it had not been blowing with such ferocity, he would be dead. Crosby fixed his eyes on the rim of the ridge, adjusting to the light and shadows, erasing everything else from his mind. He began his search along the right side, slowly moving along the edge until he reached the furthermost point.

Nothing.

He scanned back, going even slower. Still nothing. Adjusting his position, Crosby looked to his rear. There were no other source of cover. He was trapped. The sniper commanded the only high ground. If he stepped out from behind his cover, the sniper would have a clear shot, and he could not count on the wind to save his life again. The sniper would have adjusted his aim. He had to get the man to give away his position.

Crosby's mind raced along almost forgotten corridors, analyzing and comparing, reviewing situations from his past. He was certain the answer lay somewhere in his memory. But he needed the answer, fast. He reached for the Smith & Wesson in his pocket, having removed it from his shoulder holster in Aspen when he changed to the heavy winter clothing. Once the weapon was secure in his hand, he felt better, even warmer. He should have pulled it before, when the shooting started, but he had been too preoccupied with getting to safety. That had been careless.

The presence of the pistol in his hand seemed to clear his mind. There was only one way to get the sniper to reveal his position. He had to give him something to shoot at—himself. But that would be too dangerous. There had to be another way. If he was in the movies he would throw a snowball at one of the pieces of metal and the sound would cause the sniper to jump up and waste all his bullets. That was the movies; this was real. Professional assassins did not fire at sounds. They fired at targets. And they seldom fired all their ammunition; one shot was better. Multiple firings were for amateurs or when a professional was positive he had missed his target.

Crosby was positive the sniper could see the rock behind which he was hiding. He knew there was a gun trained on the rock, waiting for the slightest movement. If he could create enough movement to draw fire, and make the sniper think he had been hit, he might come down to take a look.

Careful not to show himself, Crosby worked his way out of his parka, laid it in the snow beside him, and began sculpturing a bust of snow. When the bust was about two feet high, he carefully placed the parka over it, making sure to cover the mound completely. From a distance he hoped it would look like a man's body. Then, holding the Smith & Wesson in his left hand, he began to push the mound with his right.

At first it didn't want to move, but as the base broke free of the frozen snow, it slid easily. Slowly he inched the mound to the side of the boulder. He hoped he had picked the right side—the side away from the sniper. If it was the wrong side, the sniper would have a clear view, and might not be fooled. It was not going to take long to find out. If there were no shots, the sniper would have seen through the ploy, and he was sunk.

He moved the mound past the edge of the boulder and the reaction was immediate, and deadly accurate in spite of the still-gusting wind. This time a single bullet tore through the parka just above his hand. Had he been wearing it, the bullet would have hit him in the base of the skull, killing him instantly.

As quickly as possible, without exposing himself and giving away his apparently successful ploy, Crosby shoved the bust sideways, hoping it would disappear from the sniper's view and give the impression of a man reacting to the impact of a bullet. It was his only chance. Then, it was time to wait.

He pressed himself against the jagged surface of the boulder, assuming a crouched position, his weapon pointed over the top of the boulder. When the sniper came down to verify his kill, as Crosby was sure he would do, it would all be over. Regardless of who the man worked for, some type of verification would be expected. No lone professional ever walked away without verifying that there *was* a kill.

Several anxious moments passed. It was getting colder, and he didn't have his parka. Minutes passed and nothing happened. He began to wonder if he hadn't misjudged his opponent. Maybe, he was not coming; maybe he, too, was waiting for more movement, a clearer shot. At last, he heard it—a footstep on frozen snow. It was faint, but he'd heard it. His heartbeat quickened. With one hand cupped over the pistol, Crosby released the safety muffling the click. Crosby expected him to come straight over the top, giving him a clear shot. But as an added precaution, he periodically scanned the terrain to his right and left, to make sure the sniper did not sneak up on him. Finally, the footsteps grew louder—the sniper was still moving forward, but cautiously.

The waiting was taking its toll on Crosby. He did not know how much longer he could control himself. He wanted to dash out from behind the boulder and get it over with. He was certain the sniper had seen through the ploy. He was taking too long to cover the short distance. Then, suddenly a head appeared above the boulder. Crosby fired once. That was all that was necessary. The sniper was propelled backward and upward from the force of the impact, coming to rest with a thud, arms outstretched. Crosby stood up slowly, not wishing to become the victim of a second ploy. He kept his weapon trained on the unmoving figure. He approached the body warily, then seeing the small, dark hole in the center of the man's forehead, he relaxed.

To Crosby's surprise, it was the same man he had seen earlier that morning in the motel restaurant. He had thought then the face looked familiar, and now he was certain he had seen the man before. Where, he did not know.

What was the man doing here? How could he have known Crosby was going to be at the crash site? He hadn't been followed. The man had not been aboard the plane with him, nor was he on the helicopter that had brought him. There was only one possibility. The sniper had known his destination in advance.

First things first, he thought, turning back to the boulder. It was getting even colder, and he needed his parka. The inside was damp from the snow, but it would still protect him from the wind. He threw it on hurriedly.

Retracing his steps to the dead sniper, Crosby sat down on a piece of metal. He sat silently, staring at the man's face. It was not long before his concentration was broken by the sound of the returning helicopter. The pilot must not be allowed to see the body. He could see the headlines: "Shooting Death Near Crash Site." The President wouldn't like the publicity. It was essential for him to get to the other side of the ridge for the pickup, but there was something he had to do first. Quickly, he began to search the dead man. As always in such circumstances, the man carried no identification, no labels. There was not the slightest clue to his identity. For the first time, Crosby glanced at the weapon lying in the snow. It was a Gruza.

Russian.

He turned and ran toward the sound of the helicopter. The pickup had to take place on the other side of the ridge. Snow pulled at his boots as he ran, the steep grade making sustained running difficult. But he had no choice; he had to keep going. The helicopter was not yet in sight. A little farther and his secret would be safe, at least for the time being. His legs were beginning to give out under the strain, his breath coming in long gasps, he could hear the pounding of his heart. With a last effort, he vaulted over the rim. The remaining distance was downhill.

CHAPTER 11

FUNW DENOUNCES MID-EAST STRATEGY

Washington: At a Washington rally, prominent attorney, Jefferson T. Samuels asked the question, "How much is enough?"

Samuels is the national leader of the Freeze Unnecessary Nuclear Weapons movement. In his speech, he made it clear that his movement is not simply a temporary coalition of groups that will fade away in six months or a year. Instead, he declared that FUNW is a force that must be dealt with, now, and in the future.

According to Samuels, the need for further production and deployment of nuclear weapons of any sort is unwarranted. No one in government disputes his claim that the United States and the Soviet Union possess enough nuclear weapons to achieve what the strategists refer to as MAD—Mutual Assured Destruction. The phrase itself is self-explanatory.

Confidential sources at the Pentagon tell us the United States has the capability of exploding over 12,000 nuclear weapons on the Soviet Union. In turn, the Soviet Union can send almost 8,000 nuclear warheads speeding toward the U.S.

Sources also confirm that these figures do not include thousands of smaller, tactical weapons designed for use against tank formations, battle emplacements, ship convoys and military bases.

These figures bring the total U.S. nuclear capability to almost 30,000 weapons, while the Russians have 16,000.

Samuels says, for these reasons, there "should be an immediate and absolute freeze on weapons production by both sides."

The FUNW coalition is placing its support behind congressional candidates who wish to prevent the United States from placing strategic nuclear weapons in the Middle East, at Ras Banas—a base manned jointly by forces from the United States, Egypt, and Israel.

The freeze movement has been sponsored in a Senate resolution by Sen. Timothy Fitzgerald, D–Mass., a leading presidential contender. Fitzgerald is receiving a good deal of support for his resolution, which calls for the U.S. and Russia to halt immediately the development, testing, and deployment of nuclear weapons.

"Peter, I need to see you!" came the president's voice over the intercom. It was clear from his tone that he was upset about something.

What was it today, Peter Fitzsimmons wondered? It seemed that the president found something to anger him daily. Sometimes it involved matters of major importance, but on most occasions he would be set off by the inadvertent comments of a cabinet member or some other executive branch employee who found their pronouncements in print. Askins had always felt that the media, especially print media, had been out to get him. At every opportunity, they reported comments or events that were less than flattering, while ignoring those which were complimentary. Lately, Askins seemed to be even worse—he became upset over the slightest thing.

"Peter?" The voice was impatient.

What was it today? Fitzsimmons thought. "Yes, Mr. President," he replied, depressing the intercom button. At the same time, he pressed another button placing the call on his speakerphone. He had always felt uncomfortable speaking into a small disk to an unseen person, a handle-shaped device connected to his ear and mouth. The ability to speak and hear normally from a speaker was far more comfortable, and the speakerphone never restricted his movement. Of course, Fitzsimmons was obliged to use the hand-held receiver for more private conversations, those involving national security or touchy issues, but a summons by the president was not always of strategic importance—yet.

"I need to see you immediately. There is something we must discuss." Askins's voice sounded urgent. Possibly, there *was* something important.

Fitzsimmons stopped to ponder what had crossed his desk in the last twenty-four hours—very little got past him before the president saw it. There was nothing he could think of that would account for Askins's tone—unless! Maybe Crosby had called Askins directly. Although Crosby did not have either the clearance or authorization to do so, his CIA experience might give him the know-how. The thought of Crosby bypassing him made him angry. There was also fear mixed with his anger.

"I'll be right there, Mr. President."

Commensurate with his degree of responsibility, Fitzsimmons's office was directly across the hall from the president's. With his office door open, he could easily see everyone who came and went. Most of the time the door was open for just that reason. However, the practice was unnecessary. Pat Loftus, the president's longtime secretary, had been given specific instructions to keep anyone who was not on her approved list from entering the Oval Office. Each evening, the list was compiled by Fitzsimmons and placed on Loftus's desk by six the following morning. Anytime during the day, Fitzsimmons could add or subtract from the list; only he was allowed to do so. In seven years no one had entered without having had their name placed on the list.

As Fitzsimmons entered the Oval Office, the president was, as usual, seated behind his massive desk. At least he was not pacing the room as he did when he was extremely agitated, Fitzsimmons thought. That was a good sign.

"Have you seen this article?" Again, the voice was angry. Several of the nation's major newspapers were scattered on the desk in front of him. That in itself was not unusual. Each morning the president read them—for perspective, he said—before beginning the day.

Fitzsimmons breathed a sigh of relief. Whatever the problem, it did not involve Crosby.

"Which article are you referring to?"

"The one about Jefferson Samuels. Have you read it?"

"Yes."

"Is that all you have to say? I can't understand why they even report such trash. People might get the impression there is a big movement against my Mideast policy."

"We're not exactly looking at one-hundred percent support on this issue. . . . "

"Hell. . . . If it wasn't for those assholes in Russia and that madman in Libya, nobody would care. I wouldn't even get any significant opposition out of the Arabs."

"I don't believe the article was that damaging. It was more concerned with numbers, not the location of the warheads . . . not the base."

"That damn Senator Fitzgerald is using the issue to gain support. Neither he nor any other Democrat has the slightest chance of becoming president. I'll tell them who's going to be president . . . and that's the man I decide to support . . . and it sure as hell isn't going to be a Democrat." He paused. "If I decide to support *anyone!*"

"It's a hot issue, Mr. President. He may be able to gain some support. Although most of the people agree with your proposals to achieve peace in the Middle East, I think they would like to leave out nuclear weapons." Fitzsimmons was not sure how Askins would react to this statement. The president shook his head, his eyes seemed to cloud over. Fitzsimmons was puzzled.

"There just isn't any way to achieve peace without introducing nuclear weapons. . . . It's the only feasible way to achieve superiority—superiority to a degree that will prevent attacks on Israel. There is always going to be a Qaddafi . . . if not in Libya, somewhere else." The president was not really speaking to him.

"I agree. All I am saying is that this freeze movement may cause more problems than we at first predicted. I don't think this particular article will hurt us. When you and vice president Carlson were both behind the proposal, it was unimpeachable. Now, we are weak in one area."

"Where?" the president snapped.

Fitzsimmons explained that the opposition had realized that Carlson's death left a gap in policy continuation. While Carlson was alive, there was no doubt he was going to continue Askins's policies when he became president. That certainty was now gone. No one supported the Middle East proposal to the degree that Carlson had done, no one except Askins. The freeze coalition had been given a shot in the arm. If they could delay passage until after Askins left office, the issue might die on its own. There was no assurance his successor would support the same policies.

"It always comes back to the issue of the vice president, doesn't it, Peter?" He was still seated, his head angled slightly to one side, his eyes staring at the desk. He chewed the right corner of his lip. Sadness was evident in his eyes.

"Within the next few days, we're going to have to nominate someone. I took the liberty of having the FBI do workups on the major possibilities . . . including a few new faces from the Republican governors. I hope you don't mind."

Over the past several months Fitzsimmons had been getting the feeling that Askins hardly seemed to notice what was being said to him. But, by his answer, it was clear he had heard every word.

"I appreciate the work, Peter. It seems I've been neglecting my duties . . . but you haven't."

Fitzsimmons smiled his acceptance of the compliment.

The president continued. "Did you have the FBI check on Secretary Adams and Senator Thomas?"

"I have files on both of them," Fitzsimmons replied, wondering what Askins had in mind. The next comment sent a shiver down his spine.

"Call Senator Thomas and schedule him for early tomorrow morning."

"Is there something you want to tell me, Mr. President?" Fitzsimmons responded, unable to restrain himself.

Inhaling deeply, the beginning of a smile flickering at the corners of his mouth, Askins dodged the question. "We'll just wait and see what happens in the morning. That's all for now, Peter."

Fitzsimmons returned to his office experiencing a feeling he had not had since joining the president's team. He was being left out of a major decision. Askins had always solicited his advice prior to any important decision. This time he was deciding on his own. Or, was he? Had someone silently ousted him from his exalted post of protector? After all the years and all the blind obedience, was he being pushed aside? Were the political stakes high enough to warrant offering him as the sacrifice? The office of the vice presidency, combined with Askins's desire to achieve passage of the nuclear proposal, might just have been sufficient incentive for Askins to side with Senator Thomas. It was an old cliché that politics made strange bedfellows, but Askins and Thomas were strange indeed.

But he would put up a fight. If Senator Thomas was trying to oust him, he wasn't going to capitulate. He was the man closest to Askins, and it was going to stay that way. He could use his office and the inference of presidential backing to achieve many things. He hadn't gotten to his present position by laying back when the going got tough. Just then the phone rang.

"Fitzsimmons," he said, directly into the mouthpiece. It was his practice to evaluate the sensitivity of the call prior to placing it on the speakerphone. This call was not destined to make it to the speaker system.

"Peter, this is James Denton. . . . I think you may have a problem."

Denton was an old acquaintance. They had been roommates at UCLA, and for a short time after graduation from law school had been members of the same firm. After coming to the White House, Peter had even recommended his old friend for a job with the FBI. Beginning as a supervisor, Denton's performance had earned him an appointment as an assistant deputy director. On several occasions, he and Fitzsimmons got together and shared insider stories over a few drinks. That had not happened recently; Denton felt that something in Fitzsimmons had changed. He was no longer fun to be around.

"What's up, Jim?" There was tension in Fitzsimmons's voice.

"Look, I just got a call from our office in Denver. It seems there's a new body at the crash site in Aspen."

CHAPTER 12

The security of the door felt good. There was a comfort to be found inside the apartment. A comfort that could not be found in the hallway just on the other side of her strong door, or in the elevator, or on the street outside the building. Standing, pressed against the door, Shannon detested the feeling—fear—that seemed to have overwhelmed her, immobilizing her ability to act and think. It made her want to scream, as she had done in Libya when the guards were about to kill her. The thought of being killed invaded her temporary security, and brought the reality of the last few minutes rushing back.

She had left her office at CBS about thirty minutes after the broadcast of her interview with Qaddifi ended. It had taken her that long to regain her composure. Even then, she had been unable to decide on a practical solution to her dilemma. As was her practice, Shannon waited inside the building while the security guard, stationed outside the high front doors, called for a taxi. She had developed this practice over the last couple of years while living in New York. Crime had become so widespread within the city—even on its outskirts—that it was unsafe to wait on the street for a cab to appear.

While she waited, Shannon noticed a car parked directly across from the building. Aside from its plainness, there was no reason for it to catch her eye, but it did. In the half-light of the streetlamps, she was able to discern two men. Why would two men be seated in a car parked across from CBS at ten thirty at night, she wondered. She asked Cecil, the security guard, if he had noticed the men waiting in the car. Yes, he had noticed the automobile pull up about an hour before she came out, but no one had gotten out or in. And, as far as he knew, they were not waiting for anyone in the building. Cecil added that it was common practice for people to call from upstairs if anyone was going to be waiting for them. In view of all the murders and kidnappings, security did not take loiterers lightly. Newspeople were regarded as highly visible and, therefore, certain precautions had to be taken. If the automobile had been parked on the CBS side of the avenue, a team of security personnel would have been sent out to inquire, but since it was parked on the far side, it was not felt that precautions were necessary. Policy, Cecil advised her. However, he did offer to have a security team inquire as to their business if she was worried. Hesitantly, she declined the offer—her ego would not let her show a weakness. And she considered fear a weakness.

A few minutes later, the taxi arrived and she left the safety of the building and hurried to the cab. As she gave her address to the driver, Shannon glanced in the direction of the parked car. Its lights were on and it was moving away, down the opposite side of the street. She relaxed. She was being silly. There was no reason to worry. Qaddafi didn't have the slightest idea she had overheard his conversation. Absolutely no one had seen her. If they knew she knew, they would never have let her leave Libya, she rationalized.

Suddenly, she saw the picture in a clearer light. Of course they let her leave Libya. If something were to happen to her *there*, inquiries would be made, questions would have to be answered. The death of an international newsperson would be big news, too big to be ignored. Her death would bring more attention than Qaddafi desired. Just a few days ago, she honestly believed she was in love with him, and now. . . .

No, they would wait and have her murdered here, in the United States. No one would ever know why. She would become a statistic, another murder in the Big Apple. Those men in the car *were* waiting for her. Her. She had been foolish not to let Cecil check out the occupants.

She turned to look out the rear window. The car was directly behind them. She was certain it was the same car. And, with the lights from the car behind it, she could easily distinguish the forms of two men. There was a sudden pounding in her head, her heart raced; as she spoke to the driver, her voice was barely above a whisper. "Has that ... car ... been following ... us?"

The driver looked into his mirror, but not at the car behind them. Instead, he angled the mirror to get a better view of Shannon. For the first time, she got a good view of his ugly face. That added to her fear.

"Wha' d' ya say, lady?" he asked gruffly.

She thought he sounded like a punch-drunk fighter. Whatever happened to all those talkative cabbies, she wondered. Against her judgement she repeated her question.

"Have you noticed that car following us?"

The cabbie readjusted his mirror. "What car?" he grunted.

"The car right behind us," Shannon screamed into his face. At the same time she pointed—a useless gesture since the cabbie was now unable to see her. I must get control of myself, she said silently to herself.

"How long have they been following us?" the driver asked.

"I thought you might be able to tell *me!*" Shannon replied, shaking her head in frustration. At least, a degree of calmness had returned to her voice, she thought.

"Hadn't noticed 'em at all, lady ... lots a cars in this city. . . . Don't really pay much 'tention to 'em." The cabbie's eyes returned to the street in front of him, oblivious of his surroundings.

"Idiot," she intoned. Why hadn't she let Cecil check on that car?

Twenty minutes passed, all the while she watched the mysterious car, unable to take her eyes from its glaring headlamps. At times when it came within a few feet of them, she felt the occupants could reach out and touch her. When they fell back, she somehow felt safe. Suddenly, it occurred to her that this unknown, unseen enemy was following her home. She couldn't let them know her address. There *had* to be some point of safety. Sitting in the back seat of the taxi, she felt helpless. Her heart raced; her stomach churned. What could she do? She was a newsperson not a CIA agent. But she still had to control her fears. And she had to take positive action.

Finally able to take her eyes from her pursuer, she looked out the side window. She was only three blocks from her apartment. If she was going to do anything, it was going to have to be now.

"There's a little grocery store on the corner up ahead. . . . I'll get off there." Shannon moved to the edge of her seat, and pointed at the store. She had no plan except to prevent them from following her home. The cabbie pulled next to the curb alongside the little store, its bright lights spilling onto the sidewalk, helping to lessen her fear. As she got out of the taxi, she saw the car about half a block down the street. It seemed to be moving in slow motion—bearing down upon her. Halfway out of the cab, she stood, staring, waiting—for what, she was not sure.

" 'ay, lady! A pretty thing like you ain't goin' a try to beat me outta ma fare, are ya?" The cabbie's voice startled her. "Come on, pay up."

Without taking her eyes off the approaching vehicle, Shannon quickly withdrew a bill from her purse and threw it onto the front seat. The car was still approaching—almost upon her.

The driver was saying something she did not quite catch. " . . . large bill . . . no change . . . anything smaller."

Shannon slammed the door, drowning out the voice, not caring what he was saying. Immediately, the cabbie sped away before Shannon had a chance to change her mind. The departure of the cab went unnoticed, Shannon's eyes transfixed on the mysterious vehicle. It was no more than fifty feet away. She could see two men in the front seat, but not clearly enough to make out their faces. Without realizing it, her attention shifted to the car itself—the same color, black, the same size. But she was almost certain it was a different model from the one she had seen parked across the street from her office. She continued to stare as the car drove by. To her surprise, neither of the men gave the slightest indication they were aware of her presence. They appeared to be carrying on a conversation. It was definitely not the same car. As the car passed, the face of the man nearest her came into view, its features distinct. It was not the face of a foreigner—she had been expecting someone with distinct Arabian features. Instead, the face seemed typically American. Relief flooded her body as the fear drained away. But the feeling of relief was quickly followed by one of embarrassment.

"Damn." She had been scared half out of her wits, and all for nothing; no one had been following her. No one was out to get her. The first auto had driven off in the *opposite* direction, and this one was no more than a coincidence. Her fear was making her paranoid.

Turning from the street, she looked into the store's bright interior. In her confusion over watching the approaching car, she had forgotten she had used it as an excuse to stop. But looking into the store and seeing other people made it inviting. She needed the security of being with people, even if she didn't know them, even if the danger had passed. If there had been any danger, it was over. A little personal warmth was all she required.

Shannon suddenly pictured Qaddafi. He had provided her with warmth only a short time ago. But he had turned into her reason for fear—the source of coldness and embarrassment she now felt. He was the reason she was standing on the sidewalk, confused.

That had been how she felt an hour ago, before going into Fred and Linda's Market. With the door of her apartment closed, and her back firmly against the solid wood, she was far safer than she had been after leaving Fred and Linda's. Prior to entering the grocery, she had convinced herself that she had imagined the whole thing, the first car, the second car, everything. Once inside the grocery, the people were friendly, courteous, warm—everything she needed. She often stopped at that store when she ran out of small items, instead of going to the larger supermarket several blocks away. Partly because of her television career, and partly because she shopped there, the owners always recognized her.

"Good evening, Miss Anderson," Fred called out from behind the enclosed checkout counter. "Kind of late to be out, isn't it?"

If only you knew, she wanted to say, but decided against it. Being scared out of her mind was not something she had bargained for when she decided to become a newsperson.

"I need to get some . . . bread."

It took her only a minute to make her purchase, but she was reluctant to leave. The thought of walking back in the darkness was frightening. To delay her departure, she initiated a conversation with Fred. During the conversation, Shannon watched the street to assure herself she had not made a mistake, praying that the car would not return. Finally running out of small talk, she decided to leave before Fred got the wrong idea.

Once on the street, she headed straight for her apartment. She had not gone far when a noise caused her to start. She turned. Nothing. There were no people, no cars on either side of the street. The sound had probably come from an alley cat rummaging in a trash can. But her fear soared. This was not the time of night for a woman to be walking on the street alone.

Still not seeing anyone, her control returned. In spite of her apprehensions about being alone, on foot, in New York, she found one bright note. She felt safer than when she was in the taxi. At least, she was not being followed. It *had been* her imagination.

She crossed to Sixty-Fifth, into civilization, her spirits continued to soar. There were people walking and talking, in couples and alone, along the sidewalk, and cars parked along the curb. The street was filled with the noise of traffic, a sound she had grown to appreciate. Then she saw it.

About fifty feet from the entrance to her apartment, was the car. Not the one that followed her, but the one that had been parked across the street from her office building. She *was* being followed. They had used two cars, hoping she wouldn't notice. The second car, the one that followed her to the store, had driven past to keep her from becoming suspicious. They had wanted her to *think* they were carrying on a conversation; they had purposely ignored her. At that point, the second car was no longer important. Once they had determined she was on her way home, there was no need to maintain the tail. The first car was already waiting for her. They already knew her home address. How foolish she had been to think otherwise. Had President Qaddafi really sent someone to kill her?

The fear again began to swell up inside her, a knot developing in the middle of her stomach, more severe than anything she had ever experienced. The veins in her temple pounded; she felt lightheaded. Whoever they were, they had placed themselves between her and her apartment, her ultimate safety. She could not get home without going past them.

After the initial wave of fear passed, a surprising calmness settled over her mind and body. Nothing in her background had prepared her for what she was thinking, planning. A young couple was strolling leisurely in the direction of her apartment. She fell in behind them a few paces back, making sure the men she knew were in the parked car could not get a clear view of her approach. Of course, they would be expecting her, but she was sure they had no way of knowing she was aware of their presence.

The couple she was trailing slowed down; she prayed they would not stop. In spite of her newfound determination, Shannon's breath began to come in short gasps. She had no experience with this kind of situation, and she didn't like it. It was not her style. Shannon was within a few feet of the point where she had decided to make her move. The couple in front of her seemed to have slowed even more. The lovers' feet dragged as if stuck in wet cement. They were laughing. She wondered if she would ever laugh again. Only two more steps and she would be there. One more. The time to act.

With her right hand, she pounded furiously on the window of the car, while grasping the door handle with her left. Using all her strength, she yanked at the handle. The door remained shut. Again she yanked. Still no movement. She bent down to look inside the car, expecting to look straight into the barrel of a gun. The car was empty.

Quickly, she glanced about. No one in either direction looked like the men she had seen. The couple she had been using as a shield was standing about fifteen feet away, staring at her in disbelief. Shannon knew they must think she was mentally deranged.

Without further thought as to the whereabouts of the occupants of the car, she ran the short distance to her apartment building, past the guard at the entrance, past the elevators, and up the stairs.

Her lungs were finally beginning to settle down, her heart rate beginning to slow. The powerful throbbing in her chest had almost disappeared. She wanted only to get her clothes off and jump into a warm shower. Somehow she felt the water would cleanse the dirtiness and hurt she was experiencing. She realized suddenly that her fear was being replaced by anger—an all consuming anger that was centering on Muammar el-Qaddafi.

CHAPTER 13

"This is your captain speaking," came the voice in the usual monotone. "Welcome aboard flight number sixty-five from Denver to beautiful Dallas-Ft. Worth. Our cruising speed will be approximately five hundred miles per hour at an altitude of thirty-two thousand feet. Our flying time will be approximately one hour and thirty-nine minutes. We hope you have a good flight." The voice had interrupted the conversations of the passengers, and they remained silent for a few moments—as though they were expecting something more. It was easy for Crosby to distinguish the regular air passengers from those who flew only occasionally; the first timers stood out even more. They were interested in everything happening around them. They not only listened to the captain's report, but actually followed the stewardess's recitation of the emergency instructions, tracing with their fingers the exit diagram. In contrast, the more experienced passengers paid only intermittent attention to the captain and stewardess, only wishing to assure themselves they had boarded the correct flight. That kind of apprehension always remained.

Crosby ranked himself among the most experienced travelers, having flown in all kinds of planes, to every conceivable-and some inconceivable-destinations around the world. His only concern was that they had been rerouted. Instead of flying directly from Denver to Washington, they were going by way of Dallas. And, in Dallas it would be necessary to change planes and suffer an hour's delay.

If only he could have gotten to Stapleton a little earlier, he would have been able to catch a direct flight. He had been forced to stay in Aspen because of scheduling, and his desire to look like an unconcerned, carefree tourist. He also hoped he would be able to isolate his problems to Aspen. If there was a second, or even a third killer, he wanted to stop them before he left the city.

Crosby planned to take every precaution to ensure his safety, but at the same time, he understood the importance of uncovering any new assailant. Experience dictated that he consider the possibility of a backup. In his field agent days, *he* had utilized the backup system on more than one occasion—unless, of course, the assignment was top secret. On those occasions, either he went without a backup, or a local was engaged—a drone. Locals were always left uninformed of the real purpose of the assignment, thus avoiding the danger of their being compromised. In this instance, Crosby expected a backup.

After leaving Paul's Snow Tours, where he had secured the helicopter that had taken him to and from the crash site, he had gone straight to the Holiday Inn. Walking down the crowded street, he did everything he could to make himself as conspicuous as possible. He called out to strangers, he sang, he made strange sounds—hoping to flush out a second killer. The assault never occurred, and instead of leaving early the next morning, Crosby decided to wait. It did not seem likely, but there was a remote possibility the backup might have had to await further instructions. If the problem was to be isolated to Aspen, he would simply have to allow more time. But by ten a.m. his patience was wearing thin, and he concluded that there would be no further encounters, at least, not in that place, at that time. He did not feel right about moving on, but there was nothing he could do—no action he could take to make it happen.

Reluctantly, he had boarded the next flight to Denver, and that was why he was on such a screwed up route to Washington. He was resigned to hoping that there had been no backup, and whoever had sent the killer was now in the dark as to his whereabouts. As an added precaution, he had not returned to his room at the Sheraton when he arrived in Denver. If surveillance had been established at the hotel, he did not intend to walk into a trap or pick up a tail. He could take care of his

101

remaining luggage by phoning from Washington and having it sent to his home address.

Both at the airport in Aspen and at Stapleton, he had taken up a position where he could observe everyone. No one appeared to pay the slightest attention to an eccentric, money-spending tourist. Crosby was confident in his ability to detect a tail. He had seldom encountered anyone with the degree of control displayed by the man he had left in the mountain snow. Usually, the eyes gave them away.

The lack of rest from the previous evening, and the exertion on the mountainside had exacted its toll. Crosby was exhausted; his eyelids would not stay open. He had no choice. He had to get some sleep—at least until he got to Dallas.

The changeover had gone smoothly. Delta flight four twenty-six for Washington was departing from the next gate. It went so quickly, he was able to catch a second nap while awaiting departure. Once back in the air, however, it was time to analyze what he had discovered. He had been able to get a little over two hours sleep and that had been enough to clear his mind. Many times in the past he had operated on less, and for the past three years he had gotten enough sleep to last him the remainder of his life.

When he left Washington, two days ago, he hadn't expected the investigation to become so involved. He'd been convinced the outcome would be different from the report, but he had not anticipated that anyone would make an attempt on his life—not at this early stage. It was far too soon. He didn't possess enough information to prove anything or, for that matter, he didn't have enough information to think of anything to prove. Then the obvious came to him. Either the persons responsible for the vice president's death were indiscriminate killers who needed little provocation, or he possessed more information than he was aware of.

Maybe he was getting too old to be playing such high stakes games. Remembering the metal notebook he had found in the snow, Crosby reached under his seat and placed his briefcase on his lap. There had not been time the previous evening to examine the contents. He quickly spun the small combination lock on the briefcase, his hands shaking slightly with anticipation. The briefcase was the same one he had used in the field. He admired its feel, its weight—he was alive again. He extracted the notebook. Immediately, he noticed the pungent smell of gasoline, something he had failed to notice on the mountain. As the odor filled his nostrils, he remembered that the snow around the notebook had been a dull yellow— probably fuel from the plane. Another thought struck him, and his excitement gave way to apprehension. The notebook was not designed to be waterproof, and if the contents were paper, the resulting damage could be extensive.

The simple lock on the notebook took only seconds to open. What he saw depressed him. The contents were almost completely destroyed. It was evident that not only gasoline, but some other substance had penetrated the metal cover. It contained an assortment of papers and at least three pictures. The papers were all but eaten away, making it impossible to make out what had been written on them. The pictures were in an equally bad state. The combination of gasoline and oil-like substance had destroyed the images on all but one—an eight by ten blow up of the man Crosby had left lying in the snow. The man was standing in front of some trees along with one other person who was not recognizable. Even if he were allowed access to the CIA laboratories at Langley, the face could not be reproduced, Crosby surmised. Who was the man, and what was the Vice President doing with it? Was the second man in the picture Henry Carlson or the person Carlson was investigating? And why was he investigating him? Those were the questions, and Crosby didn't have the answers. But someone must think he did. Why else would they have tried to have him killed? If he could just recall where he had seen the man he had killed. . . . Certainly, it was not recently.

How did he know Crosby was going to the crash site? The man did not follow him. Again he thought about the two people who knew where he was going when he left Washington—the president, but he was above suspicion. Of course, the president could have mentioned Crosby's trip to someone, but that person would also have to be above suspicion. And, it wasn't likely he would mention it to anyone—for any reason. Askins had clearly expressed his desire to keep the investigation secret.

The only other person who knew was Peter Fitzsimmons, and Peter had the highest security clearance. It was unlikely that he was the leak. Peter never told anyone anything. That left only one possibility. He must have picked up a tail when he went to see Mrs. Carlson. When he left, he had not checked to see if anyone saw his departure. He had not expected anyone to be watching the house or him. He realized his mistake. He simply had not expected the unexpected. He had gone stale, and if he didn't get sharp immediately he would make a mistake that might prove fatal.

Whoever had terminated the vice president must have felt it necessary to keep his residence under surveillance. Either they were expecting something, or were just taking precautions against someone like him entering the picture, uninvited. One thing was certain; whoever was behind the assassination was worried that someone might stumble upon their plans. Crosby could only speculate on what those plans might be. The answer would depend upon the men behind the killing.

He was sure Carlson had been assassinated. He did not believe that anyone would have gone to so much trouble if there had been any other scenerio. The man he had killed had been carrying a Russian Gruza, that could point to Russian involvement, but Crosby didn't think that was the case. Russians and Americans played by certain rules, and those did not usually include the killing or kidnapping of high-level government officials. It was common practice to buy or even blackmail them, but kidnapping and murder were unacceptable.

Crosby was well aware that both sides poured millions of dollars into intelligence, for their own countries and others. Both sides also gave heavy support—financial and equipment—to several terrorist organizations, internal and international. A Russian weapon, like an American weapon, could be found in the hands of almost anyone and could have been secured legally or illegally. Arms dealers throughout the world were willing to broker anything, in any quantity, for a price.

104

The presence of the Russian weapon was little indication of involvement, in fact, it might be exactly the opposite—a Russian assassin would to be smart enough not to use a weapon from his home country.

He needed to look elsewhere for a clue, but *elsewhere* didn't look too promising. It was unlikely he would be able to locate the man who replaced Jack Peters. He had probably disappeared. Up to now, those responsible had managed to cover their tracks very well. Even if he found the substitute mechanic, it was doubtful that he would know anything. He probably had been hired over the phone. Maybe he was dead by now.

Crosby was sure the substitute mechanic was not the one he had killed in Aspen; the description wasn't even close. The man he had killed was much older, much bigger. The logic pointed to some kind of conspiracy—more than one person had to be involved. Someone was behind the scenes, directing. But what was the purpose? How far did it go? What was next?

Realizing he was still holding the notebook, Crosby placed it back in his briefcase. It would still be necessary to take it to Langley for further examination. He didn't believe anything would be turned up, but it was worth a try. As he was closing the briefcase, he noticed the untouched, two-page biography of Tim Ranes, the charter pilot. Maybe that contained something of value. He picked it up and began reading.

CHAPTER 14

"Senator, I want to apologize for not being able to give you my feelings on the vice presidency," Askins said with sincerity. "Henry's death was a shock to us all, and frankly, it has thrown things into confusion. I'm afraid I have been somewhat out of touch."

"I understand, Mr. President," Senator Thomas nodded, raising his hand slightly as he spoke, a gesture similar to the thrusting movement made popular by John F. Kennedy.

"I am well aware that the presidency is an office that you have sought for several years, and I assure you it is worth the effort."

Again, Thomas nodded.

Askins continued, "I am also aware, that the person I choose to endorse is being handed the key to the presidency. That is an awesome responsibility, and I do not take it lightly."

Thomas leaned forward in his chair, mouth slightly open. He wanted the president to get to the point. He disliked his habit of pausing every few sentences—it was worse than his own southern drawl. There was no need for him to respond. It would merely lengthen the time it took Askins to reach his main point. Thomas shifted in his chair, waiting.

"Whoever I nominate for that position will have a great advantage over the other candidates. And nominating someone will constitute an endorsement. I'm trying not to fall into that trap . . . "

"I understand your concern, but . . . "

Askins glared at the senator, a silent instruction to remain quiet until he was finished speaking.

Bastard, Thomas thought. He wasn't even going to allow him

the common courtesy of pleading his case. Of course, they had talked on the subject before, but this was going to be where the points were counted, the decisions made. All the rest was simply foreplay; this was the real thing. And this bastard wasn't going to let him say anything. And anything he said later would be too late. Again, Thomas opened his mouth to speak.

Askins responded instantly. "For once in your life, Andrew, shut your mouth and listen." The president smiled, attempting to defuse the tension. Knowing he had succeeded in silencing Thomas, Askins paused for a few moments, collecting his thoughts. Then, in an attempt to make the bitter pill easier to swallow, he went on to explain the logic behind the decision. He relayed, almost verbatim, the scenario outlined by Peter Fitzsimmons, emphasizing how essential it was to nominate someone without presidential ambitions; that the nominee must also be of an age that made thoughts of future presidential ambition virtually impossible; that the person be highly respected so that confirmation would be assured; and, be willing to support the president's policies.

Thomas listened intently.

"Now, Senator, I'd like your opinion. What would your position be?"

Now, it was Askins's turn to wait. He needed Thomas's support if he was going to complete his nuclear legislation before leaving office, and that was only ten months away. .

Thomas cleared his throat, then began. "I follow your logic . . . but I do not agree with it. I think this country will be placed in great turmoil with the nomination of an obvious caretaker vice president. I concede that you are a popular man, and that your choice will have a strong impact on the outcome of the election in November. But to appoint a *caretaker* . . . I cannot agree with such a move . . . "

Interrupting, the president countered, "Senator, I need your support on this." Rising from behind his desk, he said his words slow and deliberate, "If you announce publicly that you are against it—a caretaker vice president—and do not support the nomination in the Senate, there is going to be trouble. We are both going to have trouble." He moved around the desk, never taking his eyes off Thomas's face. "You want to be president. But if I come out for someone else in November . . . someone not even in the forefront . . . you don't stand a chance in hell of winning the election. The person I support may not win, but *you* won't win. And, that's what you are after—to win."

Askins had reached the front of the desk, his eyes still on Thomas. "If we do it my way, I will remain neutral. I don't plan on giving my support to anyone. That will help you, Senator." He leaned forward. "However, I'll expect you to use your influence to promote my policies, especially those in the Middle East."

"Just whom have you chosen to nominate?" Thomas asked, hesitantly. He did not really wish or need to hear the name; he already knew it. He prided himself on being aware of everything that went on in Washington, even before it happened.

"Well, senator, I don't really believe someone from the hill would be a wise choice. Nor do I believe it would be an intelligent move, politically speaking, to nominate someone from outside the Washington circle. That really leaves me with only one choice." He paused to allow the information to sink in. He was well aware that Thomas's network of contacts had already supplied him with the name. What Askins desired was acceptance. For now. He watched as Thomas sat there, his granite-hard face, the cruel steel blue eyes expressionless. Askins did not like what he saw.

Thomas made no comment.

"I've decided to nominate the Secretary of Defense, Clayton Adams," came the president's final words.

Thomas remained impassive.

It was all a game, a preposterous, ridiculous game. Nevertheless, the president breathed a silent sigh of relief. It was over. He had officially told the man face-to-face that he was not going to nominate him for the vice presidency. Thomas was one of the most powerful men on the hill, and the one with the greatest interest in the presidency. It would be a tough fight if Askins was unable to retain Thomas's support for his nuclear strategy. There were too many people already lining up behind the coalition to freeze nuclear weapons. Just that morning, the Russians had fired another salvo in their assault on his policies. The attack had been published in the *Washington Post*. He was sure they had published it as a personal affront. He had read it seven times, and knew it by heart.

NUCLEAR WARNING

Today the Kremlin issued a strong warning to the United States, denouncing the stationing of medium-range nuclear weapons in the Sinai. Moscow also gave its clearest indication, to date, that Soviet missiles might be deployed in Cuba if such actions are taken. Mikhail Depopolov, in a rare Soviet news conference, announced that such a move would be a serious tactical error. He said, "The leadership in the United States entertain the illusion they are invulnerable. They still believe the old adage about being an island fortress. However, with today's weapons, distances must be evaluated differently. Nuclear weapons know no range."

A great way to start the day. Quickly, Askins's thoughts returned to the man before him. Thomas still had neither moved, nor spoken. But behind the calm, silent exterior he knew there was intense turmoil. Thomas was holding an internal debate concerning the president's position. Would he support him or would he oppose the nomination and his nuclear policy? As the president leaned silently against his desk, his only thought was his need for Thomas's support. It was essential to achieving his goal of placing nuclear weapons in the Sinai; the only way to bring about a lasting peace in that area of the world. However, Askins was not willing to offer the vice presidency to obtain that support.

Thomas opened his mouth as if to speak, but did not. He had not come to his decision—yet. Askins was willing to give him time. Any attempt to rush him might backfire. Political decisions were seldom made in anger, and when they were, the consequences were often far worse. Politics did indeed make strange bedfellows.

Finally the senator spoke. "Mr. President, you are aware of my feelings. As you've said, I've been after your job for a long time." Thomas stopped speaking. It was, again, his turn to fill the air with anticipation. Seconds passed. "But you've outlined your proposal to me in a very logical fashion, and I must accept the wishes of my president. Although I do not always agree with them," he added, showing a thin-lipped smile.

Askins remained expressionless.

"I've always stood behind this nation," the senator continued in a quiet voice. "I believe in this country. I feel we should maintain a strong image abroad and a solid economy at home. For these reasons alone, I am going to support you."

Again, Thomas stopped; Askins waited.

"When I return to my office, I am going to have my staff begin work on the announcement of my candidacy. The announcement should be released to the press sometime within the next few days." He looked smug and confident, the prior doubts gone completely. He had set his course.

Askins returned the look, knowing it was not the time to demonstrate any lack of confidence on his part. He had figuratively looked the man in the eye and watched him blink. He was actually going along with him. And now that he finally had the upper hand, he had no intention of letting it slip away. Control of the conversation was essential.

"I'm relieved at your decision, Andrew," Askins responded, attempting to sound as friendly as possible. "Personally, I'm getting too old to start a new political battle. And I knew, in the end, you would stand behind your country . . . I've always said that your country came first in your eyes." Almost as an afterthought, he added, "By the way, Senator, I have a two o'clock news conference scheduled to announce Secretary Adams's nomination. I hope you approve."

Thomas nodded. "I have no objections."

After Thomas departed, the president returned to the high-backed chair behind his desk. The need for the close, intimate, persuasive position was over; the battle had been fought and won. What he had believed would become a tension-filled meeting, had turned out to be a relatively easily won concession. Apparently, Thomas had made up his mind to concede prior to arriving. The rest was just for show. The whole thing had gone like it would have in the old days. He still had the knack.

Success raised his spirits. But, the feeling did not last long, his mind quickly turned to other concerns. For now, Thomas was in the past. Where the hell was Crosby? he wondered; it had been three days since he sat here in the Oval Office telling his story, and no word since. He had talked with Peter, who hadn't heard from Crosby either. Askins prayed that nothing drastic had happened.

Crosby *had* to be wrong. It had been nothing more than a simple plane crash—a mechanical malfunction. The initial report from the FBI, released to the press, had said as much. Crosby was not going to discover anything new; there was *nothing* to discover. Askins did not wish to dwell on the implications if a murder had actually taken place. There were too many terrorists, and if it came out that they had succeeded in killing the vice president of the United States, they would run rampant. Although he had made some progress in reducing terrorist activities and organizations, he had not come close to eliminating them. Far too many countries were willing to use terrorism to promote their policies until death and destruction had become a way of life. If Carlson had been murdered, it could get decidedly worse. When the leader of a nation, such as Qaddafi, called for revolution and the death of other world leaders, and it happened, others would be encouraged to try even greater acts of terrorism. And Askins's purpose had been to discourage them.

If he had known about Qaddafi's interview with that Anderson woman, and what Qaddafi was going to say, he'd have done everything in his power to keep the interview from airing. Shannon Anderson was not high on his list of beautiful people. She would never be allowed to interview him. The president caught himself. He had been talking aloud. He had to put the

111

whole thing out of his mind and get on to the daily functions of government—his projects.

As on all previous occasions, the phone rang only once, the time of the call having been preset. The words were few on both sides. They were powerful.

"Deathblow," came the single word from the man answering the call.

"The subject is aboard Delta flight four twenty-six from Dallas to Washington. Expected time of arrival, nine-fifteen this evening. Any further instructions?" The voice was matter-of-fact, expecting no other conversation. There was none.

A simple reply was spoken softly into the receiver. "Bring him in."

CHAPTER 15

The warm shower had helped calm Shannon's frayed nerves. She was still angry and afraid, but not to the same degree she had been only an hour before. The hot spray had succeeded in relaxing her tight muscles. With the tension washed from her system, she could now sit down and think. But first, what she really needed was a drink. With only a towel covering her she made her way through the apartment to the bar. In spite of her lingering fear, she experienced a sense of pleasure as she walked through the apartment. It had cost her a small fortune, but before moving in, she'd had it totally redecorated. She had wanted something that was distinctively hers. So, she created it.

Each time she walked barefoot through the rooms, she reveled in the feel of the soft, shaggy, gray carpet. It reminded her of home, when she was a child. On summer mornings, she used to walk barefoot through the little meadow behind her parents' house, the soft grass caressing her feet. Her past seemed strange now; to go barefoot in the meadow, she had had to slip by her father. He had been adamant about not permitting young ladies to run around barefoot, especially in public. To get caught doing so resulted in harsh words or, on some occasions, even a spanking. He wanted her to be so perfect, and she'd tried so hard.

The apartment always evoked strong feelings of home, in Mississippi. But yet, it was so different. The white leather sofas, with the chrome and glass accessories gave the room a modern look—a sharp contrast from Mississippi, where everything was so tied to the past. One of her friends from back home who had come to visit her had described it as antiseptic. But Shannon liked it. And *that* was what counted. The frantic activity of New York was nothing like the South, and the people were so different. Southerners even moved at a much slower pace. Shannon often thought they were so much more real, so much more sincere than Northerners; they were more concerned with their fellow man—and woman. If she had it all to do over again, she would still choose Mississippi as the place of her birth—the charm, the tradition, the history. It had been like living a dream. That feeling had lasted all through college. Even finding a job had been easy. The combination of high academic standing and her good looks—to say nothing of her parents' connections, had helped her land a high-paying television news job.

Shannon reached the white oak bar, her hand going straight to the bottle of Chivas. She was grateful that she could drink and eat without experiencing a weight problem. Of course, she gained weight when she binged—just like everyone else—but she had no trouble losing it. She mixed a Chivas and water, sat down on the sofa, and drew her legs up under her. Curled up comfortably with a drink in hand she felt safe. Perhaps it was from thinking about home, she thought. Her confidence was returning. It was time to decide what must be done.

She had no way of determining the identity of the men who had followed her home. All she could hope was that they were not in the building. Even if they were, the security was good. Or, it was supposed to be, she thought. Anyway, she was safe for the time being. But how was she going to leave for work in the morning? Surely, they would be waiting.

The horror of the experience kept returning, making concentration impossible. Terrifying pictures of what might have happened, had she been caught, flashed repeatedly through her mind. She wasn't sure how much more she was willing to take. She had already done things, like attacking the parked car, that she had not thought herself capable of. Her parents would have been shocked by her behavior. Her father had wanted her to be a boy, but he had raised her as a lady, and ladies did not do such things.

Shannon tried to rid her mind of the images, a tightness was

114

beginning to grip her chest. Again, control was slipping away, the feeling of dread threatening to overwhelm her.

She took a long drink of scotch, followed by several deep breaths, and the tightness eased, the fear subsiding with it. She must remain calm. She had been through too much, and she wasn't going to be any good to herself or anyone else if she didn't stay calm, and think. The idea of placing a transatlantic call to Qaddafi suddenly came to her, and just as quickly it was rejected. If, indeed, he had *sent* those people . . . he wouldn't admit it to her. He would just be nice . . . and sweet . . . and she would believe exactly what he told her, and those men outside would eventually kill her.

Well it wasn't going to happen that way she decided, taking another long swallow. The glass was empty. She got up and mixed another Chivas and water, drinking it straight down, barely tasting the strong liquor. She poured another.

Back to the sofa; back to her position of safety. The rapid intake of alcohol began to have its effect. The fingers of her right hand holding the drink were insensitive to the cold glass. Her lips tingled. A numbness centered in her chest and spread throughout her body, down to her toes. Alcohol would help calm your nerves, an inner voice seemed to be whispering.

For a long time, she sat there, slowly sipping her drink, staring across the room. She was convinced she needed help. She was in over her head, but who could she turn to? Who could she call? If she called the police, they would think she was paranoid. There was nothing she could prove. Nothing had really happened. Maybe she *was* paranoid! No one would have reason to have her followed, and the more she thought—and drank—the more she understood that it was impossible for anyone to know she had overheard Qaddafi and Jadallah.

Before she had left, she had spoken with Jadallah and the president, both on a formal level. The presence of their staff had prohibited any personal goodbyes. And, neither had given the slightest indication that anything was amiss. They had been extremely polite. Then who was following her? *Why* were they following her?

It was time for another drink, she thought. As before, she

115

drank the first drink straight down. Then she poured another. By then the alcohol had taken its full effect. Returning to the sofa, she heard a voice. It sounded far away, muffled. Wherever it was coming from, it was difficult to focus in on. She listened—it stopped. Then it started again. Finally, she realized the voice was her own. She had been talking out loud, saying someone's name. "Clark Welch."

The fog began to clear, as if a soft light had been switched on. Maybe there *was* something she could do to get help.

"That son of a bitch Clark Welch would help," Shannon declared directly to a rubber plant on the table beside her. He was a good man. She could definitely call him for help. Under that hard crust there was a soft, caring gentleman. He had always helped; he would do anything for her.

Shannon took her drink with her into the bedroom and sat down on the bed beside the phone. From the drawer of her vanity, she withdrew an address book. With some difficulty, she thumbed through the pages.

"Ah!" she rejoiced aloud, attempting to place her finger under Welch's name. "ere it is," she stammered.

Slowly, careful to maintain her balance, she reached for the phone and punched out the numbers. She was surprised at the difficulty she had in pushing the correct numbers; they seemed to move as her fingers sought them out.

After several rings, a sleep-filled voice answered. "What!" It was not a question.

"Do ya always answer yer phone 'at way?" she slurred.

"Who is this?"

"Shannon. Who ya think it is?"

"Shannon?" he replied, disbelief evident in his voice. He did not speak immediately. "Have you been drinking?"

"A course, I 'en drinkin'. I think . . . I might be drunk!"

"What's wrong, Honey?" Welch responded in a voice that rang with authority and concern.

"I need . . . some 'elp . . . , Clark," Shannon said slowly, making a concentrated effort to enunciate clearly.

"What kind of help?"

116

"I need ta talk ta ya." Her voice again slurring. "Somethin's very wrong. Someone's tryin' ta kill me."

Welch did not reply.

"Clark?"

"Are you sure the alcohol hasn't gotten to you? This sounds like some prank you'd pull."

The comment irritated her, shocking her into a resemblance of soberness. "This *isn't* a prank. I need help. Are you going to help me or not?"

"Of course, I'm going to help!" Again, the concern was evident. "But, I need to know what's wrong."

"I can't talk to ya over the phone. It's just too important. I've got to meet ya somewhere."

Welch looked at the clock beside his bed for the first time since answering the call. Two in the morning. "Why don't we meet at the office in an hour," he suggested.

"Ok," Shannon replied quickly. Then she remembered the car parked in front of her building, and the occupants who were undoubtedly waiting for her. "I can't do that . . . could you meet me here, Clark . . . at my apartment? Soon?"

Welch hesitated for a moment, then agreed. Both hung up, neither saying goodbye. Welch got quickly out of bed and dressed hurriedly. It was unlike her to drink, to excess anyway. Whatever was wrong, was serious.

In her apartment, Shannon sat back, sipping her drink.

Someone was pounding on the side of her head; the sound echoed from side to side. It was those men. They were back. They had somehow broken into her apartment while she slept. Again the pounding.

Shannon stirred; the motion caused some of the cobwebs to clear. No one was hitting her. She had simply fallen asleep while waiting for Clark to arrive. The pounding was repeated.

Shannon forced herself to concentrate on the sound. Someone was at the front door—knocking. It must be Clark. She stood, steadied herself, and staggered into the living room.

"Who's there?" She yelled.

117

"Clark," came the voice from the other side of the door. "How many people are you expecting?"

A feeling of relief swept over her, a feeling so strong that even the effects of the alcohol were dimmed. She covered the remaining distance to the door in two long-legged leaps. Her fingers tore at the triple locks. When she finally got it open, she threw herself into his arms.

"Wooo, Honey!" he exclaimed, catching her.

"I'm so glad you're here!" she gasped. After a few seconds, she let go of him and stepped back into the room. "Come in and close the door."

As he entered, she looked both ways down the hall. No one was in sight. He closed the door, and relocked it. Then he turned to her and said, "What's the problem, Shannon? I . . . ." He stopped, and stared at her. His steady gaze forced her to look down at herself. She began to blush. She had forgotten to dress. All that covered her was a bath towel.

"Excuse me," she gasped and walked unsteadily from the room. "I'll be back in a minute," she added at the bedroom door.

Welch continued to stare at the bedroom door. What a sight! he thought. She sure was something. He looked around him. He had never been inside Shannon's apartment. He *had* given her lifts home when some of the staff got together after work for drinks, but she had never invited him up. Clark wasn't sure he would have come even if he had been invited. It wasn't a good idea to get too close to your employees. But this was different—she was frightened. She needed help.

His eyes surveyed the room. Nice, he thought. He would have guessed she had taste; it showed in her clothes and the way she wore her hair and makeup—just enough to accentuate her natural beauty. His gaze settled on the bar across the room from the doorway, where he still stood, too startled by Shannon's appearance to proceed into the room. Anyone shaken out of a sound sleep at two in the morning deserved a drink, he decided.

Just as he'd finished fixing himself a double, Shannon returned. She was now dressed in blue jeans and a sweat shirt. Her movements were still a bit unsteady, and her hair was stringy and matted from having failed to comb it after her shower. Nevertheless, she looked beautiful. She *needed* to be taken care of.

Welch motioned her toward the sofa. "Sit down, Honey, and tell me what this is all about."

Shannon did as directed.

"I'd ask if you wanted a drink, but from the sound of your voice over the phone, I'd say you've had enough."

He leaned back on the sofa and waited, as Shannon told her story. It took her an hour to recount the circumstances that had prompted her late night call. She began with her trip to Libya and ended when she arrived home that evening, leaving out only the details of what she had overheard. All Clark needed to know was that the information involved the security of the United States. She did tell him she believed it was essential for someone in the government to be told, but she was not sure who to contact, or how much to tell them. She also apprised him of her fear that if she told anyone, she would be killed. Then she realized that the issue had been settled anyway, with the presence of the men outside. They had been sent to kill her, regardless.

A small twinge of guilt ticked at her stomach. She didn't like keeping information from him. He was going to help her. Shannon reasoned that the little she held back had no bearing on the outcome. Clark could help her decide what to do, and how best to do it, without having to know every detail.

For most of the time, Welch simply sat back and listened, half disbelieving. He kept thinking that if he had not known Shannon as well as he did, he would chalk the whole story up to the drinking and go home. But he had never known Shannon to lie about anything.

Welch sipped his drink. He could think of no reason for her to concoct such a story, and he was certain she had not wanted to lure him to her apartment in the middle of the night. With her looks she could have anyone she desired. She sure didn't need a fifty-five year old has-been like himself. No, something as absurd as this had to be true. His thoughts were interrupted by her question.

119

"Did you see anybody when you came in? Was there anything suspicious on the street?" Even Shannon didn't really know what she meant by "anything suspicious," but she had to ask.

Welch thought for a moment before answering. "No. But then, I wasn't looking for anything. Or, anyone."

"What am I going to do, Clark!" she cried, holding her head in her hands. He didn't like what he was seeing. He preferred the tough girl he saw at the office. That one was willing to do anything to get a story; she did not cry.

"Let me think for a few minutes," he said, rising from the sofa. "You need a drink." It was more of a command.

"Yes, I think I could use one."

Welch looked around for her glass, but didn't see it, and she didn't seem inclined to tell him. He took the remains of his drink from the coffee table, and went to the bar, thinking as he went that he would get her a new one. It was silly to waste time thinking about such a simple thing, but his mind did not want to dwell on what she had told him. The story was just too unbelievable. As he fixed the two drinks, he thought how un- usual it was for a woman to drink scotch. Everytime she ordered a drink at a staff get together, it surprised him. Scotch was a man's drink. How things had changed. In the old days he might be in a woman's apartment in the middle of the night mixing drinks, but he sure wouldn't be listening to tales of interna- tional intrigue.

Handing Shannon a full glass, he said, "I'm not exactly sure what we should do, but we do need to get in touch with someone from the government. And that *someone* is going to have to be pretty important. We've got to think this thing through."

They sat in silence, Welch trying to formulate a plan, Shan- non, again assessing her situation.

"Where's the phone, Honey?"

"Phone?"

"Yes. You know, the thing you hold to your ear and talk into," he said smiling, but Shannon did not reciprocate. "I need to make a call. I've got an idea."

"Over there." She pointed to a phone near the bar.

Not really knowing what he was going to say, or even more

importantly, what he wasn't going to say, Clark walked over to the phone. As he did so, he removed an address book from his inside coat pocket, and located the home number of one of CBS's attorneys. Forrest Robertson acted as liaison with the government on sensitive stories involving national security. Welch was positive he could obtain the name and number of someone high enough in the vast governmental hierarchy to guarantee action. Although Shannon hadn't given him the specific details, he was certain it was too important to be delayed or possibly buried in bureaucracy. He didn't want the name of some flunky.

Glancing at his watch, he saw it was not quite four. He regretted having to call at that hour, but speed was essential. If Shannon was right, it might indeed be a matter of life or death.

Within five minutes, he returned to his seat on the sofa beside her. She had not moved. On a slip of paper torn from his address book was the name of a man in Washington they could call. Welch's friend in the legal department hadn't been especially pleased to hear from him at such an early hour, but he had been cooperative. There had been few questions, which Welch appreciated. All he had been required to say was that the matter was confidential and should remain so. His friend had agreed.

"Honey, I got the name of a man in Washington we can call. He will help," Welch said, handing her the slip of paper. "But we're not going to be able to get hold of him until . . . probably eight o'clock. So, why don't you go in and get some sleep. I'll sack out here on the sofa."

"That sounds like a good idea . . . this has been a *long* day."

Without taking the time to remove her jeans or sweat shirt, Shannon slid between the sheets of her bed. The soft mattress felt good under her tired body, and the satin sheets were comforting. She prayed she would go right to sleep, but sleep did not come. Images of Qaddafi on top of her, loving her, kept entering her mind. These images were followed by feelings of guilt—confused, distorted images, flashing in and out of her mind's eye. How could she tell the United States government he was plotting to kill the president. Surely, she had misunderstood. She was confused. She *had* to have misunderstood; but she *couldn't* have misunderstood. The inner dialogue replayed itself in her head. She would never forget the words. *"He must be shot! Everyone around him must be shot! But what will be the reaction of the new American president?"*

The words were erased by another image—Qaddafi smiling; his mouth smiling; his eyes smiling. He was loving her. The idea was impossible to cast off. But he had used her. He had used her television interview. He used everything and everyone. If she could just maintain that attitude, Shannon was sure it would be easier to tell her story. There would even be satisfaction in being the one to overturn his plot. She would use *him*. With that thought, the fear and images were dispelled, and exhaustion took over. She fell into a deep, dreamless sleep.

Half awake, Welch heard a soft tapping on the apartment door. He waited several seconds before deciding to act. There was no evidence of movement from the bedroom. Evidently, the knocking was too light for Shannon to have heard, or her sleep too deep. If he had been through what she had, he would probably sleep through a tornado, he thought. The tapping came again.

Rising, Welch shook the effect of the alcohol from his brain. Making his way through the darkness to the door, he wondered who could be visiting at such a late hour. Possibly Shannon had called someone else and forgotten to tell him. He stopped.

"Who is it?"

"Police," came the muffled reply.

Shannon *had* called someone else. What was he going to say to them? Their involvement would only complicate the issue. The first thing that needed to be done was to talk with the man whose name he had given Shannon. He'd say something to get rid of them. Maybe he could tell them she had been drunk when she made the call. That *would* be the truth.

Welch opened the locks hurriedly, not wanting the officers to become impatient and ask more questions than were necessary. What a city—people had to barricade themselves in their own apartments. It was ridiculous. Finally, he opened the door. There were two men dressed in suits, detectives, plainclothesmen, he thought. The man on his right had his hand outstretched; he was smiling. As Welch reached out to take the hand, he saw the gun, but it was too late. It was in the outstretched hand, aimed at his chest. Before he could react, the gun exploded. In the narrow hallway, the sound was deafening. It shook the door, the walls, the very air around them. The impact of the bullet propelled him back into the room. For a moment, he hung on the edge of a chair, then collapsed to the floor.

In the bedroom, Shannon was awakened by the sound of Welch calling out to someone. She had been unable to hear the reply, but instinct told her whoever was at the door meant them harm. Jumping to her feet, she had rushed to the bedroom door, hoping to stop Welch from letting anyone into the apartment. Too late. She heard the apartment door being opened. There was no need to wait and see who was on the other side. Shannon knew. Instantly, she slammed the bedroom door and locked it. For the second time that night, Shannon Anderson found herself with her back against a door—a very flimsy door. Again she felt the tightening in her chest, the sickening feeling in her stomach.

The explosion made her jump. Her skin crawled. It had finally happened. They had killed someone. Clark Welch. And she was next. But she wasn't going to let them get to her—not without a fight. Shannon's eyes shot around the room in search of something she could use to defend herself. Nothing. Those men were coming for her. Any second they would be breaking down the door. Her eyes came to rest on the only window in the room. The fire escape. She had always hated it in the past. The rusty, archaic monstrosity ruined an otherwise excellent view of the city. But suddenly it was her only chance to escape. She ran to the window and raised it as quietly as possible. Easing herself outside onto the small, black platform, she felt the cold, metal grating against her bare feet. Standing on the fire escape, she turned and without thinking, closed the window

123

before she heard the first sounds at the bedroom door. She began to run down the steep steps, two at a time. Then came two shots in rapid succession. The lock was being shot off her door.

By the time she had descended four of the eight stories, the men had gained entrance to the bedroom. Thank God I closed the window, she said to herself. It'll give me time. She descended the last section of stairs, and felt the pavement under her feet. She turned east, running wildly, not sure where she was going, only knowing she needed to get away before the window opened and they started shooting. She turned onto Sixty-Fifth Street a half-second before the window was thrown open.

On Sixty-Fifth Street, she hesitated, uncertain of her next move. Surely, the men would come after her. A cab! She could take a cab to a hotel. They wouldn't look for her in a hotel. They would expect her to go to a friend's.

She began walking, hoping to go unnoticed. There might be others, waiting for her on the street, but they would expect a hysterical, running woman. For the first time, she became aware that she was barefoot, but she still did not feel the cold pavement. Her only thoughts were to thank God that she had been too tired to remove her clothes before going to bed. She walked almost three blocks before a cab finally appeared.

"Where to, lady?" the cabbie asked as she climbed into the back seat. It was obvious he had noticed her bare feet and sloppy dress, especially her hair.

"The Marriot," she replied on impulse. That was as good as anywhere else, she thought.

The cabbie looked questioningly at her in the rearview mirror, but he only said, "Any particular one?"

"In Queens," she shot back. "The one near JFK." That should be far enough away.

"That's a long ride, lady."

Shannon did not answer. There had been three shots. That left little doubt that Clark was dead. The idea of his dying because he had been kind enough to come to a woman in trouble brought tears flooding from her eyes. She had been so concerned with her own safety, she hadn't had time to think about Clark.

After the cab had gone a few miles, she began to regain her composure. She had to defend herself. And suddenly she was angry again. She wanted to fight back.

CHAPTER 16

The radio alarm on the table beside the bed went off on schedule, eleven-thirty. Crosby liked to be awakened by the alarm. His first wife had told him he was crazy; an alarm was a shock to the nervous system, she had said; music awakened you gently. But he liked to be jarred from sleep, the "kick-start" helped him charge through the day. It got his heart pumping quickly.

Crosby stretched his entire body, feeling more rested than he had expected. His body felt refreshed. The previous three days had taken their toll. When he arrived home, late last night, he had been exhausted. Both of his legs and his right arm ached from the strain on the mountain, but that was expected. He had allowed his muscles to deteriorate. While in Aspen, he had made a mental note to start a regular exercise program. Maybe he would join one of those health clubs, play some racquetball—like many of the others around Washington. But that was going to have to wait—first things first.

It had been after midnight before Crosby had retrieved his car from the airport parking lot at Washington National. His plane had landed before ten, but for over two hours he had invented reasons to stay around the airport. The time had been spent observing the people around him, those waiting in lines, reading newspapers, loitering. After the first hour, he had been certain that no one was watching him. But he stayed a second hour. Finally, he had been satisfied and gone to his car, and home.

The White House, particularly Peter Fitzsimmons, had no way of knowing he was in town. He decided to use the opportunity to catch up on his sleep before contacting the office.

126

Now, however, it was time to call in and notify the president of his findings, and his suspicions. He dialed the familiar number, somewhat relieved that his assignment had come to an end. It had been "fun," but he was glad the investigation could be turned back to the FBI. It was their job.

"Fitzsimmons," came the standard response. Peter's idea of efficiency often bordered on rudeness.

"Allen Crosby," he replied, matching the other man's curtness.

The next words he heard shocked him, especially their intensity. "Where the hell have you been?"

"I'm here in Washington . . . . Why?"

"We've been wondering if something had happened to you. That's why!"

Crosby could not understand why Peter was angry. There had been no orders for him to check in, periodically or otherwise. Why was Fitzsimmons so concerned with his whereabouts? Did *Peter* have men looking for him? Someone undoubtedly did, and that person wasn't exactly friendly.

"What could have happened to me, Peter? I was only on a routine investigation."

Fitzsimmons ignored the question. "Have you been in touch with your secretary?"

"No. You're the first one I've called. No one else even knows I'm in town."

"Then you haven't heard."

"Heard what, Peter?"

"I think you need to come in and talk."

"Heard what?"

"You had better come in, Allen. Everything will be all right if we can talk."

"Why don't you tell me what's wrong, Peter? I can tell something has got you upset," Crosby ventured, keeping his voice calm.

Silence.

Finally. "Allen, you have to come down here . . . to the White House . . . my office. Now." The voice was commanding. He was pulling rank.

"Maybe we could meet somewhere," Crosby countered, his suspicion growing. "What's the rush for me to come in?"

"What's the rush?" Fitzsimmons repeated, his voice rising. "You're conducting an investigation for the president of the United States . . . . You go to Aspen and leave a body behind . . . . You tell *me* what's going on!"

Crosby decided to feign ignorance, stalling for time. How did Fitzsimmons know there was a dead body in Colorado? How much did Fitzsimmons know? Was he more involved than Crosby had been led to believe?

"Dead body?"

"Yes, dead body. Denton, over at the FBI, gave me a call. Apparently there is a new body at the crash site. He got a call from some helicopter service; the one that helped in the removal of the original bodies. They found it yesterday . . . . "

"What were they doing at the crash site?"

"The owner of the service decided to go up and check after a free-spending tourist paid to be taken up there just to take pictures. He thought the man was crazy; acted crazy; talked crazy. And I assume you were the tourist."

"I *was* the tourist."

"Then, who the hell is the dead man?"

"I was hoping you could tell me," Crosby said lamely. "Have you checked on the identity . . . fingerprints?"

"Not yet, there hasn't been time. The body is being shipped . . . under guard . . . in the strictest confidence." A pause. "What happened up there?"

"Someone tried to kill me," Crosby said flatly, and waited for Fitzsimmons's reaction.

"Are you sure?"

What a stupid question, he thought. "Peter, let me assure you, when someone is trying to kill you, you know it."

"I suppose so." Fitzsimmons replied flatly.

Fitzsimmons was too remote, too cold, too detached. Crosby did not like that.

" . . . Allen?" Fitzsimmons had been talking, but Crosby had not heard. "When are you coming over to see me?"

There it was again, that demand to return; come in from the

field. They always wanted him to come in. Why was Fitzsimmons so worried about him coming in?

"I . . . I'm not sure, Peter," Crosby found himself saying. There was new input that needed to be examined. He couldn't be too cautious. Someone had given the details of his movements to the assassin in Colorado. "Did you tell anyone I was going to Colorado . . . about the investigation?"

"No. Of course not. The president ordered it to remain secret. No one knows."

Was there something in Fitzsimmons's voice, something that shouldn't be there? Or was *he* just a little strung out? It had been a long time since anyone had tried to kill him—maybe he was overreacting. For the first time in the conversation, Crosby lost his temper.

"Someone sure as hell knows or there wouldn't be a dead body on its way back from Aspen."

"Calm down," Fitzsimmons said, lowering the volume of his voice.

"You've got a lot of nerve . . . telling me to calm down. I'm the one some asshole tried to kill." What was he saying? He was losing control. He was not even sure the man knew his agenda. It was just as likely that the man had followed him from Carlson's house.

The outburst surprised Fitzsimmons. Maybe a change of subject would be advisable, Peter thought. "Were you able to find anything that might help the investigation? Was Carlson killed?"

"I'm sure he was assassinated. At least, the plane crash was no accident . . . . "

"How do you know?"

"The presence of the assassin confirms that! And I found something that belonged to Carlson."

"What?" Fitzsimmons almost yelled.

That voice again, the extra degree of concern. He decided to let the issue dangle. It was his turn to ignore a direct question. "Have you spoken with the president?" Crosby asked.

"I haven't had a chance to tell him anything. He's been too

129

involved with the nomination of Secretary Adams and his Mid-eastern stategy. He doesn't know abut the man you killed."

Crosby had seen the headlines about Adams in a newspaper at the airport. A good choice, he had thought at the time. He turned his attention back to Fitzsimmons. "I want the president informed."

"If it's okay with you, Allen, I think we should keep this between us for a couple of days . . . "

"It's not okay. I want him told!" Crosby was now shouting, the comment having caused his suspicions to soar.

With that Fitzsimmons had had enough. "Listen, Allen, you sound very upset. Why don't you come in to your office and we'll discuss what you've got. Maybe we should get the FBI involved—they're involved now—with that body."

Crosby fell silent again. Was Peter considering taking him off the investigation? Was he trying to cover up something? Crosby felt the frustration, the anxiety pressing in on him.

"I don't understand you, Peter," he said bluntly. "*I* uncovered this thing, and *I'm* acting on it . . . under the direction of the president. Now, it seems you're trying to divert my efforts . . . "

"No. Don't get the wrong impression," Fitzsimmons interrupted. "I just feel we should keep it quiet . . . you know, for political reasons."

"No. I don't know . . . "

Before Crosby could continue, Fitzsimmons cut in, the tone of authority increasing. "Allen, I'm going to send some people out to pick you up. They'll be there in about thirty minutes. You just wait for them!"

Crosby slammed the phone into its cradle, cracking the receiver. After a second's hesitation, he vaulted from his bed, ran to the closet and threw on some clothes. Grabbing a tennis bag, he quickly filled it with extra clothing. Packed, he hurried to the library, went straight to the safe, which like the gun cabinet, was concealed among the bookcases. Quickly he extracted large bundles of currency totalling sixty thousand dollars. In the field, immediate access to cash was an essential element of survival, and keeping some around was a habit he had been unable to break. The money had been placed in the safe right after the house had been completed. Up to that moment there had been no need for it. From behind a small door inside the safe, he removed a small plastic case containing several bank books. Each represented a savings account, each account located in a different country.

Halfway out the door, he stopped. He had almost made a potentially deadly mistake. With a renewed sense of urgency, he returned to the bedroom, strapped on his shoulder holster, adjusted the Smith & Wesson, and pulled on a light jacket for cover.

Not until he had reached the safety of the woods behind the house was he able to relax. He glanced at his watch. It had taken less than fifteen minutes to make his exit. It took only a second to assess the situation. He was directly behind the house, about one hundred feet from the rear door, barely ten feet inside the tree line. The woods bordered the house on three sides leaving only the street side open. The woods were dense enough to conceal anyone not wanting to be seen, and Crosby did not wish to be seen. But he did wish to place himself in the best possible vantage point to observe anyone approaching the house. That would be the east side, the one nearest the driveway. Anyone coming to "pick him up" would undoubtedly park in the driveway; the house sat too far back from the street to make roadside parking practical. Yes, that would give him a clear view.

He picked a spot from which he could see but not be seen. The only thing left to do was wait.

The wait was not long.

An unmarked car came racing down the street and turned into his driveway, coming to a halt no more than thirty yards from where he stood. He had an unobstructed view of the two occupants. Neither man was familiar. They emerged from the car, weapons drawn, intent on reaching the front door as fast as possible. It was obvious they were professionals—the way they moved, the way they carried themselves, the cut of their clothes. It all fit a pattern. These men were not with the government—not the United States government.

When the two were within ten feet of his door, Crosby turned

131

away; he had seen enough. He had found the leak. The surveillance had not been picked up at Carlson's house or anywhere else; it had been with him from the start. But he needed proof. A burned-out, ex-CIA agent did not start throwing accusations at the chief of staff without concrete evidence.

The first thing he had to do was to uncover the country involved. Someone of substantial power had to be behind the assassination of a vice president. Fitzsimmons was not acting alone; he was not the type to initiate the orders. And he had nothing to gain. Fitzsimmons was no more than a mole—placed in a high government position.

Even before he left for Colorado, he had called Combs at the CIA. He needed details on the plane crash, and now it was essential that he speak to Combs before the word was out on him. Fitzsimmons could be counted on to alert the intelligence community that he had gone over the edge or over to the other side—whoever *they* were this week. After that, he would be sanctioned, terminated. He quickened his pace.

Crosby sat alone at the rear of the small diner. He had just finished his third cup of coffee; he did not feel like eating. But having made the mistake of mentioning to the waitress that he had not eaten breakfast or lunch, she pressed him to order more than coffee. She was evidently the motherly type. He had chosen the diner not for the quality of its food, which he doubted, but, for its appearance. The lettering on the window had all but disappeared; a neon sign above the door flickered, crying out for repair. The torn seat covers, the cigarette burns—he had made a good choice. It was unlikely that anyone he knew would be coming in for a meal. Maybe no one came in for meals; the place was practically deserted. He was able to select a booth at the rear. From there he could observe anyone entering from either the front door or the door to the kitchen. He wasn't expecting anyone, but he could never be too careful.

He had been sitting in the booth drinking coffee for over an hour. He was in no hurry. He had arranged a meeting with Jerry Combs for nine that evening, and it was only four in the afternoon. Four hours had passed since he'd been in the woods watching the two assassins Fitzsimmons had sent to pick him up. Crosby had thought it best not to mention his troubles to Combs when he had phoned him earlier. Besides, it had not been necessary. Either Crosby had moved too fast, or Fitzsimmons had moved slower than he should have. No order to sanction had been issued. His identification, his clearances, had still been intact when he spoke with Combs.

He had expressed surprise that the call had not come a couple of days earlier. Crosby's original call had hinted at urgency, and to accommodate him, Combs had rushed to secure the information. When Crosby didn't call, Combs had wondered if something had happened to him. Why did everyone think something had happened to him? Was there something he didn't know?

According to Combs's findings, there was no doubt about the identity of the bodies. They were, indeed, the vice president and his staff, including the pilot, Tim Ranes. All records at the White House matched, teeth, bonebreaks, scars—everything. And the information supplied by the charter service at Stapleton confirmed that it was the body of their pilot. There was no longer the question of identity to consider; one less area of concern. And it confirmed Crosby's suspicions. Combs was also able to confirm that the cause of the crash had been engine failure. The pilot had been unable to make the plane climb as it approached the mountain. What Combs had added further dispelled his doubts.

The Company laboratory in Langley had uncovered evidence of foul play. Someone had tampered with both the altimeter and the navigational system, causing the pilot to fly off course, into higher mountains. To prevent the pilot from saving the plane at the last second with a sudden burst of power, a governor had been placed on the engine. One of the Company investigators had discovered a device that had been fused to the carburetor. It was extremely sophisticated, designed to activate at an altitude about seven thousand feet, thus preventing discovery during takeoff. That was what had prompted the frantic conversation between the pilot, Ranes, and the control

133

tower. There had been no advance warning. Although the pilot would have seen the mountain, he would not have panicked. From experience he would have known that he could pull up and go over it. But by the time he realized the plane was not responding, it was too late.

Crosby had asked Combs why that fact hadn't been discovered in the initial investigation, and Combs had explained that there had been no reason to look for it since all indications were that the crash had been an accident. The file indicated that a request had come from a very high level—they'd assumed the White House—that a speedy confirmation was all that was desired. Fitzsimmons obviously, but he still needed proof—something with his signature or a tape.

Combs had gone on to tell him about a call he had received early that morning from Shannon Anderson, the television newsperson. She had been upset—not hysterical—when she told him what had happened to her over the previous twenty-four hours. She had left out most of the details, but from what he could make out, a man had been killed in her apartment, and his murder had something to do with a plot to assassinate the president.

Crosby had asked if there'd been a recent assassination attempt that had been kept secret, or if Anderson could have been mistaken and been referring to the vice president instead. But Combs had made clear that Anderson was referring to a future attempt, and she had requested a meeting to fill in the details. That had set off the bells inside Crosby's head. A future assassination attempt on the president could easily be linked to the vice president's death. He needed to hear more. He had to get proof, and Shannon Anderson might just be the key.

Crosby and Combs had agreed to rendezvous an hour before the scheduled meeting with Anderson. That would allow him sufficient time to tell Combs what he wanted, and an opportunity to assure themselves that no one suspicious was loitering around the meeting area. At first, Combs's invitation to join the meeting had surprised Crosby, but the more he considered it, the more it made sense. Combs had always liked him. In the end, it had been Combs who had recommended Crosby for a position on the White House staff. And Combs knew that what Anderson had to say might benefit his investigation. Combs had always been a team player.

Sitting in the diner, Crosby was still unsure what he would tell his friend about the present situation. Prior to breaking off the conversation earlier that afternoon, he had instructed Combs to keep their conversation confidential. He knew Combs could be trusted to remain quiet—he had trusted him with more in the past. By the time they met, he calculated the word would be out that he was to be terminated. If it wasn't out by then, it wasn't going to happen. Maybe Fitzsimmons didn't have the guts for it. But that was unlikely—Carlson was dead. On the other hand, it was possible that Fitzsimmons was unable to act without orders. That would give Crosby more time, and time was something else he needed.

Still, Combs was going to have to be told something. Crosby needed his help. Combs might recognize the face of the man in the picture or be able to locate him in the Company's elaborate files. He needed answers. Crosby rose from his seat, tennis bag in hand, and walked to the cash register. It was time to begin. First, he would need a car, and there were no rental agencies in this area of the city.

CHAPTER 17

The mood in the Oval Office was somber. As the morning progressed, those who had appointments with the president found him increasingly distant, preoccupied. His words were clipped, his questions short and straightforward. He did not seek extended conversation or welcome it. Earlier that morning, Askins's chief political advisor, Malcom Hamilton, had informed him that another influential senator had aligned himself with the forces opposed to placing nuclear weapons in the Sinai. Campaigning in California, Senator Kortland, in response to statements issued by the White House, had clarified his stance on the nuclear issue. Much to Askins's irritation, Kortland had told reporters he was not against nuclear weapons or their strategic positioning. What he was against, "was President Askins's asinine proposal to place weapons in the Middle East." The statement had made Askins furious.

Kortland was only fifty-two years old. However, he was not a newcomer to the national scene. He had been in the Senate for over twenty years, achieving office shortly after attaining the minimum age of thirty. Since his election, he had consistently placed himself in the forefront of national issues. Kortland had not always been on the popular side of every issue; he had always taken a strong stand on issues to which he was committed. After twenty years of placing himself in the national spotlight, Kortland was now the Democratic frontrunner. And, with his full support being thrown behind the congressional movement to prevent the placement of strategic nuclear missiles in the Middle East, approval would become more difficult, and probably cause further delay.

Askins would not tolerate delay—time was running out. It

was this mood Peter Fitzsimmons encountered when he briefed the president on the Carlson investigation. He was waiting for the opportunity to speak. It finally came.

"Mr. President, I have had word from Allen Crosby."

Askins stopped what he was doing and looked up. For two days he had been preoccupied with Crosby's investigation. Askins did not appreciate being unable to contact the people who were working for him. He demanded regular updates. He insisted on being in control.

"Has he uncovered anything? When can I see him?" The president responded quickly.

"I can't answer that," he said simply.

"What is that supposed to mean? You're the person he works for . . . what did he say?"

Possibly, I should have withheld the information altogether, just as I told Crosby I was going to do, Fitzsimmons thought. Political considerations should always remain paramount; that was a fact he must never forget. This was certainly not the proper time to bother the president with the Crosby issue. Yes . . . it *was* becoming an issue. An issue he had to resolve —alone.

"He didn't really say anything . . . he just called to let us know he was back in Washington. He sounded paranoid . . . as if someone was after him . . . trying to kill him."

"Is there?"

"Not that I know of. After my phone conversation with him, I sent two FBI agents to pick him up. They weren't able to get to his house for a couple of hours, and when they arrived, his front door was wide open. No one was home."

"Something may have happened to him."

"I don't think so," Fitzsimmons replied confidently.

Just a few hours before the meeting between the president and Fitzsimmons, a telephone on an antique desk rang. As before, there was only the single ring—and the one word answer.

"Deathblow."

137

"Our man was gone when we arrived. Evidently, he is aware we are after him," a gruff voice responded.

"Do we know his present whereabouts?" Deathblow asked, his voice remaining calm.

"No," came the simple reply.

Deathblow did not wish to lose track of Allen Crosby. Even if he could not eliminate him, he could at least neutralize most of his actions *if* he could control his movements. Neutralization, if not death, was the objective.

"Find him. Kill him. Now."

Deathblow hung up the receiver and sat back in his chair. For several moments he was lost in thought. Crosby had to be isolated, but there was another issue that required attention. And time was running out. He picked up the phone again. The call was answered on the first ring. Deathblow gave the instructions—for the second assassination to be carried out without delay. A team of experts was to be assembled within the hour. The death had to appear to be from natural causes. There could be no further investigations.

The cab pulled up to the front door of the Marriot, the brick canopy blocking out the sunlight, allowing Shannon's eyes to focus on the approaching doorman. Shannon was out of the cab and on the drive before the doorman was able to reach her. The driver was also getting out, concerned about his fare. As she walked toward the front door, past the waiting doorman, the cabbie said something. She was unable to distinguish the exact words. Turning, she said, "Pay him, please. And put it on my bill, along with a tip for yourself."

The doorman stared at her less than elegant attire and bare feet. For a moment he did not move, but her matter-of-fact tone signaled that she was accustomed to being catered to, and the opportunity to set his own tip put him in motion. He paid the driver without comment.

Shannon continued through the lobby to the front desk, satisfied with her behavior thus far. She was no longer self-conscious, in spite of her appearance. Behind the reservations desk stood a young male clerk. From the look of awe on his face, it was evident he recognized her. They always looked that way, she thought.

"You're Shannon Anderson . . . aren't you?" The clerk stammered. "At first I wasn't sure." He looked embarrassed.

Flashing her most winning smile, she replied, "I'm flattered that you recognized me. I didn't think anyone could . . . not looking like *this*."

"What happened?" The clerk inquired, hoping to discover something about the private life of a celebrity.

"You really wouldn't want to know." She smiled again. "I believe I need a room."

Shannon explained that she wanted the bill sent to her office. The clerk readily agreed, knowing that her network had an account with the hotel. Registration complete, Shannon headed for her room, thankful she had encountered no real problems.

It was mid afternoon—time to get going. Most of the day had been spent sleeping. At first, she hadn't thought she would be able to sleep, but having stayed awake most of the night and the lingering effects of the alcohol had produced a tiredness that would not be denied. She felt better now, almost relaxed.

Earlier that morning, after only a short nap, she had placed a call to Jerry Combs, the man Clark Welch had suggested—her contact with the government. She had told Combs only enough to pique his interest, saving the rest for when they got together. She believed that more could be accomplished through personal contact. And, in this particular instance, the story she had to tell was so unbelievable it had to be told face to face. She could be dismissed too easily as a crackpot. Besides, everyone said she was at her best in person, and she was too much of a realist to care that it was her beauty that got her the initial attention. It was important to get people to listen, and after the initial meeting her intelligence took over.

Jerry Combs had agreed to meet with her that evening in Washington, which had been fine with her; she wanted to get out of New York. After completing the call, feeling ravenous, she called room service. A short time later, a large breakfast was delivered. She loved breakfast in her room; coffee shops were always too noisy and crowded.

After she had eaten, Shannon decided she'd better attend to her wardrobe. There was only one thing to do—buy new clothes, and the idea buoyed her spirits. But that was short-lived. A sense of guilt washed over her. A dear friend had been killed, and she was thinking about clothes. Guilt or not, she could not go to a meeting in Washington dressed as she was. Slowly she opened the door to the hallway, looking in both directions before going out, and closed the door firmly behind her. She realized she was too jumpy; she knew she would have to remain in control.

The hotel dress shop was in the lobby, across from the registration desk, situated among several speciality shops whose main patrons were the more well-to-do customers of the hotel. Many of the shops had to be subsidized by the hotel. Within a half hour she had purchased everything she needed, including a small, brown, leather case. Then she simply charged everything to her room.

Leaving the boutique, a smile of satisfaction on her face, Shannon realized she would need cash. How was she going to pay for the shuttle to Washington? Suddenly, an idea struck her. Earlier that morning, when she checked in, the clerk had informed her that several out-of-town network employees stayed at the hotel. That probably meant they had a sizable account, and sizable accounts deserved special treatment. The manager would surely want to do everything possible for a star employee. She would discuss her problem with the manager, without, of course telling him of the circumstances that had led to her predicament.

Although the clerk behind the desk was not the same one who had helped her when she arrived, she was again recognized. She asked for the manager and was told he would be right with her. This time, however, she did not get away from the desk without signing some autographs. She tried not to let her nervousness show; she was attracting far more attention than she desired. It had been a mistake coming to the desk at that time of day; there was too much traffic. She should have asked the manager to come to her room. Finally, he came—a portly man, with an ingratiating smile. He rushed to greet her.

"Well! Well! What have we here? Miss Anderson, I believe," he said expansively. "Our humble little home is honored by the presence of one so famous . . . and, so beautiful!"

Shannon returned his smile, thanking him for his compliments. Within seconds, he directed her to his office, away from the still gathering crowd. As she walked toward the safety of the office, her arm in his, her nervousness began to subside. Ten minutes later, Shannon was out of the office with one thousand dollars in her suitcase, and her plane reservation for the shuttle confirmed. Both the cash and the plane ticket would be added to the bill and sent to her office. All that was left was to pick up the ticket at the airport. It was all too simple.

On her way to the elevator, she noticed a stack of morning newspapers lying on a table. She picked up a copy and seated herself on a loveseat opposite the table. Quickly, she leafed through the pages, scanning all the headlines, large and small. It would be a major news story. There would be questions, more people looking for her—the authorities. Maybe the police were looking for her right now. The thought frightened her. Maybe she should call her office, check in. Surely, they had been informed by now. There would be questions about Clark's death, about her. But she was not sure it would be the right thing to do. Shannon put the idea aside and continued looking through the newspaper. Nothing. Perhaps the police and media had been notified too late for the story to make the early edition. She would return to her room and catch the television news.

That had been several hours ago, and since returning to the room she had left the television on. Although she had gone back to sleep, she had only catnapped, bringing herself fully awake whenever a newscast or news bulletin came on. Still, nothing. Her first thought was that someone at the network might be sitting on the story until she could be contacted, but she quickly discarded the idea. The other networks would not cooperate. They would be stumbling over each other in their rush to release the story.

141

Something was not right. Shannon concluded that her decision not to call her office had been a mistake. It was time she took some action, sitting back and waiting was not her style. She slid across the queen-size bed for the phone and called her office. Her secretary answered on the fourth ring.

"Shannon! I thought something had happened to you," Bettie responded in her usual cheery voice.

Astonished, Shannon could not reply immediately. Bettie had been very close to Clark Welch. How could she sound so unconcerned? When she was finally able to speak, Shannon's tone was guarded. She didn't wish to reveal anything that wasn't already common knowledge. "I'm not going to be able to . . . to come in today . . . I don't feel well."

"That's okay, Shannon," came Bettie's still cheerful reply. "Clark isn't here either."

"I guess that makes me lucky," Shannon answered, hoping her tone did not betray her.

"It sure does . . . you know how he doesn't like us to miss work. His brother called and said there had been some type of accident in the family. Clark was called to the West Coast. He apparently asked his brother to call for him."

Shannon was unable to speak. Clark Welch did not have a brother. He had told her all about his family at one of their weekly staff get togethers. But Bettie had no way of knowing. It made no difference. *She* knew . . . she thought she knew . . . she had not seen . . . he had been killed in her apartment. Could he have gotten away? The facts as she thought she knew them were beginning to fall apart.

Shannon heard herself telling Bettie that it would be a couple of days before she returned to work. Bettie mentioned that since Shannon's next show had already been taped and that nothing else was pressing, a couple of days off would do her good. If anything did come up it could wait until she returned; Bettie would cover.

Mechanically, Anderson hung up the phone, her body numb. She sat staring at the television screen, not really seeing it. She stared for a long time, wondering. Someone had called in for Clark, and that someone was not the person he said he was.

142

Clark was not on his way to the West Coast. He was dead. There had been too many shots. He had been killed when he opened the door. He never had a chance to escape.

So, a coverup was already in progress. She had to go back to her apartment; that would be the only way to find out for sure. But there wasn't sufficient time. If she didn't hurry, she would be late for the shuttle and her meeting with Jerry Combs. She had to go to Washington. When she returned, in the morning, her apartment would be the first place she would go.

Slowly, she raised herself from the bed. As quickly as she could make her numbed body respond, she prepared for her upcoming journey.

By the time the taxi dropped Shannon off at the airport, her mood had undergone a complete turnaround. The negativism had been overcome by the realization that she had bested those who were out to get her. She walked swiftly to the ticket counter, taking no notice of the people she passed. Her thoughts were focused on her upcoming meeting in Washington, her opportunity to enlist help. She took no notice of the two dark-skinned, casually dressed men, standing nearby.

As she left the ticket counter, she overheard them discussing the delays caused by the increasing air traffic and the American habit of overbooking. As she headed for her gate, one of the men fell in behind her at a distance. The other proceeded to a bank of pay phones.

The plane was already in the process of boarding when Shannon reached the gate, and without looking back she started down the long tunnel to the waiting plane. The man behind her turned and retraced his steps to where his companion waited.

The short flight barely gave Shannon time to read the magazine she had brought from the hotel. Not wishing to spend any more time than absolutely necessary in the airport, she was among the first to deplane. She secured her luggage and arranged for a rental car. Within twenty minutes she was leaving the terminal.

143

Outside, in the rental parking area, Shannon located her car, placed her one suitcase in the backseat, and climbed behind the wheel. The engine roared; she felt the power. It was a good feeling; she had always enjoyed driving—fast. She backed the black Datsun 300 ZX carefully out of its slot, and headed for her meeting. She planned to get there early, being only slightly familiar with the area of the city in which the meeting was being held. It was an out of the way location, and she had been there only once.

She was not sure why she had chosen it; it meant nothing to her. She was surprised she had even remembered it. At first, she had asked Jerry Combs to meet her at the Lincoln Memorial, but later decided that was not a good location. In fact, it seemed ridiculous. The Lincoln Memorial was where they always met in the old spy films. Her second choice was much better.

She'd had a date with a young congressman a couple of years ago, and it was he who had introduced her to the secluded spot. He took her to what he had described as a beautiful oasis within a slum. And it was. When they had reached the vicinity of the bridge, Shannon had begun to wonder if the congressman was playing a joke on her. The area was not one of the city's most fashionable, and might even be dangerous. But she soon saw that a special parks project, providing employment for minorities, had indeed produced an oasis. Trees and shrubs had been planted, gravel laid along one bank of a small river, creating a sort of lovers' lane that attracted young couples from all over Washington.

Shannon felt comfortable going there, now. It was not an unlikely place for a rendezvous. She would be safe. She failed to notice a car, carrying two occupants, pull into the lane behind her as she left the airport.

CHAPTER 18

Crosby parked the rental car several blocks from the designated meeting place, a precaution that had become second nature. He was aware that most rental cars could be recognized as such, and he wanted to avoid doing anything that would alert any potential adversary to his presence. Walking would provide a better opportunity to survey the meeting place. It would also enable him to plan a route of escape, which was often easier on foot than by car, especially under the cover of darkness.

Stepping out of the car, he removed the Smith & Wesson from his shoulder holster, checked the safety, and replaced the weapon with a practiced smoothness. The warm metal felt good in his hand—it always felt good. He didn't expect trouble, but he wanted to be ready if it came. He covered the distance in less than five minutes, the brisk walk winding him. A few days ago, on the mountainside in Colorado, he had learned he shouldn't run; he did not want to be out of breath when he arrived. Maybe I worry too much, he thought.

Slowly, he began working his way down the long bank of the river, the dense trees creating a blackness that not even the street lamps along the nearby bridge could penetrate. He appreciated the darkness. It would provide added cover while he listened to what Anderson told Jerry Combs. He continued, to a place about thirty yards from the base of the bridge. From all indications, he was the first to arrive, so he sat back against the base of a tree and waited.

His wait was not long. He heard the person approaching long before he was able to see anything. Instinct told him it was

Combs. The man was taking little precaution to be quiet, obviously expecting no one except possibly Crosby.

Their meeting place was a so-called lovers' rendezvous, and from what Combs had said over the phone, he was fairly familiar with the location. It was the proper place for a meeting of this nature. There was little chance they would be interrupted. The people who went there kept pretty much to themselves. Combs had also advised Crosby that he was not taking Anderson's story as the strict truth. She was a newsperson, with a reputation for digging out stories, and this might be an attempt to do so. Crosby did not agree.

In spite of his feeling that Combs was the man approaching, he withdrew his pistol and held it pointed at the ground, safety released. The figure of a man came into view, barely discernible in the sparse light. Crosby was now certain it was Jerry Combs. Although he engaged the safety and put his weapon back into the holster, a shiver ran the length of his spine. He could not help wondering if an alert had been put out. Had the termination order been given? Had Jerry Combs been given the go ahead on him?

When the man was within a few feet of where he stood, Crosby spoke. "Good to see you, Jerry." The words were soft, spoken not to carry in the stillness.

Combs's reply came in the same quiet tone. "It's been a long time, Allen. Too long."

Neither man moved to shake hands. They were truly friends; handshakes were for acquaintances. But, more than that, they were professionals, and professionals limited their movements when exposed in the open, keeping their hands free.

"Yes, it has," Crosby agreed.

"How's the White House been treating you?"

"Pretty good. I've been conducting this investigation I spoke of . . . it's sort of like old times."

"Ya, I was thinking the same thing driving out here . . . Us working as a team—meeting this Anderson woman. It *is* like old times."

There was a moment of silence. Crosby did not know what

146

Combs knew about him. If the order had been given, would Combs carry it out?

"Do you have something for me?" Crosby finally asked.

Combs reached inside his coat, withdrawing several folded sheets of paper. "Here's the report we discussed," he said, handing the sheets to Crosby. "All it amounts to is the written version of what I told you over the phone."

"I appreciate your help," Crosby replied.

"You're on to something pretty big here, Allen. I don't know where it's going to lead you, but be careful—don't get burned. Since I haven't heard anything about it, I can only assume the investigation is top secret. The president is probably involved . . . would be my guess."

Crosby nodded—his movement barely discernible in the darkness. He was willing to allow his old friend that much.

Combs continued, "I'm sure you would tell me more if you could. I just want you to know I'm willing to help you any way I can."

Crosby was grateful for that. He knew he could count on Combs's help, and his discretion. And now he was becoming more confident that Fitzsimmons had not issued the order for his termination. For the time being, he had to rid his mind of the thought.

"Were you able to uncover anything else that might be of help?" Crosby inquired.

"No, I'm afraid that's it. I wish I had more for you."

Again, silence.

"I sure hope Anderson shows on time," Combs went on. "I've got some other things to do this evening, and I don't think this is going to amount to much. The more I thought about it, the more I believe it's just some trick to get a story."

"I'm not so sure about that. What I am working on might be directly related . . . she may have some pretty valuable information."

"You really think so." It was not a question. "About the death of Carlson!" Again, it was not a question.

Crosby remained silent. Both men stood without speaking for several minutes. Because they had worked together in the

147

past, they understood when it was time to talk and when it was time to wait. They remained standing there, knowing that silence was important to their safety, and the safety of the woman they were about to meet.

As they stood there, cars filled with high school and college-age girls and boys drove up, one by one, down the short road to park along the river bank. Several years ago, the city had dumped gravel into the soft mud, creating a quasi-beach. People came to swim and picnic; lovers came to park.

An hour passed.

Seven cars were parked, at varying intervals, along the river bank. Crosby had carefully scrutinized each one as it entered the little park. None contained a lone passenger, and he doubted Anderson would bring anyone with her. Crosby raised his arm to check the time; she was ten minutes late. Maybe Combs was right. She could be just another hysterical woman who thought she knew something, but really didn't, and when it came down to the final moment she had backed off. Or maybe she *was* after a story, and something else of more importance had come up. She was a newsperson—a good one, but the more he considered it, the more he rejected the idea that she was just a hysterical woman. Her reputation as a detached, analytical person belied such a conclusion. It was obvious, however, that Combs did not share his view.

Crosby became aware of Combs's restlessness. Every few moments he shifted his weight impatiently.

Still, neither man spoke. They remained unseen and unheard by the young lovers. Again, Crosby checked the time. Thirty minutes late. He knew from previous experience that Combs would wait only thirty minutes more. When people were late for appointments, they usually had problems, he reasoned, and he did not like for others' problems to become his.

Just then the lights of a car appeared on the bridge above. Twenty seconds later the lights turned onto the little gravel road, headed for the beach. Like those before it, the car would have to pass within a few feet of them, their presence concealed by the trunk of a huge tree. They waited. The lights continued down the narrow road, creeping closer, seeming to take much longer than any of the others that had preceded it.

Once it passed, both men stepped forward for a better view of the interior. There was only one silhouette, but in the darkness it was impossible to determine if the driver was a man or woman. Immediately, Crosby noted that the automobile was a rental. It was doubtful that it was being driven by someone just passing through. The car was new; it stuck out like a sore thumb. None of the other cars parked along the river bank were less than five years old. Their woman had finally arrived.

But neither man moved as the car worked its way to the end of the line of parked vehicles. It stopped in the exact spot where Anderson had told Combs she would park. Crosby and Combs began moving silently toward the car. When they were still some distance away, Combs whispered to Crosby to remain where he was, out of sight. He would meet her and bring her back beyond the rear of the car. Conduct the interview. Crosby would remain behind a tree, just close enough to overhear what was being said.

As Combs walked forward, Crosby took his position. In the light from the opening car door, Crosby was able to see the occupant clearly. It was, indeed, Shannon Anderson. Her auburn hair and smooth skin shone in the light. Her slender, graceful form emerged from the driver's seat elegantly clad in a creamy silk blouse with mandarin collar, soft, grey, wool slacks, and high heels, which further accentuated her long, shapely legs. She looked as if she were dressed for a television appearance. She was the most beautiful woman he had ever seen, and he had seen them all over the world.

Swiftly he erased the thoughts from his mind. He had to focus on the job at hand. Crosby watched as Combs made contact. The introductions were brief, and he could not hear their words because they were too far away. Then they moved back toward him, stopping within five feet of where he stood. He listened. Her story was incredible. What she had been through—how had she stood up.

It took Shannon a while to tell her story, and even as she did so, he kept alert to his surroundings. He noticed only two

149

vehicles cross the bridge. Neither slowed; neither stopped. He felt certain that no one had followed any of them. He began to relax. Her story was coming to an end, and Combs was talking about her safety.

Then it happened—the one thing a field agent feared most. Crosby *felt* more than saw the man approaching from up river. Swiftly, he reached inside his coat, but before he could draw his pistol, there was an explosion. Then a dull thud, followed by a low moan. Directly in front of him, Combs fell backwards to the ground.

Crosby spun to his right, at the same instant, aiming his weapon in the direction of the fire flash. There was a second explosion, followed by a scream. Crosby had found his target. The man had failed to take a fundamental precaution when firing a weapon at night; he had not moved after firing. From the scream Crosby knew he was not dead. But there was no way to tell how badly the man was wounded. A second shot would be useless. Simply by falling, the man had removed himself from the line of fire.

Turning his attention to Shannon, he saw she had not moved, apparently immobilized by fright. He had to act swiftly. He sprang toward her, bringing her to the ground with a flying tackle. As they fell, a third shot split the still night air, only this time the shot came from the direction of the bridge. Combs was already dead—one down, two to go.

Crosby's mind raced. Had the killers followed her from the airport? Or had they intercepted her call to Combs, and simply driven to the meeting place and waited. Suddenly, he had a frightening revelation. Were these men after him? Had he been the cause of Combs's murder? Was he responsible for endangering the life of an innocent civilian? His heart pounded—from fear. And just as suddenly, it subsided. He had regained control of himself.

Silently he steered Shannon toward her car, gambling that the side near the river would provide the greatest cover since it was between two vehicles. He heard the sound of car doors opening, as the young lovers emerged, shouting to one another and wandering aimlessly about. The whole area was a confu-

150

sion of bodies and voices. Why hadn't the killers used silencers, normally a standard practice? he wondered. They must want to create as much confusion as possible, he answered himself —to use it to *their* advantage. And men who were not concerned about concealing their actions would not hesitate to shoot an innocent bystander, if they thought it necessary. Their only concern was achieving their objective.

It was time for action. Quickly, he duck-walked to the front of the car, keeping his head down. Shannon remained huddled against the rear tire. Easing around the front fender into a half-kneeling posture, he pressed himself against the bumper. Even in the darkness, he could make out a figure on the ground about twenty-five feet away. There was no movement. He crawled toward the man, weapon ready. When he reached him, he realized that his bullet had done the job. The man lay in a deep pool of blood. There was no doubt; he was dead. He had almost forgotten the effect of the weapon. Crawling, Crosby made his way back to the protection of Shannon's car. She had not moved.

"Shannon," he whispered, "did you see the second man?"

For a moment she just stared at him. When she finally did speak, her voice was strong, steady—not at all what he had expected. "No. I don't think there has been any movement except from the people in the cars." She paused. "You don't think they are involved?"

"No."

"Where have you been?"

"I went to check on . . . he's dead."

Shannon looked up at him. Another dead man . . . two dead men. Everyone she asked to help her got killed! But this time there was a difference. Finally, she was on the side doing the shooting instead of the running. As she looked up at him, she suddenly felt a sense of security.

"We're going to have to flush the second one out," he was saying.

"How are we going to do that?"

"I'm not sure, yet. He's out there somewhere . . . among those people . . . or just behind them, waiting for us to make a move."

151

Shannon said nothing. Crosby moved his mouth close to her ear. "What I want you to do. . . ."

CHAPTER 19

The long, sharp scream had drawn the couples from their cars. After milling about, they grouped together in a semi-circle, talking excitedly among themselves. In the darkness, no one had noticed Combs's body until Shannon's screams brought them to it.

"Over here! Over here! Someone's hurt!"

They rushed over to where she stood, everyone talking at once. A woman screamed, "A body!"

Crosby watched silently as the crowd gathered around Shannon. She began talking rapidly. Crosby could hear the steady cadence of her voice, but not the actual words. He was confident she could keep the diversion going, and he moved to a more strategic location. He hoped the second killer's attention would be drawn to Shannon, at least for the few moments it took him to change his position.

There was no movement from anywhere except the crowd. Satisfied, he waited. In spite of the murmur of the voices, the night seemed still. He doubted the man would have run, his mission incomplete, and Crosby doubted he'd had time to mix in with the crowd. But the man *was* out there somewhere. He knew the target was either himself or Shannon; Combs had simply gotten in the way. It happened.

Crosby pressed closer to the car and listened. Finally, the sound he was waiting for came—from his left, near the river's edge; from the direction of the bridge. It was faint, but it was there, the raking of a misstep on loose gravel. He leveled his pistol across the hood of the car, his movements slow, measured. He was careful to make no sound. The man came into view, silhouetted by the light of the moon emerging from behind a

153

cloud as he crept out of the shadow of the bridge. So intent upon his goal, he took no notice of his exposed position.

Crosby was certain the man was unaware of his presence. The ruse had worked.

Half a minute passed, a minute, two; still Crosby waited. His hands and arms began to tingle. At last, the figure came to a spot close enough. Crosby took careful aim. The moment had come. His finger pressed slowly against the trigger. Suddenly he released the pressure. Should he take him alive? he wondered. Maybe he could supply some answers.

He reset the safety and reholstered his weapon. He measured the distance with his eye, took two steps and propelled himself into the air. The force of his body knocked the killer's gun from his hand. It flew into the air, landing with a splash in the river. The impact carried both men into the water. As they fell, the killer spun in midair, grabbing at Crosby's throat.

Crosby pounded at the man's stomach with both hands, but the force of his blows were weakened by the water. The man's hands remained locked on his throat. His lungs began to burn. He needed leverage; it was his only chance to break the death grip. Crosby twisted his body, kicking his feet beneath the water, finally finding solid ground. With solid footing beneath him, he brought his knee up into the man's groin. The killer cried out in pain, his grip broken. He doubled over. Crosby caught him just above the nose with a second kick, knocking him unconscious.

Exhausted, several seconds passed before Crosby was able to react. He stood waste deep in the cold water, gasping for air, his right hand massaging his swollen throat. He had to rest, but there was no time.

Wading into the river, he grabbed the man by the collar and pulled him to shore. The effort drained his last ounce of strength. He knelt on all fours, his breath coming in short gasps. Shannon broke away from the crowd and ran to him.

"Are you all right?"

"I . . . I . . . I'm not sure," he panted.

She helped him to his feet, and as she did, she glanced down

154

at the unconscious man. His face was not familiar. The crowd rushed up, shouting questions.

Leaning close to Crosby, Shannon whispered, "Who is he?"

"I don't know . . ." Crosby gasped. "Let's get him in the car and get the hell out of here."

"What about your friend?"

"I'll check, but I'm sure he's dead."

"I know he's dead . . . I checked. But what about the body?"

"We'll have to leave it," he said.

Back on his feet, Crosby summoned all his energy and lifted the man onto his shoulder. The crowd parted, sensing that at last someone knew what had happened and what to do about it. Crosby headed straight for Shannon's car.

While he dumped the man into the passenger side of the front seat, Shannon climbed in from the opposite side, sliding onto the console. Crosby got into the driver's seat and turned on the interior light. They saw the killer clearly for the first time. He was olive skinned and slight of build. The engine of the Datsun roared into life and Crosby drove off, gravel spewing from the rear tires.

Neither of them had spoken since leaving the scene of Combs's murder. Crosby had literally been driving in circles for almost ten minutes. He knew it was important to get out of the area, but he needed a plan—and none had come to him. He was unable to concentrate.

"Who are you?" Shannon asked, breaking the silence.

The sound of her voice startled him. He turned in his seat, looking straight into her eyes. "My name is Allen Crosby. I'm with the White House." He hesitated for a few seconds, not sure he should continue. Then he went on. "I was with the CIA. . ."

"What were you doing back there?"

"You mean in the park?"

Shannon nodded.

"I came as the backup . . ."

"Backup for what?"

"For Jerry Combs . . . his *protection*. In the event something unexpected happened . . . there has to be more than one person to handle the situation. Agents try to plan for the unexpected."

He knew what she was thinking. If he had done his job properly Combs would still be alive. He had failed. There was no excuse. But her next words came as a surprise.

"I'm glad you were there. You saved my life."

Expecting condemnation, it was good to hear words of gratitude, even praise. Feeling it necessary to say something, he responded, "I think I saved mine, too."

"What do you mean?"

"I overheard the story you told Combs. I was only about five feet away. You're not the only one who has had attempts on their life over the past few days."

"Shit, you're going to be a hell of a lot of help!"

"Hey, easy, lady. There's no reason to talk like that."

Shannon Anderson glared at him in the darkness. Crosby stared straight through the windshield, watching the reflective road markers disappear under the car. He wanted to tell her, no matter who she was, that he did not like that kind of talk from his women. *His* women. . . . Why had he thought that?

Fortunately, she changed the subject. "I hope you know where you are going." The softness had not returned to her voice.

"I'm not sure . . . I'm working on a plan."

The words sounded hollow, and he knew she could sense his indecision.

"Shouldn't we be getting as far from here as possible? They might come after us."

"Of course we should get out of here!" Crosby replied angrily. "Don't ask so many damn questions." Again, he felt his control slipping away.

Shannon did not reply, instead, she sat in silence, thinking. Why was this man so easily angered? She had to find out what was on his mind. She risked another question.

"Were you very close to Combs?"

In a low voice, he replied. "Pretty close . . . we worked together several times in the past."

"I'm sorry."

156

"It wasn't your fault."

Suddenly, there was movement on the passenger side. The man was reaching for the door handle. Crosby slammed on the brakes and lunged across Shannon, but he was too late . The man had shoved the car door open and jumped out. In a matter of seconds he was lost in the blackness of a nearby alley.

"Damn! There goes our answers," he said.

The same feeling of helplessness she had experienced after Welch was killed swept over her. "We've got to do something! I don't know what happened to *you* . . . who's trying to kill *you* . . . but I think those men were sent to kill *me*."

Even in the half light of the street lamps, Crosby could see the fear etched on her face. He wanted to reach out—to comfort her. Instead he straightened himself behind the wheel.

"I'm sure they were part of the group that killed Clark. They probably followed me here from New York."

"You mean you believed someone might follow you when you came here?" Crosby asked in disbelief.

"Of course I didn't *know* they would," she declared. "I wouldn't have come if I did. I got lost trying to find the park, anyway. That's why I was late." Her intensity increased. "If someone had been following me, I would have known, and I would *not* have come!"

Trying to sound calm, Crosby said slowly, "You don't always know when someone is following you. These people are professionals—they're good."

"Can't we just get out of here." She replied, not intending the words as a question. There was still anger in her voice.

"Right now!" Something clicked in his brain. "Where did you get this car?"

"I rented it at the airport."

"In your name?"

"Yes."

"We have to get rid of it, quickly. They'll be looking for this car—if you were followed. I'm going to drive back a couple of blocks where I have another car. It's near a phone booth. You can call the rental agency . . . tell them you've had car trouble and you want someone to pick it up. Tell them you have a cab waiting—that may help throw them off the trail."

Crosby pulled to within half a block of the phone booth, and jumped out. While she placed the call, he went to his own car and quickly backed it down the block to the booth.

"Any problems?" he asked, as she climbed into his car.

"No. And I told them a congressman friend of mine was waiting for me. They were very cooperative. Say, this is a rental car, too."

Not knowing what she expected, Crosby only nodded in agreement, but he could feel her eyes boring into him. Then, he realized what she was thinking. She was about to learn a lesson.

"Can't they trace us through *your* car?"

"No."

His curt response irritated her.

"Why not?" she asked, sarcastically.

"Its not rented in my name."

"How did you do that?"

He looked at her in mock surprise. "Surely, an ace reporter like you should know that CIA agents have to use other names."

"Oh." She sat back in her seat and stared out the window. She wondered if she liked this man. He seemed to lose his temper too quickly . . . and he looked too old to be running around playing spy.

Crosby was also staring out the window. Every few minutes he would glance over at her. His first impression had been correct; she certainly was the most beautiful woman he had ever seen. For a moment, he wondered how he could have such thoughts in the midst of such danger, but he looked at her again—the long, auburn hair, the hands and face like silk, the long legs. He *knew* how he could have such thoughts.

The silence hung like a curtain between them, neither knowing what to say. Shannon's thoughts turned to their destination. Crosby had not yet told her where they were going.

"You want to let me in on where we are going?"

"Richmond."

"Virginia?"

"Yes, we can go there . . . find a motel and sort things out."
He spoke with authority. "No one will be expecting us to go
there . . . we have no reason to." Crosby decided further explanation was necessary. "From what you told Combs, we can't
go to your apartment in New York, and I'm sure they've found
your room at the Marriot and are waiting for you to return. I
can't go back to my house here in Washington. So, Richmond
is the place."

She had no comment.

CHAPTER 20

For most of the drive to Richmond, neither spoke. She stared out the window, reviewing the incredible events of the past few days. The road markers flicked by under their headlights and she thought of death. Clark Welch had been killed and now two more people were dead—and it was her fault. Her shoulders slumped forward from the weight of the responsibility.

Crosby was barely aware of the road in front of him. The past week had turned into a nightmare after the initial exhilaration at accepting the assignment from the president. That feeling had been replaced by an agonizing fear; fear that he was slipping back into the anxiety-ridden pattern of his last years with the Company.

Regardless of how hard he tried, he could not remember his last two years with the CIA. The psychiatrist had told him he'd come close to adopting the personality of one of the characters he was portraying. He had become a danger to his country—not fully rational, not dependable under stress. They had had a long name for his condition, but he could never remember it. He had not wanted to remember it. Apparently the president had thought he was cured of whatever had been wrong with him—if anything really had been wrong. Why else would he have given him the assignment? And that had been good enough for him—he was satisfied if the president was satisfied.

The one hundred five miles to Richmond raced by, the needle of the speedometer never falling under eighty miles per hour. They pulled into the gravel parking lot of a roadside motel, just outside the city limits. It was neither luxurious nor run-down. Peering through the windshield, Crosby decided it was just right. The outside was clean, but not too clean. It was the kind of place where the owners would not be concerned about the identity of their guests; questions of marital status would be unthinkable.

Normally, Crosby would not have concerned himself about cleanliness, but Shannon Anderson brought out another side of him—a side that had been submerged in his many years with the Company. He wanted to do everything possible to take care of her.

He felt the hardness against his spine, the cold and pain evoking images from his past—a cold, cement floor in Vladivostok, a narrow wooden beam in the jungles of Vietnam. Nightmares. But this time it was different, something associated with violence and torture was missing. The smells. Absent, was the stench of a bucket overflowing with human excrement, the pungent odor of blood from skin punctured by bamboo sticks. The ultimate smell—of death—was not there; just the musty smell of a second-class motel room.

Slowly, avoiding any movement, Crosby opened his eyes. If danger was present, he did not wish to alert anyone that he was awake. The light from the sun rushed at him through the flimsy curtain, bringing him back to the present. The events of the past evening came stabbing back into his brain. He remembered where he was.

The pain he felt was caused by the hard motel floor. He also began to notice the intensity of the cold. Although it was spring, the temperature remained in the low 30s, and to make matters worse, his clothes were still damp. Exhausted, he had neglected to turn on the heater when they arrived. Fortunately, he'd gotten an extra blanket from the night clerk. Crosby wrapped it close about him.

There was a low cry from the bed. Shannon was having a nightmare—little wonder considering what she had been through. He also had been living a nightmare, but, he was much better equipped to handle such situations. Yet she was not just a frail woman. What a woman she was. And there she was, only a few feet from him, asleep, wearing very little. But there was more to her than her beauty. She had a quick mind, a spiritedness that evoked what he'd thought were long-lost feelings. She made him feel younger.

As had happened too often recently, Crosby's thoughts swiftly changed course. His concerns returned to his immediate problems. There was a job to be done. If indeed there were assassins from Libya in the United States, there was no time to lose. But who could he trust? Who could be counted on to come through when he needed them? Combs was dead. The thought sent a stab of guilt through his mind. Peter Fitzsimmons could not be trusted. He had to clear his mind—make a plan.

He decided he needed a good breakfast and several cups of coffee. Then he could talk to Shannon—get more facts. He threw off the blanket, and raised himself to a sitting position. He looked at Shannon's face, sharply defined against the white pillow—her smooth, tanned skin. But he had no intention of falling back into the trap of fantasizing about her.

Shaking his head, he stood up. Pain shot through his back muscles. The sight of Shannon Anderson might make him feel younger, but not young enough to spend the night sleeping on a cold, hard floor. He had to get back in shape, he admonished himself.

Rounding the bed, he headed for the bathroom, taking a last look at the beautiful face.

It was 8:27. Less than an hour had passed since he had awakened. Now, Crosby and Shannon were seated in a small diner two miles from the motel. While checking out he had asked the day clerk to recommend a place for breakfast. The man had been polite and cooperative. He had asked the standard questions about their stay, and Crosby used the opportunity to plant some misinformation. He casually informed the man, that they were on their way to Florida even mentioning their specific destination. If someone was trying to pick up their trail, maybe they would buy the story.

Across from him, Shannon sat in silence, fidgeting with her silverware. Crosby also sat in silence. He wanted to start a

162

conversation but didn't know what to say. What was it about this woman? They had not had a meaningful conversation since they had left the park.

Crosby looked at her, and she raised her head and looked directly into his eyes. He saw the fear. He knew it. He had seen it many times before. She had hidden it well; it was not in her voice, not in the way she carried herself, but it was in her eyes.

"Are you going to be all right?" he asked, simply.

"Of course, I will!" she replied, defensively. "I'm not going to be pushed around by these people."

Her reaction surprised him. He had sensed she was a strong person, but he had not realized how strong. He knew it had taken a lot to achieve her position. If she hadn't been tough when she started out, she had to be tough by the time she got there.

"I didn't mean anything by it."

"Oh, I'm sorry," she replied, more softly. "Clark Welch was a good friend . . . then, the two men last night." A sadness spread across her face.

It was evident that she cared deeply, but no tears came to her eyes. She wasn't breaking down; she was only confused. He was not sure he would have been as strong if their roles had been reversed.

She went on, a semblance of a smile parting her lips, "I know this is a terrible thing to say, but in spite of it all, the experience has been . . . well . . . exciting." She stopped, realizing he might take her wrong; he got angry so easily. "I really can't explain it."

Crosby looked deep into her eyes, hoping to find a clue to her true feelings, to the real Shannon Anderson. Her eyes were filled with concern, but they were still sparkling. She wasn't about to let anyone know what she was thinking. No one was going to get her down for long.

"The work is exciting all right. But the important thing is who walks away afterward—who survives."

"Maybe, I've gotten in over my head. I didn't ask for this . . . anyway," she replied.

"We have to find some answers, Shannon. Right now, I'm in

163

the same position you are. I'm not too sure who I can trust. And from what you said last night, you don't think you can trust anyone."

"I don't really know what's happening," she shrugged. "Everyone I get involved with gets killed." And then almost in a whisper, she mention. "I hope you don't."

"Well, we agree on one thing," Crosby replied, laughing nervously.

Shannon smiled. For a moment, the seriousness of the situation vanished.

"That's good," he said, "you still have a sense of humor."

Before they could say more, the waitress appeared with their breakfast. It took her only a second to place the plates in front of them, but that was all it took for their moment of closeness to pass.

"Shannon," Crosby began again, his tone now serious, "I don't want you to take this wrong, but from what I overheard you telling Jerry Combs, you have known about this assassination plot for several days. What I can't understand is why you didn't get in touch with someone earlier."

At first, there was no response. Looking at her, Crosby could not determine what she was thinking. She started to speak and then stopped. Finally, she whispered, "I was afraid. . . ."

"Of being killed?"

"That was part of it," She said, looking down at the table. "But that wasn't the main reason."

Crosby did not respond.

She went on. "You see . . . in my line of work, you're involved with governments . . . you hear a lot of things. Your reputation is everything." She stopped speaking. Crosby was staring at her, trying to make sense of what she was saying.

"I wasn't positive about what I heard . . . I . . . I couldn't believe that he was plotting to kill the president. It didn't make sense. He's not that kind of man."

Crosby was still staring at her. "Shannon, he's killed indiscriminately before. . . ."

"Okay," she screamed, "I was having an affair with him. Is that what you wanted to hear?"

164

Crosby was unable to speak. Shannon saw the hate building up in him.

"Don't judge me too quickly," she said, her voice like that of a little girl.

Crosby still could not respond. He could not find the words to express what he was feeling.

"I guess . . . I didn't want to believe what I had heard. But when I watched the interview on television—I saw him for the first time for what he was. Those men following me! I knew I had to tell someone, even if I was wrong."

"You should have told someone . . . someone in the government as soon as you returned. That should have been your first priority."

He wanted to say something about her and Qaddafi, but it was none of his business. They were nothing to each other. But still . . . there was a sense of betrayal. He put the thought out of his mind.

"I made a mistake. Now, I've told you, and I need your help in correcting it." Shannon looked hard at him. "What are we doing here in Richmond, instead of Washington? We should have driven to Langley last night and reported what was going on!"

"Let me clarify something. . ." With that, Crosby went on to explain his involvement, omitting his reasons for leaving the Company. He also held back the purpose of his assignment —conducting an investigation for the president.

She sat there, not saying a word, her head tilted slightly to one side. The change in subject made her feel better. Her relationship with Qaddafi was over! It should never have happened.

Crosby noticed she was looking at him with the same intense expression she used on celebrities when she was getting them to reveal all.

She spoke in soft tones. "I've been interviewing people for a long time, and I can tell when they're holding back. And you're holding back."

"What makes you say that?"

165

"If you're no longer with the CIA what were you doing backing up Jerry Combs?"

"That's simple." The lie came easily to his lips. "The White House is very interested in matters involving the president, and Combs called me. I thought it might be something we should look into."

"The president knows?"

"Not yet."

"Then who sent you?"

"I came on my own."

"Does *anyone* at the White House know you're here?"

"No."

"You're still not telling me everything," she stated flatly. "I can't believe you came to a meeting about something as potentially important as the assassination of the president and didn't tell anyone."

"I saved your life last night, give me a break, will you. I'm not totally convinced those men where there because of you, but I'm certain they would not have hesitated to kill you."

"What do you mean . . . you don't think they were there because of me?"

Immediately, Crosby realized he had said too much.

"I just don't believe you!" she exclaimed. "Last night you gave me a lecture about being followed, and now you tell me it was *you* that might have been followed. Why would they be there because of you?"

"Let's forget it, for now," he said, trying to divert her. "There's no reason to go any further into it."

Strangely, Shannon was willing to halt her questioning. He would slip again, and, then she would find out everything. The newswoman in her sensed a story—a story that might well be the biggest in her career. "What do we do next?"

Seizing the opportunity, Crosby answered quickly. "First, I think we better get you somewhere safe."

The statement came as a shock. "What do you mean, get me somewhere safe? I'm in this as much as you are."

"I don't think so! It's too dangerous."

"Listen, a good friend of mine has been killed . . . two others

166

were killed last night." She lowered her voice. "I don't think there is anywhere safe. If you don't take me with you, I'm going to call the story in to the network and make sure that it makes the lead story on the six o'clock news."

A young boy appeared at the table, carrying a canvas bag filled with newspapers. "Care for a newspaper, Mister?"

"Sure," Crosby said, glancing up at the intruder, showing little interest.

Crosby reached absently into his pocket, retrieved the proper coins, and handed them to the carrier. The boy laid the paper flat on the table in front of Crosby. He glanced down; the headline glared back at him.

SECRETARY ADAMS FOUND DEAD IN GEORGETOWN RESIDENCE

CHAPTER 21

Suddenly, he felt nauseous. Another death. Another murder? Whoever was behind it was determined that the office of the vice president would remain vacant. The president would surely be the next target. Then chaos. He had to do something—immediately. How many times he had thought that recently, and still he had done nothing?

His body felt weighted, paralyzed. Wild thoughts ran through his mind. He had always been a man of action, yet he continued to sit there, transfixed. He suddenly felt very depressed. Minutes passed, seeming like an eternity. Still, he did not move. He had no idea what to do.

Finally, he raised his head, slowly, his strength returning. He looked at Shannon—a look of horror frozen on her face. All color had drained away; her eyes were glazed. For the first time, he felt sure Shannon was in real danger, but he was unsure why. He had never doubted the truth of the story she had told Combs, but he was convinced the two killers in Washington had somehow followed him to the park. He and Combs were practically the same height and build. In the dark it would be impossible to tell the difference. They had simply mistaken Combs for him, and killed the wrong man.

Of course, there had been an attempt on Shannon's life, and one person was dead as a result of it, but he didn't see how that incident was connected to Washington. Maybe that was it. He could be overlooking something. Maybe everything was connected and he just didn't know how to fit them together.

Shannon raised her eyes from the newspaper and saw Crosby staring at her. Immediately, the glazed look receded. She did not want Crosby to think she was weak, to pity her. She returned his look with such intensity he had to avert his eyes. She knew he was deeply involved—that he knew far more than he had been letting on. She had to know what it was.

Shannon caught herself. She was letting her instincts as a reporter take over. This wasn't just another *story* she was after. Lives were at stake—including her own.

Crosby reached for the paper.

The sudden motion startled her. She had to find out what he knew as quickly as possible. A decision had to be made. Should she wait and let him read the story or should she jump in before he had time to collect his thoughts. His guard was down now. Crosby was already leaning back, snapping the paper straight. She decided not to press him.

"Tell me what it says," she said anxiously. Several seconds passed before Crosby said anything. Then he began reading parts of the article. His voice was unsteady.

Secretary Clayton Adams, only yesterday designated the vice presidential nominee, died last night in his Georgetown home of an apparent heart attack. According to sources inside the White House, the attack came suddenly . . . The secretary, who has been a widower since the death of his wife in 1981, was found early this morning when his valet came to awaken him . . . Adams had had a long history of heart trouble, having had major attacks in 1977 and 1980. . . There has been no word from the White House, nor has a statement been issued on a possible replacement for the secretary.

Crosby stopped.

"A heart attack?" Shannon asked.

Crosby was shaking his head.

"What's wrong?" Shannon asked, already knowing the answer.

He did not reply, continuing to shake his head, not seeming to have heard her. He knew that heart attacks were not always the result of natural causes. More than once he had been involved in assignments where a death had to look as if it happened naturally. It was fairly easy to simulate a heart attack; a variety of chemicals were available on the open market.

This was madness. They had assassinated another top official. But who were they? The Libyans? Fitzsimmons? He needed answers. The sense of urgency had now become almost unbearable.

Shannon was still staring at him. She could no longer hold back, "How are you involved in this?"

This time he heard her. "What makes you think *I* am involved?"

"The way you look," Shannon shot back. "It's written all over your face. You don't think the secretary died of a heart attack. You're thinking murder. I can see it."

"It's your imagination. You've been hanging around newsrooms too long."

"Don't give me that crap! I didn't get where I am without being able to see something that's right in front of me. You're scared. You know the secretary was murdered, and you know why. You might even know by whom. Is the CIA involved in this?"

"Now you're really way out on a limb," he said. "You're after another damn news story, trying to promote your pretty ass. . ."

"Thank you," Shannon interrupted. "Thank you for the compliment."

Crosby just shrugged.

"Come on, tell me what's going on. Who's involved?"

The newswoman in her had taken command of the conversation. She was interviewing him again, and he did not realize it.

It happened a lot in her profession. She took control of the interview with her searching questions, and many people, especially men, got caught up in her looks and answered, telling much more than they had intended. That was one of the qualities that made her a good interviewer, and she knew it. She kept the questions coming.

"Is the CIA involved in something domestic?"

"No," was his immediate reply.

Just as she'd hoped, he had not thought about his answer.

"The CIA isn't involved in anything domestic as far as I know. . ." He stopped. "I'm not with the CIA . . . I told you, I'm with the White House."

"Then how are you connected? Is there some kind of a cover-up? Another Watergate?"

Crosby's stared at the table, expressionless. "I really don't know."

"You still haven't told me how you are mixed up in this," she went on, sensing he was confused. She intended to help him think out loud.

"I'm involved because of the president," Crosby heard himself saying.

"The *president*," she almost shouted. "What does he have to do with this?"

"Nothing . . . really."

"Come on!"

"It's just . . . I'm in charge of an investigation for the White House. And if you do something for the White House, it is *for* the president." Crosby hoped the half-truth would satisfy her. He knew he could not tell her the whole story, but it was becoming obvious he was going to have to tell her something, if he were to get some degree of cooperation from her. He continued, "Look, why don't we just discuss this calmly, and you can stop your questioning."

"Okay, if you'll tell me," she agreed.

Over the next hour, and five cups of coffee, Crosby told her the story of his involvement. He left out very little, rationalizing that she could provide the help he needed. He was almost certain that help would not be forthcoming from the White House—not in time to avert further deaths. When he finished, Shannon, true to her nature, had more questions.

"What do you think the White House is doing about this?" she said, pointing to the newspaper on the table between them.

"I really can't answer that," he sighed. "I don't know for sure if Peter Fitzsimmons is involved. I don't know how much the president knows. If he has not been kept up to date, he's surely going to have questions. He's got to know that the deaths of two top officials cannot be a coincidence."

"You're sure?" she asked, her head tilted to one side.

"Of course, I'm sure. The vice president was murdered. That wasn't an accident."

"How do you know that?"

Crosby told her about the report he had obtained from Jerry Combs the previous evening.

"That man in Colorado *did* try to kill you, not just scare you away?"

"There's not much doubt about that," Crosby chuckled. "When you're being shot at, you know it." It occurred to him that she had asked the same question Peter Fitzsimmons had asked. Coincidence.

"I can believe that. Why don't you just call the president?"

"Its not that simple."

"Why not? *You* could get through to him."

"Well, yes, I could get through to him, but I'd have to go through Fitzsimmons."

"And he's not going to let you! Right?"

"I'm sure he won't. He'd ask me to come to his office and talk. After I spoke to him the last time, within thirty minutes there were people breaking down my door—with guns drawn."

"I see what you mean. What are you going to do?"

Again, that was the ultimate question. He'd never had a problem deciding on a course of action. He'd been able to adapt to events; that was not happening now. He had read that one of the first things to go when the mind was about to snap was the ability to organize oneself, to make decisions. Maybe that was what was happening to him. It was a frightening thought. He *had* to make a decision, quickly. Shannon could help him.

". . . is there anyone else at the White House you can call?" she was asking.

Crosby thought for a moment. Who could he call to get a message through to the president, bypassing Fitzsimmons.

"I don't know," he replied.

"What about your secretary?" Shannon persisted. "Surely, you have a secretary."

Why hadn't *he* thought of that? Why hadn't he thought of that a long time ago?

172

"I guess . . . I could call her."

"Can you trust her?"

"Yeah! I think so." His voice was filled with hope.

"Let's do it," Shannon said, rising.

"Wait a minute. Wait a minute," Crosby responded, raising his hand. "Let's not go off half-cocked. First I have to find another person in intelligence who can give me some information. I have to check out some things."

"What?" she exclaimed.

"I'll show you." Crosby pulled out a piece of paper and placed it on the table before her. It was the photograph of the man he had killed outside Aspen. "I have to identify this man."

"I don't know him," Shannon said automatically.

"No, I didn't expect you to." He laughed.

"This is the man you shot in Aspen! What happened to the rest of the picture?"

"I found it among the wreckage of the vice president's plane. Gasoline must have eaten away the rest of it. I'm hoping the CIA lab can help. Maybe they have his picture in their files. But with Combs dead I'm not sure I can get any cooperation. There may not be anyone left there to trust. But I do know one thing about this man."

"What's that?"

"I have seen him before."

"You have?"

"But I can't remember where," Crosby said, shaking his head. "I'm sure it will come to me eventually. I know I've seen him."

They sat in silence for a few moments. Then Crosby said softly, "I know I've been rough on you, Shannon, and I'm sorry." He realized he needed to arrive at some common ground with her, but at the moment he simply wanted to neutralize her—she was in control of the airwaves. Deep down he wanted to understand her. "What finally made you call the CIA? The death of Welch—your friend?"

"No." Shannon replied frowning. "I had decided before that. I guess it was always in the back of my mind . . . that I had to contact someone. When those two men started following me,

I knew something had to be done . . . immediately. When I saw those men, I guess I finally realized Qaddafi was serious."

"I admire your work, Shannon."

"You don't have to say that," she said, looking away.

"I'm not just saying it," Crosby countered. "I really do admire your work."

"Then I thank you. From what you've said up to now, and the way you've said it, I didn't think you liked me at all."

He looked straight into her eyes. "How could anyone not like you?"

She smiled. It was the first real smile he had seen since he'd met her. He smiled back.

"We need to find a phone," Crosby was saying as he eased the car onto the side road, the cafe still visible in the rearview mirror.

"Why didn't you use the phone in the restaurant?" Shannon asked.

"We need a secure phone."

"Secure?"

"One where I can talk and not be traced easily. An outside phone booth would be satisfactory. I don't want anyone around to overhear me. And if the phone call is traced back to its source, there won't be anyone around to identify us. At this point, I'd rather you and I not be linked together."

"There seems to be a lot I need to learn about this spy business," Shannon replied.

"A hell of a lot."

"Let me ask you something. These people from Libya, Qaddafi, Jadallah, why do they want to kill the president? Why do they want to cripple the government?"

"That's a complicated question, Shannon. And, I'm sure you already understand some of it. First, there is the president's nuclear strategy—a strategy, the Libyans don't like. Qaddafi wants to control the Middle East—all of it—and doesn't want any interference from the United States. If the president is able to place nuclear weapons at Qaddafi's back door, under the Tri-parte agreement between Egypt, Israel, and ourselves,

174

Libya's power will be drastically reduced. The total balance of power in the area will be affected. And, it gives Israel the outward appearance of superiority.

"Qaddafi cannot stand for his position of power to be weakened. It would mean a terrible loss of face. He's spent almost twenty years building a base from which to spread terrorism and his own form of manifest destiny. He's trying to become another Nasser. . ."

"I understand that. He believes he can unite the Arab people to a greater degree than Nasser."

The second thing that frustrates the Libyans—and I'm sure it goes back to Qaddafi—is Askins's stand on terrorism. He's come down hard, and terrorist acts have been sharply reduced in the past eight years. Qaddafi promotes much of the world's terrorism with oil money. Libya has a lot of money to throw around. Of course, it also receives a good deal of aid from Russia. . ."

"Is Russia involved in this?" Shannon asked, unable to restrain herself.

"What 'this' do you mean, Shannon?"

She hesitated for a moment. "Let's leave it at the assassination, not the attempts on my life."

"Well, I really can't answer that. It does seem plausible. The man in Aspen carried a Russian-made weapon, but they're sold all over the world. Sold and resold. It could have been purchased by anyone, anywhere. My guess is no. We don't go around assassinating Russian leaders, and they don't come over assassinating ours. We *do* play by some rules. But the smaller nations . . . they don't handle their foreign affairs in the same way as the superpowers. They have less to lose if they get caught behind a major assassination plot, but a superpower would lose more than prestige, it could be disastrous. A nation the size of Libya could recover. They're known as a rebel anyway.

"I guess a third reason Qaddafi might want to bring Askins down is because he's a strong president. He has stood up to Qaddafi; ordered the Americans out of Libya; placed a freeze on Libyan oil imports; dropped bombs on Libyan soil. Maybe that's why he finally decided it was necessary to deal with Askins in the only way he knows."

"But, with Askins leaving office in less than a year, wouldn't it all be a waste?" Shannon interrupted. "Why would he want to shoot him now? He could just ride it out."

"I don't know. I haven't been able to figure that one out. I've been going over it in my mind since I heard your story. If *I* were Qaddafi, I'd wait. But, of course, we don't think like he does."

"That's for sure," Shannon said in a half whisper, not really speaking to Crosby.

He looked closely at her. Why had she said that? Why had she said it that way? Was she thinking of her affair with him?

Half a block ahead, they spotted a phone at the side of a convenience store. Without further conversation Crosby parked at the side of the store. He quickly got out of the car and placed a call to his secretary in Washington.

Crosby heard the familiar response.

"Drenda, this is Allen. . ."

"Allen! Where are you? Peter has been asking me every hour if you've called. He wants to talk to you about something very important."

"Did he say what he wanted to talk to me about?"

"No. What's going on?"

"Drenda, I need you to do me a favor."

"Sure, Allen. What do you need?"

"I want you to get a message to the President."

"Wouldn't it be easier to call Peter and have him speak to the president for you . . . Or better yet, I can make an appointment for you. . ."

"No! I'm working on a special project for the president. It's important that Peter not be told that I called or that you are giving the president a message from me. Can you do that for me?"

"Of course, Allen."

Not wishing to stay on the phone long enough for someone to trace the call, he quickly gave her the instructions. She was to arrange for the president to receive a confidential call at precisely two that afternoon. Crosby would make the initial call to her, and she was to patch it through to the president. He made it clear that the president was to inform no one of the call, including Fitzsimmons.

The conversation completed, he hung up and ran to the car. He wanted to put as much distance between himself and the phone booth as quickly as he could.

At that moment, a man seated in a basement near the White House also broke his connection, and released the record button on a tape machine. He lifted the receiver of a second phone and dialed a North Carolina exchange.

CHAPTER 22

Assistant Deputy Director James Denton of the FBI sat in his dark brown, leather, Queen Anne chair trying to conceal his nervousness. He was positioned directly in front of Peter Fitzsimmons. Every time he was summoned to the White House, which was seldom, in spite of his long career, his palms became sweaty and he developed a slight catch in his voice. He had a habit of repeatedly clearing his throat, which he assumed irritated those around him. Denton was thankful he did not report directly to the president; he was not certain he could take the pressure. Still, Peter Fitzsimmons had the ear of President Askins. It was rumored around Washington that Fitzsimmons made many of the decisions for him. Whether true or not, Fitzsimmons was still a powerful individual, and Denton wanted to do everything in his power to cooperate.

Even though their relationship went as far back as college, he had not felt comfortable with Peter after he took the White House position. Although it worried him, and at times even made him more than a little angry, Denton had seen it happen before, and he understood—any position connected with the White House did something to the person who took it. They instantly became self-important and invariably enjoyed exercising their new power.

"Tell me what you've turned up on this Aspen situation." Fitzsimmons said.

"Peter," Denton began, unsure if the informal address was proper. As chief of staff, Fitzsimmons had made few friends. "We have reviewed every aspect of our investigation into the death of Vice President Carlson. I don't know quite how to say this, but I'm afraid we made a mistake."

"A mistake? A mistake about what?"

At first, Denton didn't reply. He knew Fitzsimmons was aware of their error. Basically, it was due to *his* inquiries that the investigation had been reopened. Of course, there had been an interagency request from Jerry Combs at the CIA to examine the plane wreckage and do a body identification check, but that had been prior to the reporting. Denton assumed that Fitzsimmons was unaware of any CIA involvement, and he was having trouble deciding if he should be the one to tell him.

"In reexamining the wreckage, we discovered that the vice president's plane had been sabatoged. . ."

"How could something of such magnitude have been overlooked?" Fitzsimmons replied angrily but without raising his voice.

"I don't know."

Fitzsimmons's face turned red. In a move that startled Denton, Fitzsimmons shot forward in his chair, slapping both hands on the desk. "That is *no* answer." His voice was strained. "You are supposed to be experts. Mistakes like this don't happen . . . unless. . ."

His words hung in the air. Denton didn't like the implication. "Unless what, sir?" Denton replied, his voice no longer friendly. He would make Fitzsimmons say exactly what he meant. He knew then that the man could no longer be called a friend.

Fitzsimmons stared hard at Denton. For several moments neither man spoke. Growing impatient, Denton broke the silence. "How extensive of an investigation would you like . . . *sir?*"

With a coldness that equaled Denton's, Fitzsimmons responded, "How extensive of an investigation will it take to find some answers? And I don't mean asinine answers like what went wrong with the damn airplane. I want to know who is involved . . . I want to know the identity of that body in Aspen. Do you understand what I mean, Assistant Deputy Director?"

Denton understood the threat. If he was not willing to cooperate, Fitzsimmons would have his job. He would also see to it that Denton would be unable to find work—for a long time.

The real question in Denton's mind was how much was he willing to help—to cooperate.

"I will personally surpervise any further investigation. All you need to do is let me know how extensive you wish it to be." Fitzsimmons's threat and accusations were forgotten. Denton's mind had raced on.

"The first thing I want to know is who was killed in Aspen, and who the killer was. . ."

"I can answer that right now. We haven't been able to match his fingerprints with any in our files."

"Find them," Fitzsimmons ordered. "The second thing I need to know is the whereabouts of Allen Crosby."

"Who's Crosby?" Denton replied immediately, before recalling the name. Now it came back to him; a burned-out CIA agent taken in by the White House and given some cushiony job. The connection hit him with a jolt. Jerry Combs just murdered. . . Crosby conducting a priority investigation . . . Combs was the man who got Crosby to the White House. Something was wrong here, and Denton intended to find out what it was. Fitzsimmons was just completing his explanation of Crosby's function, but Denton had not been listening.

"After you locate Crosby," Fitzsimmons continued, "I want you to get in touch with me—any hour of the day or night."

"You want him picked up . . . brought in?"

"No, *just* call me."

The intercom on Fitzsimmons's desk buzzed. He grabbed at the receiver and at the same time, dismissed Denton with a look and a nod.

As Denton was leaving the office he heard Fitzsimmons say, "Yes, Mr. President, I will be right there."

A powerful man, Denton thought. Too powerful. He would need to be very careful if he had to cross him.

Opening the door to the Oval Office, Fitzsimmons immediately recognized the deep, slow, self-confident voice of Senator Thomas. Thomas had not had an appointment. From the tone, he could tell there was some disagreement. What could Askins want from Thomas, he wondered. Everything had been agreed upon earlier—two days ago. Whatever the discussion, it was certainly of great importance.

"Senator, I didn't expect to be having this conversation with you, but we are both grown men. We have been through many political battles together, and I realize we haven't always been on the same side of the fence. Regardless of that, we have always acted in a manner which we believed best for our country. I am only asking you to continue on that course . . . for the good of the country."

Silently, Fitzsimmons moved to the nearest chair and sat down heavily. His plans were going awry. No one acknowledged his presence.

"Robert, we have known each other a long time, and not all of that time has been pleasant. I am sure you have thought through all the possible ramifications before making this offer. Only a few days ago, you explained your reasoning to me. I understood why it would be wisest to consider another man. And I know how hard it must be for you to make this offer at this late date. But you must understand that I am just as reluctant to accept. A few days ago the office seemed a much greater prize. . ."

"If the threat of danger worries you, I can assure you that you will be given maximum protection," Askins returned quickly. "Besides, that's another reason why you should accept. Your courage is above question."

"It's not the danger. . ." the senator began, raising his hand so he would be allowed to continue.

But Askins went on. "I think the danger involved, if you accept my proposition, is worthy of discussion. That is why I called for Peter." At that, he nodded at Fitzsimmons, acknowledging his presence for the first time. "Peter and I have a former CIA agent making some discreet inquiries regarding Carlson's death. And, Crosby—the agent—believes Carlson was murdered."

Thomas did not react. Fitzsimmons shifted uneasily in his chair.

"When I heard that Secretary Adams had died, supposedly in his sleep, I began to believe Crosby. For some as yet unknown reason, someone does not want a living vice president. The damn thing is making me a little paranoid. I'm probably the next target." Askins then turned to Fitzsimmons. "Have you asked Crosby to look into the secretary's death?"

"I haven't been able to speak with him as yet, Mr. President."

Askins turned back to the senator. "I need your help for more than just the vice presidency. I need you to help me achieve my ultimate goal of achieving a lasting peace."

With that he proceeded to tell Thomas as much as he knew.

"I can't believe anyone . . . a foreign government . . . would have the audacity to assassinate the vice president of the United States then the vice presidential designate. Who do you think is behind it? Russia? The Arabs? Sombody in Central America?"

After Thomas's outburst, several hours were spent speculating on which country or individuals might be involved. The possibilities discussed ranged from an internal group of extremist dissidents, to Bader-Meinhoff, to the Brigate Rose, or a combination of these groups.

"What about the interview that Anderson woman had with Qaddafi? Did you see it?" Thomas asked the president.

Askins nodded.

"That man called for your assassination. Right there on national television. He called you a terrorist. That interview should never have been allowed to air. Your office should have been informed in advance . . . given a chance to cancel its showing."

"We haven't been too lucky at manipulating them," Askins interjected, his contempt for the press evident.

"If these deaths *are* assassinations as you believe . . . and I'm not saying one way or another . . . it is clear that the future of the country is at stake."

What bullshit, Fitzsimmons thought to himself.

"As I understand it, only the three of us are aware of the possibility of foul play." Thomas hesitated. "Of course, your man . . . Crosby is aware."

Fitzsimmons still did not volunteer his knowledge of the new FBI investigation.

182

"I think it essential we keep access to this information limited to those who already know. If the general public were to learn of it . . . of a plot to kill the top leadership of the government . . . there would be a panic."

Both Askins and Fitzsimmons sat in silence as the senator went on.

"Equally important is our internal stability in the eyes of foreign powers. We cannot be seen as weak. The leadership of the United States cannot be seen to waiver. Nations such as Russia or China or even that God-awful Qaddafi would eat us alive. We could find ourselves ripe for a foreign takeover."

Each of the three participants agreed on the gravity of the situation and the need for secrecy. The conversation ended and, as if on cue, the senator rose to leave. As he left the Oval Office, Thomas told Askins that he would seriously consider his offer and provide an answer within the next few days. Neither man wished to make an announcement so close on the heels of the death of the secretary.

Askins agreed to the time limit. Although Askins did not voice his thoughts, he sensed that Thomas might still be somewhat reluctant to accept the nomination because of the danger.

Left alone, Askins and Fitzsimmons did not speak for several minutes, both absorbed in their assessment of the conversation. Askins was concerned with the apparent disappearance of Allen Crosby or more likely, his unwillingness to stay in touch with him. Fitzsimmons was worried about Senator Thomas. He was not happy about his joining the administration, and certainly not in a position of such stature—a position with more power than Fitzsimmons now possessed. If the senator was trying to unseat him, there was going to be a fight, a fight like the senator had never seen before.

CHAPTER 23

Crosby noticed that his hands were shaking as he punched out the unfamiliar numbers. Calling one's own office was always strange when it was done infrequently. The fact that his hands were trembling made him glad he had asked Shannon to wait in the car while he made the call. Why were his hands trembling? He had been through too much for something as simple as talking to his secretary to be so unsettling. But deep inside, Crosby knew that talking to Drenda West was not the issue. If he was unable to contact the president through Drenda, he would be cut off. Communication with command center was always essential; the president had to be told what was happening; new orders had to be issued. Askins had to be made aware of the disloyalty among his staff. How far did it go? How many others were involved?

Crosby was smart enough to know he needed help, but he wasn't about to tell Shannon. That helpless feeling of three years ago was trying to creep up on him. He shuddered, and the sensation retreated.

An unfamiliar voice answered on the fourth ring. A renewed feeling of helplessness swept over him. He asked for Drenda.

"Mrs. West is not in. May I take a message," the voice replied.

Crosby hesitated. He had not expected anyone else to answer. Drenda was expecting his call. He had told her the exact time. She should have been there, waiting. Instinctively, he looked at his watch. Maybe he had made a mistake; there was no mistake; it was two p.m. He looked at Shannon waiting for him in the car, watching him. She could be of no help. Finally, he spoke, "This is Paul West, her husband. Is she at lunch?"

"No, Mr. West. A friend called and said she would not be

returning for the afternoon. I believe she is ill. You might want to check at home. I hope it isn't anything serious."

"Thanks. . ." Crosby barely managed to reply, his voice hardly above a whisper.

He ran to the car. He had to get as far away from that phone booth as possible. They would be coming after him—and her. Someone had betrayed them. Again.

Without stopping to tell Shannon what had happened, he gunned the engine and sped off. Shannon watched as he drove, noticing that his hands were shaking badly.

"Are you okay?" she asked without thinking.

Allen looked at her, his eyes blank, his words coming in a rush. "My secretary didn't return from lunch. Someone must have overheard the call and gotten to her . . . I don't know of any other way to reach the president."

After a few moments, she said determinedly, "Let's just drive to the White House and demand to see the president. We'll tell him everything we know."

"If Fitzsimmons is involved, he won't let us get near the president. I don't think it would be too far off the mark to say that he would guard the president with his life."

Shannon shook her head.

"But if I'm wrong, and Fitzsimmons is not involved, everyone will think I am a crazy burned out ex-CIA agent. No one will believe me."

"What about me!" Shannon interrupted. "They'll believe me."

Suddenly Crosby regained control of himself. He said calmly, "It's not that easy. The White House, the CIA, none of the agencies trust the media. They'll treat you like just another reporter trying to get a story, or creating one. And that's not the least of it. Whoever is involved will have both of us killed."

"Can't we just present them with the proof we have?" Shannon replied; desperation evident in her voice.

"What proof? All we have are two dead bodies, one in Aspen and one in Washington. And we can't *prove* what happened —except that I killed someone."

"How about Welch's body? That will prove he was shot. Would that help?"

185

It just might, Crosby thought. At least it was the best idea so far.

"Allen, I don't want to sound stupid . . . but can't you call the president? Isn't there a code you can use to obtain access to people?"

"Code numbers are changed every few weeks. My information is over three years old, even if I could remember the numbers . . . which I can't. And there's no one I can call to get current information."

"I'm sorry," she smiled.

"Don't be sorry. You were trying to help." His voice sounded more reassuring than he felt. The pressure inside him was still there., but it had eased—when she'd called him Allen. "There's only one thing we can do. We're going to your apartment in New York."

"Agent Pierce, this is James Denton. How are you doing on the identification of our mystery person from Aspen?"

Standing in the corner of the totally white room, Sam Pierce held the phone, which was also white, close to his ear. Several others in the room were in various stages of examining corpses. It was noisy.

"I'm afraid I haven't had much luck on a name, but I can tell you that he was of medium build, of Italian extraction, and was quite familiar with weapons."

"What makes you say that?"

"Callouses. The inside of his index fingers are heavily calloused from contact with the trigger of a gun. Both index fingers. *That* is unusual."

"What's the holdup on matching his prints? We should have this joker's prints on file. If we don't, I would think Interpol does." Denton replied.

"That was my impression, too, but it seems that someone has removed his file."

"There's something mighty fishy about all this. I'll get back to you," Denton said, hanging up.

CHAPTER 24

In sharp contrast with its usual shroud of evil, for him darkness could, at times, provide a comfortable cloak of safety. Crosby had decided to utilize that cloak to stakeout Shannon's apartment. Standing in the darkness, a darkness made deeper by two aging brick buildings towering on either side of him, Crosby was safe from detection by passersby. Shannon stood beside him, in silence—waiting. He could feel her tension. He had felt it as soon as they left the car.

Their car was parked two blocks away, but it had not been that simple for them to reach their present position. Crosby did not wish to be detected, he did not want anyone to know where they were going or how they got there. As a precaution, he had employed a circular route, always staying a minimum of two blocks from his objective. Almost two hours had passed before he brought their journey to an end, covering the last several blocks pressed against dirty walls, sliding along dark alleyways. Their progress had been slow, but it had been important to be seen by no one. Someone along the streets could be waiting for them—anywhere.

Beside him in the cool darkness Shannon had not moved for several minutes. She was intent, trying to convince herself that the elaborate precautions had been necessary. Certain precautions, of course. But sneaking through dark, dirty alleyways seemed uncalled for. One thing was certain. This man took his spy business seriously.

From where they stood, close to a wall, the street in front of the apartment building was in full view. Anyone coming out or going in had to pass their line of sight. When Crosby saw anyone he thought suspicious, he whispered to Shannon for recognition. Thus far, she had been able to pass everyone—all potential enemies were no more than longtime residents.

As time crawled by, Shannon grew more and more restless. Crosby was aware of her impatience, nevertheless, they kept their vigil for over three hours. People continued to move in and out of the building, up and down the street. Finally, Crosby decided the street, as much of it as they could see, was telling him nothing. It was time to move further into the open. He wanted a better view of the area on the side on which they stood. He was certain there would be telltale signs of surveillance—a shoeshine boy, a wino, a man innocently reading a newspaper by the light from a street lamp, or possibly lovers on a nearby bench, even a woman near the front door.

The drones had made errors, errors that had allowed both him and Shannon to escape on more than one occasion—there would be no further slipups. Those behind the assassins would take every precaution to assure success. Viewed in that light, he and Shannon's chances of success were limited. Unless. Unless they were not expected.

The decision made, Crosby edged forward. Shannon hesitated, then followed. They continued along the alleyway until their view encompassed the entire block. To Shannon's surprise, some of her impatience subsided with the movement. She was not exactly sure what they were looking for—suspicious-looking people, she guessed—but they were moving, and the view was getting better. She was no longer staring at one wall, and some of the darkness had been dispelled by the faint glow of the street lamps. The light, regardless of its faintness, seemed to chase away some of the cold. Crosby did not share her warm feelings.

No one was near the entrance. No one was across the street. There was no movement in any direction, no pedestrian traffic, no loiterers. For a moment, his mind stopped functioning. He was more than certain the building was being watched. They were sure to know Shannon would return. She had to, eventually. All they had to do was wait. He knew he was coming to *them,* but where were they.

Although uncertain of his next move, he continued to lead

her forward, each step bringing them closer to the street, more into the light. Just before the nearby street lamp totally erased the shadow of darkness, he stopped.

"We're going to wait here for a couple more minutes, then make our way down the street . . . parallel to your building." His voice was soft—it did not carry. To Shannon, he sounded like he knew what he was doing. Maybe he was overcautious at times, but it *was* his field.

Several minutes passed before Crosby felt further progress was warranted. Finally deciding to move into the light, he took Shannon's small hand into his own and began swinging her arm back and forth. At first, Shannon was startled by the action, but quickly realized what he was up to, and swung her arm with his. They emerged from the shadows as two lovers out for a late-night stroll, having stolen a couple of moments alone in a dark alley. Gently he slid his arm around Shannon's waist as they leisurely strolled the length of the block. Both periodically laughed aloud, occasionally stopping for a tender embrace—their progress slow, but steady. All the time, Crosby's eyes never stopped scanning the streets.

The "lovers" crossed the street at the end of the block and started back down the other side. Crosby made his decision. He turned Shannon into the front entrance of her apartment building, still holding her and laughing. Once inside, he quickly glanced around for the nearest stairwell. Spying an "exit" sign, he directed Shannon to the door, and after a quick check, followed her through. A small wire mesh and glass window in the door afforded him a view of the building's entrance. With minimum risk of being seen by anyone entering the building, they stood, silently, in the small enclosure, watching.

Five minutes passed. Ten minutes.

The door did not open. Crosby could not believe his luck. They had gained entry to the building without being detected. He turned and started up the stairs.

"What are you doing?" Shannon exclaimed in a half whisper.

"Going up to your apartment." He smiled.

"I live on the *fourth* floor!"

His smile broadened. "I know."

189

After a brief hesitation, she walked past him and led the way up the stairs. Halfway to her floor, Shannon turned to face Crosby, "Why are we using the stairs instead of the elevator?" She could readily see that he was tiring after only two flights. What would he be like after four?

"The reason we're . . . not using the . . . elevator . . . ," he said, puffing "is because I don't want to . . . step onto the fourth floor . . . with nowhere to go."

She looked puzzled.

"If anyone is waiting for us, we would be trapped on the elevator. Once the door opens we've had it. There's no place to run. At least on the stairs we can maneuver. And these doors," he pointed to the one connecting the stairwell with the hall, "are not only fireproof, they're practically bulletproof."

She smiled. He *did* know what he was doing.

Once on the fourth floor landing, Crosby peered through the small window in the firedoor. He saw no one, and he had learned from Shannon that there was nowhere to hide, no turns, no alcoves. Still, he made no move.

At the far end of the hall was a second door leading to the opposite stairwell. It would be necessary to check out those stairs before it would be safe to remain in the hallway. As quietly as possible, he eased open the heavy door and moved quickly down the hall. He had instructed Shannon to remain in the stairwell and listen, in the unlikely event they were being followed from below.

Shannon watched him as he swiftly covered the short distance between the two doors. In spite of the fact that he was not in the best of shape, his movements were quick and athletic, she thought. She had felt the muscles of his back and arms when he'd held her. Allen Crosby was definitely a good looking man.

Shannon was shocked by her thoughts. Sure, they had been together steadily for the past forty-eight hours, but she really didn't know him. But she could not deny the strong attraction she felt. Before she could ponder the matter further she saw Crosby waving to her. He was standing in front of her apart-

190

ment door. Apparently he had checked the other stairwell while she had been daydreaming.

"Everything's all clear on my side. How about yours?" He asked as Shannon approached.

"Didn't hear a sound," she replied with a smile. She was beginning to feel safer than she had felt in several days. But the feeling passed quickly. When she saw the apartment door, she was immediately gripped by fear. The emotions of the night Clark Welch was killed came rushing back. A tightness in her throat made breathing difficult, her head felt light. Crosby was staring at her, waiting.

With a shudder, she turned the knob and gave a slight push, her eyes closing involuntarily. The door did not budge. She opened her eyes and turned to Crosby, unable to speak. She had to mentally prepare herself for what lay beyond the door. Now, there would be a delay.

"I don't have the keys!" Her voice was shaky. "I left too fast . . . We can't get in . . . Someone has locked the door."

Ignoring her, he stepped in front of her and tried the door. Then he reached inside his coat pocket and retrieved a small packet. It contained an assortment of lock picks. In seconds the door was open. It gave him a feeling of satisfaction to discover he had not lost his touch.

A feeling of terror swept over Shannon as the door swung back on its noiseless hinges. For several seconds she stood there transfixed, her eyes closed. A voice penetrated her fears.

"Let's get inside," Crosby was saying.

She moved slowly into the room, guided by Crosby's hand on her arm. At any moment, she expected to trip over Clark Welch's body. She could envision him lying there on the floor in a pool of dried blood, staring up at her, eyes open wide. Crosby closed and locked the door, and guided Shannon to the sofa in the middle of the room. She sat down heavily.

The room was immaculate. It looked as if it had just been cleaned; nothing was out of place. Her eyes moved to the door where she still expected to see Welch's body. Nothing. A closer look at the carpet disclosed no evidence of blood. She got up and ran to her bedroom. The bed was made. The window was

191

closed and locked. The door she had expected to find in pieces was intact.

"The police must have cleaned and repaired everything," she announced.

Crosby looked at her, not believing what he had heard. Either this woman was incredibly naive or her fear was causing her to reject the inevitable. "The police do not clean," he said grimly.

Shannon's expression told him she understood. It was now obvious to her that what she saw—or didn't see—was part of the coverup. Those involved had gone so far as to manufacture a fictious brother to explain Welch's absence. They were good. And they were thorough. He was back to square one. The only real facts he possessed was an unidentifiable picture, a possible assassination plot overheard by Shannon, and Mrs. Carlson's belief that her husband was gathering information on someone inside the government.

Shannon returned to the sofa while Crosby stood, lost in thought. But it did not take long for him to notice her. She sat with a distant look in her eyes. She had been through so much. He could assess their position later. He spied the bar.

"Care for a drink?" he asked, attempting to sound casual, upbeat.

Shannon looked up at him and nodded, almost imperceptibly.

"What's your pleasure?" Still upbeat.

She understood, and appreciated his obvious attempt to bring her out of her depression. A horrible nightmare that had happened only seventy-two hours ago had been obliterated. Wiped away like it had never happened. Had it been just that, a *nightmare? Had she dreamed it?* The more she tried to focus on reality, the more unreal everything seemed. Did Allen believe her? Of course, he did. They had been through a great deal together.

"Chivas and water," she said flatly.

"That's a strange drink for a woman."

Shannon began to cry, not uncontrollably; she would not allow herself that luxury. No one was going to see her lose control completely. Such release of feeling was for private moments, moments when her pillow was her only friend. Instead, the tears slid silently down her cheeks, leaving crooked streaks in her makeup. She made no effort to cover her face. She did not feel ashamed. What had happened was enough to make anyone cry. She was entitled to let go—a little.

Crosby stood behind the bar, a drink in each hand, not sure what he could do for her. Finally, he went to the sofa where she sat, tears flowing from her eyes, and placed the drinks on the table beside her. Then he sat down next to her and without hesitation, took her in his arms. It felt good to hold her, to feel her warmth, her helplessness—yet her strength. Selfishly, he hoped she would need him to hold her for a long time. Shannon returned the embrace, resting her head on his chest. Silent tears continued to spill from her eyes. For a long while they remained in each others' arms.

He could not tell how much time passed. Their drinks remained untouched. They were lost in themselves, their fears, their hopes. He was the first to speak.

"Try some of this."

Shannon accepted the drink, remaining close to Crosby even after the embrace was broken. A great deal had changed. The terror they had shared, their need for each other, the physical attraction had drawn them together.

"Come to bed with me," Shannon whispered.

Crosby woke first. The cool sheets felt good against his skin. It seemed an eternity since he had slept in a bed, yet, it had only been three days since he'd slept in his own bed, in his own home.

He longed to be there now, with all this behind him. Next to him Shannon stirred, a slight sigh escaped her lips. As she turned toward him, a smile spread across her face. In that instant, it all became clear. He knew what he must do next. For days he had been uncertain about everything. But now he knew what he had to do. He arose swiftly with a confidence he had not felt in days.

He was out of the shower and partially dressed before Shan-

193

non became fully awake. Her eyes opened wide when she saw he was getting ready to leave.

"Where are you going?" she asked, surprised. As she sat up, the sheet fell to her waist. She took no notice. He turned to her but said nothing. At first, she tried to ignore the alarm that was going off inside her head, the uneasiness in her stomach. She felt like screaming at him, but she knew she had to stay in control. If he was running out on her, she must, at the very least, keep her dignity.

Allen's gaze shifted from her eyes to her exposed body. The dark blue of the sheets and pillows accentuated her golden brown skin, and creamy white breasts, which rose and fell in her excitement.

Allen Crosby realized he had never cared so much for anyone. The feeling had revitalized him—filled him with a new determination. Misunderstanding his silent admiration, Shannon was experiencing the hurt of one betrayed. She had been to bed with other men, but those experiences had not been the same. True, they were experiences to be remembered . . . some, even cherished . . . but she wanted to keep this man. He was not just another adventure, and now he was walking out on her. Crosby began moving toward the bed, reaching to embrace her. She moved to receive him, her body filled with excitement, hope.

"I thought you were leaving me," she breathed, pressing hard against him.

"Never," he whispered.

Relief flooded through her.

It was early morning and the sidewalk in front of Shannon's building was deserted. A spring chill filled the air. Crosby was the first to exit. Although he had stood behind the double glass doors for a full ten minutes surveying the area and saw no one, he was still cautious. If he was wrong and someone was waiting, he wanted them to strike when he appeared, and to assume that Shannon had remained inside or was not with him. He had decided to avoid the rear of the building with its dark and narrow alleyway. He and Shannon had been able to utilize the safety of darkness the previous evening, but in the morning it would work against them. They would be the ones emerging from the lighted building, their eyes unaccustomed to the darkness; anyone waiting would have a clear advantage, and a clear shot.

When he felt sure there was no one there, he summoned Shannon and they walked rapidly toward the car. They were within half a block of the car, and the only person they had seen was a wino lying against a lamp post, asleep. The man didn't look suspicious, but Crosby's instincts were alerted. He quickened his pace; Shannon responded by grasping his arm and keeping stride. Then Crosby saw the second man. He had stepped casually from the shadows across the street. There was a weapon in his hand, as he raised his arm to fire, Crosby yanked Shannon to the ground. The bullets thudded against the stone building behind them. The man took Crosby's bullet in the upper chest, and fell backwards.

Glancing up and down the street, Crosby saw the drunk rising to his feet—quickly. Crosby pointed his weapon just as the man pulled his from under his dilapidated coat. Crosby's bullet ricocheted off the lamppost alongside the man's head.

"Damn," Crosby muttered, setting off a second round. Too late. He had scurried for an alleyway and was out of sight.

"Let's go!" Crosby yelled, rising from the sidewalk, and pulling Shannon with him, shoving her in front of him. Crosby kept looking back as they ran.

"You drive," he commanded.

Shannon slid behind the wheel and started the engine. As she put the car into gear she realized that Crosby had not gotten in. He was standing behind the open door pointing his pistol at the alleyway.

"What are you doing?" She screamed.

"Gun the engine," he ordered, in a low voice.

Shannon pressed the gas peddle to the floor and held it. The roar of the engine echoed between the buildings. The man, minus his cumbersome coat, stepped out onto the sidewalk. He looked startled. The car was still at the curb, and there was

Crosby, facing him. He was positioning himself to shoot as Crosby's bullet struck his chest.

Shannon watched in terror as the man stumbled backward clutching his chest. Blood had begun to run through his fingers when the second impact knocked him to the ground.

Crosby ducked into the car and slammed the door.

"Drive!"

CHAPTER 25

The phone rang only once. The man who answered had been sitting at his desk for two hours waiting for the call. He expected important news, good news. His plans had been laid so carefully. He had spent the last five years perfecting his idea. Everything was finally in place. Patiently, he had sat by while others made mistakes. At times it had been difficult, but timing was of utmost importance. The time was *now*.

"They have escaped. Two men are dead." The report was delivered without emotion. At the receiving end, shock, replaced in an instant by rage.

"Where are they, now?"

"We don't know."

There was silence. The assassin waited, his profession had given him patience. He had expected an outburst. He deserved the wrath of his employer, whoever he was. Several attempts to eliminate Allen Crosby and Shannon Anderson had failed, and it was his fault. In the beginning, they had been unrelated targets. He had expected little trouble from Anderson; she was *only* a woman. Crosby, on the other hand, had presented a problem. He was a professional. The caller had been instructed to send his best man to Colorado. That man's corpse was in the hands of the FBI. Shortly after the assignment had been received, Anderson and Crosby had teamed up. He was not certain how or why. That was all he knew. Possibly, Jerry Combs was responsible. But Combs was dead. That made him unavailable for questioning.

When Deathblow decided to speak, the voice was harsh, but matter-of-fact. "I want them found . . . I want them found *to-*

day. And I want to see pictures of their bodies." He paused. "Is that clear?"

"I understand."

"No more foul-ups. I don't care what it costs or what it takes. I want it done."

The caller was concerned with his reputation, nothing more; Deathblow was frustrated at not being able to close a small hole in a well-designed plan. *Deathblow* sat back in his chair. Crosby was a problem that had to be dealt with; the sooner the better. In the beginning, the Anderson woman had been unimportant to the success of his plan. Looking back, it might have been a mistake to involve her any earlier than was absolutely necessary. No matter, he mused, those working for him understood that it was in their best interests to carry out his instructions. Anderson and Crosby would not remain a problem for long.

"Son, I've been on the phone, here," Senator Thomas paused to point to the beige instrument on his massive desk, "talking to some of ma' friends. They seem to have mixed emotions 'bout me acceptin' the vice presidential nomination. Some a ma' backers think the president in tryin' to pull the wool over ma' eyes. They want me ta wait. 'Wait for what,' I asked. Well, they think I can be elected president of these here United States all on ma' own. They're afraid I might get myself associated with the wrong policies if I hook up with Askins. Now, I for one, don't think our ole president is tryin' to pull the wool over anyone's eyes. Hell, I don't think he's smart enough to pull anything over anyone's eyes, 'specially mine. What's more, I don't think those policies are all that bad. At least, he's giving that terrorist Qaddaffi a rough time. After all, we're all in the same party. That asshole hasn't done anything that a little southern fine tunin' can't fix. What da ya think, boy?" The senator relaxed in his chair, waiting for the younger man to speak.

Jason Gherhart sat across from Senator Thomas listening intently. He had been an aide to the senator for seven years, coming to him straight from law school. He knew him as well as anyone, and Thomas valued his opinions.

"I don't know if it's just coincidence or what, but everyone connected with that office has died. Maybe it's jinxed. . ."

The senator interrupted. "Jinxed . . . Why, son, I've been around a long time. I've seen a lot of people come, and a lot of people go. Some have left office after a long and successful career. Some have resigned in disgrace and run home with their tail tucked between their legs. And, yes, some have left in a pine box. You young people look at things differently from us old folks. We're talking about ole me here—heart attacks, plane accidents—it's just coincidence them dyin'. There is no such thing as a jinxed office."

Thomas looked straight at his young aide. He had no intention of telling Gherhart of his conversation with the president about the deaths of Henry Carlson and Clayton Adams. That information, and the necessity to keep it secret, might be too much of a burden for the young man. Thomas had always lived by the principle: If you don't want important information leaked don't tell anybody. He continued. "Besides. If ma' country needs me, I must serve. You can't let yourself run scared everytime there's a little danger. The next thing ya know, you'll look back and find you've run yourself right out of sight."

Bullshit, thought Gherhart. He had been around Thomas long enough to understand that the senator never did anything for anyone unless he could get something out of it. That included his country. Hell, that included his accent. Either the president had performed a snow job on Thomas like nothing Gherhart had ever seen before—something he had not thought possible—or Thomas had some important piece of information that he was withholding. It was impossible to tell. There was one thing he was sure of—Thomas was not acting out of love of country.

Regardless of the senator's reasoning, Gherhart quickly made up his mind to support his apparent decision to accept the nomination. He knew it was far more prestigious to be an aide to a vice president than to a senator. To be close to a man who just might become president was too good an opportunity to pass up. He didn't intend to be the one pointed to as being faint of heart. Look at those clowns who had hung around Carter. Almost everyone of them had landed an important job after leaving office—jobs none of them were qualified for, or would have been considered for if they had not been in the White House. The experience *did* open doors.

"You've waited a long time for this opportunity, senator," he said. "It would be regrettable if you decided not to accept. I have every confidence that you would make a fine president."

Thomas smiled warmly. "One step at a time, boy. One step at a time."

Sitting with his feet on the corner of his desk, hands clasped behind his head, office door open wide, Peter Fitzsimmons was masking his true feelings. Under his calm exterior was a man experiencing great inner turmoil. He felt he was losing control of the situation. For almost an hour he had been sitting there, staring at his phone; it did not ring. He did not hate Thomas, but he did not like the man. He was not to be trusted. The last thing he wanted was for Thomas to be nominated for the vice presidency. What had the president been thinking when he made the offer? Normally, he would have consulted with him before making such a major decision. But there had been no communication whatsoever. The president was beginning to make more decisions on his own. He had to do something to get back into the process. Thomas would just get in the way. He had known Thomas was trying to oust him, but he never thought it would happen. There had been no hint of trouble. Fitzsimmons wondered what Thomas had said to cause him to be exiled. He was going to find out.

But that was not the worst of his problems. Where was Allen Crosby? He had to be found; he was making a shambles of Fitzsimmons's credibility. Another question that continued to plague him was whether Crosby had been able to contact Askins directly. The fact that he had been with the CIA might give him that capability. He had to find Crosby before he spoke with the president.

"I'm becoming paranoid," Fitzsimmons said aloud, to the

empty room. "What do I care if Crosby talks to the president. What could he say?"

In another part of Washington, Deputy Director James Denton sat staring at the the picture on his desk. It was a full frontal view, clearly defining the man's hardened features. That was all he had to go on. The team working to identify the mystery person had discovered very little. He went over the profile again.

Approximate Age:	52 years
Weight:	178 pounds
Height:	5'11''
Hair and Eyes:	Brown
Ancestory:	Italian
Distinguishing Marks:	Absence of identifiable fingerprints (altered by acid treatment), scar left leg (possible bullet wound), scar left side (possible bullet wound)
Cause of Death:	Head wound (bullet)
Identity:	Unknown

Almost a week had passed. There were too many questions. Why had Crosby killed him? What connection did he have with the death of the vice president? Denton sat in silence pondering the situation.

It was his assumption, that the man had followed Crosby to Colorado to kill him. But Crosby had killed him instead. Crosby had left the body, then disappeared. Later, he had been in a gun battle, where Jerry Combs, an old friend of Crosby's, had been killed. Although there had been a great deal of blood, no body other than Combs's had been found. Eye witnesses said three people had left in a car, two men and a woman. One of those men presumably was Crosby. Who was the woman, and what connection did she have with Crosby or Combs?

Two days ago Secretary Clayton Adams had been found in his bed. He had reportedly died of a heart attack. Rumor had it there was more to it than that. Although Fitzsimmons was pressing him for a renewed investigation, the secretary's death was being ignored. Fitzsimmons had turned a cold shoulder to any questions Denton had raised. What did Crosby have to do with that death?

Denton felt the frustration. He was getting nowhere, but he couldn't help feeling that all the information pointed in the same direction—to Crosby and Peter Fitzsimmons. The two men were deeply involved. Fitzsimmons wasn't telling him all he knew, and he couldn't locate Crosby. Crosby might have the answers.

Two soft rings, indicating an outside call on his private line, interrupted his thoughts.

"Jim, we've got a shooting up here you might be interested in." The voice was that of Mike Palmer, a special agent in New York.

"Tell me."

"A witness said a man and a woman were assaulted by two men. . . The man killed both attackers."

"What's so unusual about some citizen protecting himself?" There was irritation in Denton's voice.

"Well, when the witness went to call the police, someone removed the bodies."

Denton sat upright in his chair.

"Furthermore, the witness recognized the woman as one of her neighbors. . ."

"Who was it?" Denton responded, anxiously.

"Shannon Anderson . . . the newswoman."

The man sat alone. Waiting. At exactly the prescribed times the four calls came—exactly one minute apart. Instructions were given. It was *not* the time for action.

CHAPTER 26

Shannon was alone in the motel room. She looked about, deciding it was the cheapest looking motel she had ever seen or been in. It was even worse than the one in Richmond. The more she thought about the room, the more it personified their troubles. Nothing in her life had prepared her for what she was now experiencing. If anyone had told her a month or even a week ago, that she would be forced to live in such surroundings, she would have laughed.

But she would not let the surroundings depress her. She turned her thoughts to Crosby. He was out ditching the rental car, explaining that it would be too dangerous to leave at the airport. Whoever was after them might locate it and trace it to them. Boarding the plane without being identified would be difficult enough. He was certain the airports were being watched.

This was the first time either of them had left the room since they'd arrived early the previous morning. They had even sent out for food—pizza. One consolation. She loved pizza. So did Allen. That counted, she thought, and immediately felt silly. She was acting like a young girl with her first boyfriend. But she knew he also cared.

Yesterday, for the first time, they had actually discussed things other than their current danger. They discovered mutual likes and dislikes; even their backgrounds were similar. Crosby had told her of his manuscript, resting on his desk in Washington. At first, he had been embarrassed. Although he held authors in high regard, he felt self-conscious saying he was working on a book. He felt there was a vast difference between those who had writtern a book and those who were only working on a book.

She had told him she was proud of him for having the fortitude to sit down and write. Giving himself to a task as time consuming as writing—especially a book-length manuscript —was something he should be proud of. He had asked her to help, and with that invitation her heart had soared. From there, the conversation had drifted into their pasts and their plans for the future—at present an uncertain future at best. Neither had wished to discuss their immediate problems.

Four sharp raps on the motel door told her that Crosby had returned. She now knew he tried to leave as little as possible to chance. She quickly unlocked the door. Just as quickly, Crosby entered the room, shutting and locking the door behind him.

"I left . . . the car . . . where no one . . . will find it," Crosby gasped.

"Why are you so out of breath?"

He held up his hand, signaling her to wait. When he'd caught his breath, he continued. "The car is safely hidden. I left it in the alley of a rundown area. Within a couple of hours, the neighborhood car thieves will have taken it apart and sold the parts."

Shannon looked around the room. What area could possibly be more rundown than this? she asked herself.

Crosby went on. "After I got rid of the car, I didn't want to take a taxi. If anyone did trace the car, the first thing they would check into would be if anyone had called for a taxi from anywhere nearby. So I walked."

"Was it far?"

"Far enough. I just don't have the old stamina."

"You still have stamina for some things," she responded quickly, her eyes sparkling.

Crosby smiled back. "It's time to go."

"Where are we going?" Shannon asked, knowing he had developed a strategy.

"To Libya," came the quick reply.

"Libya! Didn't you listen to anything I told you?"

Crosby had listened, very closely.

Still over the Gulf of Sidra, the TWA flight began slowing for the long descent into Tripoli International Airport. Sitting beside Shannon, Crosby was thinking about how easy it had been getting to the airport and boarding the plane undetected. The first phase was completed.

On the premise that their enemies had been able to place a contact inside Shannon's office, she had phoned her secretary, telling her their plans. However, Shannon had told Bettie that she and cameraman Paul Brookes were leaving for Libya in two days. Crosby had even gone to the added precaution of making flight reservations for that day. Instead, they left only two hours after Shannon had talked with her secretary. The bait had been taken.

Crosby had even considered calling Fitzsimmons and telling him the same story, but had decided against it. Let Peter work for his information. He could be dealt with after they returned. Crosby felt he would have a great deal more information and be in a position to prove his accusations by the time he returned.

To assure their reception in Libya, Crosby instructed Shannon to wire Qaddafi, informing him of their actual arrival time. The wire had not been sent, however, until they were ready to board the plane. Qaddafi would not be able to alert anyone in the United States of their departure until they were on their way.

He was not sure what they would discover in Libya, but it was the only way to communicate with Qaddafi. He also felt that Qaddafi would be less likely to do anything to them while they were in his country. Shannon's position would assure them that much. Regardless of the risk, whatever happened couldn't be much worse than being constantly hunted as they were now.

Just as on her previous trips, a private plane was awaiting Shannon's arrival. But unlike the previous visits, she refused to accept the condition that she leave her cameraman behind. As Shannon argued with the man sent to escort her, Crosby stood silently, smiling. After several minutes of heated discussion, the man relented.

During the short flight from the airport to the summer house, Crosby remained silent. He refused the offer of food and drink by the flight steward, and spoke to Shannon on only one occasion. "Nice plane," he had said, shortly after boarding.

They had gone over his plan several times, and Crosby was convinced Shannon would be able to carry out her part.

Neither Shannon nor Crosby spoke during the limousine ride from the small landing strip to Qaddafi's residence. No one came to greet them, a fact which Crosby thought odd—unless Qaddafi knew they were on to him. As they rode, Crosby took note of the security—it was awesome. His plan would have to work perfectly, and they would still need a great deal of luck.

The limousine came to a stop in front of the well-lighted residence. It, too, was awesome. It was a veritable palace. And security forces were everywhere.

Crosby watched as Shannon exited opposite him, then he stepped out of the limousine, he made note of the guards— all heavily armed. Each carried a light machine pistol. He knew the weapon. They had been manufactured in Yugoslavia—a strange source for someone as dependent on Russia as Qaddafi was reported to be. Maybe it was nothing, but Crosby made a mental note. In addition to the pistol, each soldier carried ammunition belts and hand grenades. They looked formidable, but had these men been tested under fire? he wondered. He knew they had been trained either in Russia, at their commando camp outside Murmansk or in Libya, where the Russians operated a similar camp near Zillah. Their knowledge of the martial arts could not be questioned. But, it was face-to-face combat that mattered.

As Shannon stood and watched, Crusby was ordered to stand beside the limousine, hands stretched across the top. It was obvious he did not understand the words spoken by the gruff-voiced guard, but the accompanying gestures left little doubt as to their meaning. The search was quick, lasting less than a minute. Afterwards, the same soldier gestured for him to proceed up the steps. Without a word, Shannon fell in beside him. Evidently, they trusted her or had been given orders that she was not to be subjected to the indignity of a search.

Once inside, Crosby took in the details of the vast entry—still more troops, and the metal detector that Shannon had described. He caught his breath. Shannon had told him the detector was supersensitive. In spite of the air conditioning, sweat formed on his brow as he passed through the small tunnel. From all sides, the guards watched them.

Crosby passed through quietly. Immediately, the tension in the room seemed to dissolve. He strode to one side of the room and leaned against the wall farthest from the detector. Their moment of truth was about to come. Within the next few seconds, he would know how good the security was. Shannon was next.

Just as he had suspected, Shannon's attractiveness and the troops' familiarity with her lowered their level of alertness. And she helped by turning her fabulous smile on one of the soldiers, one she obviously recognized. Crosby noticed that he was a colonel, most likely the man in charge of the palace troops.

At that instant a piercing sound echoed through the room, repeating, sirenlike. The soldiers raised their weapons in unison. But Shannon never stopped smiling or staring directly into the colonel's eyes. His eyes stayed riveted on her as she continued through the small tunnel to within two feet of him.

The alarm continued to sound. Slowly, Shannon reached inside her coat, pulled out a gold cross pen, and handed it to the startled colonel. At that, they all broke into relieved laughter.

Crosby awoke early. He had slept well, but he was wide awake the moment he opened his eyes. Ten minutes later, he stood looking out the large bay window of his bedroom, a cup of hot coffee in his hand, from the pot he had found on his bedside table. The sun was just easing over the horizon, illuminating a vast garden containing a large variety of vegetation. Shannon had described it to him as an oasis in the middle of the desert. She had been right. He guessed the house sat in

the center of almost a square mile of cultivated land, surrounded by a ten-foot high stone wall.

A sharp rap at the bedroom door drew his attention back to
the large room. Securing the belt of his robe, Crosby walked
quickly to the door. It was too early to expect Shannon.

"Who is it?" There was no reply. Then he realized that the
door was so thick, he could not be heard. The whole room had
probably been soundproofed, and it was just as likely that it
was bugged. If that were true, he had to assume there would
be hidden cameras.

He opened the door slowly.

"Let me in."

It *was* Shannon. Out of habit, he opened the door only wide
enough for her to pass through.

"What are you doing up so early?"

"I just had to talk to you. I couldn't wait any longer. . ."

Crosby placed his finger against his lips, and motioned her
to follow. He went directly to the bathroom and turned the
faucets on full force.

"That should be sufficient to cover our voices if we speak
softly. . ."

"What's going on?"

"Listen carefully. Our rooms may be bugged, and there may
be cameras. We only have a short time before someone comes
to find out what we are doing."

The idea of someone watching her as she undressed infuri-
ated her. "Tell me what we do next. I want to get that bastard,
Qaddafi."

"First, we need to set up the interview. Tell Qaddafi that I'm
here to get some special shots. Tell him the network insists
that the photographs will be essential to the program. Make
him think the story will make him a hero."

Shannon nodded. Leaning close, she whispered, "I have the
gun with me."

Crosby smiled. She had carried it off brilliantly—getting his
pistol through security. No one had suspected the pen to be a
ruse.

208

"Bring it to the interview. They might search me, but I doubt they will search you."

Crosby wondered if he looked as ridiculous as he felt. For fifteen minutes he had been dancing around like a drunken ballerina photographing Qaddafi from every conceivable angle. To make him look like a professional, periodically he adjusted the angle of the lights. He aimed their bright glare directly on Qaddafi's face, and then took them off him completely. To that point everything had gone as planned. Just as he had surmised, he was searched before being allowed into the room, Shannon was not.

Qaddafi had been seated when they entered. He had greeted Shannon warmly, but barely glanced at Crosby. The only others present were two guards, armed with the same weapons as those outside. Someone had had the foresight to station them at opposite sides of the room.

The room itself presented problems. One entire side was glass. The guards who periodically goose-stepped past could see everything that was going on. The only consolation, Crosby thought, was that the glass was probably bulletproof.

While Crosby took the pictures, Shannon conducted the interview. He was surprised at the ease with which she was able to talk with him—how she was able to control the hatred she had expressed earlier. And Qaddafi never took his eyes off her.

Qaddafi suddenly rose from his chair. The two guards came to immediate attention, the crack of the heels of their boots Nazi-like.

"This session is over," he announced in clear English. Turning to his guards, he said something Crosby was unable to understand.

Turning slowly in the direction of the nearest guard, Crosby waited as he approached. One more step. Then, with the movement of a punter. Another. He caught the unsuspecting guard directly under the chin with the side of his foot. The force of the kick sent the guard sprawling back against the wall, where he crumbled unconscious to the floor.

The second guard hesitated before raising his weapon. A

second kick landed directly under his nose, driving the cartilage into his brain. He was dead before he hit the floor.

Crosby turned to Qaddafi, who stood before him almost casually, his arm hanging loosely at his side, a small-caliber pistol in his hand. Crosby didn't understand. Why hadn't Qaddafi shot him. And then he looked at the still-seated Shannon. His Smith & Wesson was pointed directly at Qaddafi's chest. The expression on her face left little doubt that she was ready to use it. Crosby had never seen such hatred in a woman's eyes.

"Do *not* shoot," Crosby said evenly, keeping his eyes on Qaddafi. "Stay calm. Mr. President, I would like you to drop the pistol on the carpet and be seated." Qaddafi obeyed in silence. "Shannon, hand me the gun. Everything is under control."

Shannon Anderson looked up at him. He was not sure she even saw him. The look in her eyes was still there. Then, her body shook for an instant, and she handed him the gun. Crosby walked to one door, threw both deadbolts into place, and proceeded to do the same with the second. Satisfied they were secure for the moment, he took the guards' weapons and ammunition, placed them next to a chair, and sat down.

CHAPTER 27

"Now, Mr. President, its time we get some answers," Crosby said calmly, his gun pointed at Qaddafi's chest. He couldn't help admire the man. He showed no fear. Even when it seemed that Shannon would shoot him, he had not flinched. Strangely, Crosby found himself understanding what Shannon had seen in him. There was a certain strong-man mystique about him that women might find attractive.

Crosby looked at Shannon. She sat quietly, watching his every move.

"Start talking," he said, turning his attention back to Qaddafi.

Expressionless, Qaddafi responded. "What would you like me to say?"

"How about telling us why you have been trying to kill us!" Shannon suddenly said, almost shouting. Although it was there only for a moment, Crosby caught the change in Qaddafi's expression—the eyes.

"Don't just stare at me! I want to know how you could do such a thing. What did I do to you?"

"Not so loud Shannon," Crosby said, gesturing toward the door.

Shannon slumped in her chair. She had not intended to lose her temper, but he had tried to have her killed.

Still without expression, Qaddafi replied. "Why would I want you dead, Shannon? And your cameraman . . . or whoever he is? Why would I want to harm him? I don't even know his name."

"Let me put it to you this way," Crosby replied. "We know you gave the orders."

"What proof do you have, Mr. . . . ?"

"Crosby."

"Mr. Crosby, I ask again. What makes you believe I wish either of you dead?"

"Simple. Shannon and I stand in your way of assassinating the leadership of the United States. . ." Crosby stopped. Two soldiers were marching by the glass wall. He held his breath, waiting for them to look into the room. After several agonizing seconds, the soldiers passed by without even turning their heads. Crosby turned back to Qaddafi.

"Let me put it to you as directly as I know how. If you don't talk, you're dead."

"Mr. Crosby, I really don't know what you are talking about. If Shannon, whom I know to be in possession of her senses, wasn't with you, I would think you were insane—a crazed terrorist. You come into my country—into my very home—asking ridiculous questions. Point a gun at me. Injure, possibly even kill my security guards. And *I* am supposed to have the answers. This is not America where people run loose with guns killing one another. You have committed a great crime and you. . ."

"That's enough," Crosby shouted. He felt the room closing in around him—uncertainty crept down his spine. He shuddered. No. He was not about to listen to a lecture as long as he had control of the situation. They might not leave Libya alive, but they didn't have to sit through a propaganda lecture while they still had some control of the situation.

Qaddafi stopped. Suddenly, Crosby heard a sound near the door. He spun around, leveling his gun at the door. Seconds ticked by; nothing happened. No further sound. Had it been his imagination? He looked at Shannon; she was staring, but not at the door. Her eyes were riveted on Qaddafi—eyes filled with loathing. He turned back to Qaddafi.

"Mr. Qaddafi, it seems ridiculous to me that you insist on denying your involvement in the attempted assassination of United States government officials, or of Shannon and myself. The last time Shannon was here, she overheard you and one of your aides discussing the plot. Shannon speaks fluent

212

French; she understood every word. And she had her tape recorder with her."

Qaddafi's eyes widened, a small smile appearing on his lips.

The French airliner was still one hundred miles from Boston when Shannon raised her head from Crosby's shoulder. She had been sleeping for a couple of hours, the strain of the last days finally catching up with her. A long rest would do her a world of good, he thought, only there wasn't time. It was a miracle they had been able to get out of Libya alive. In retrospect, it probably had not been wise for them to go, but they had gotten useful information. Although they still could not be sure who was behind the events surrounding them, they were relatively certain who was not.

He could still hear Qaddafi's words: "Although I respect your ability to penetrate my elaborate security, I am not very impressed with your analytical abilities. It appears you do not understand the total impact of an assassination on the world community. The two of you perceive my desire to control greater territory as a complete negative. That is not correct. The fact that I am a rebel does not mean I can or would carry out any act. It is true that someone—someone of great importance—is out to assassinate the top leadership of the United States. I have been privy to this information for several months. In fact, I have periodically attempted to sell the information for the benefit of my country, but I have been unable to do so. Your assumption that I am behind such a plot is absurd. I must admit that you are not the only persons to harbor this view. However tempting such a task might be, I cannot bring it to fruition.

"The international community is unstable. Many nations, including your own, sponsor terrorist organizations. Each of these organizations has been responsible for the murder of innocent people. *Innocent* people. They are victims who carry no real significance. They are the things of which international headlines are made. Not wars. And with the exception of the Israelis—Massad, Hagannah—these deaths are soon forgotten by all concerned. Not so presidents and kings. Contrary to what

213

is written by the United States news media, assassinations are seldom the result of a conspiracy. It is not the business of one nation to order the killing of the leaders of another. Look at the furor that resulted when it was discovered that your nation was involved in assassination attempts in Central and South America, the Mideast. Similarly, enormous problems were created for the Soviets when they were suspected of overzealous support of the assassination of foreign diplomats—even the attempted assassination of the Pope.

"Regardless of our sovereignty, we cannot always do exactly as we wish. The death of your president—even of those around him—would be of no benefit to my country. It would be disastrous for our image in the international community. Even those nations with whom we have close relations would turn away. I cannot afford such a loss. It would be detrimental to my goal of Pan-Arabism.

"As it now stands, some world leaders view me as too much of a loner. They say my country is too prone to use violence to achieve its goals. I believe we are no more violent than any other nation—the U.S., the USSR. If I were behind an attempt to assassinate the leaders of the United States, I would become an outcast. A leper. Even the Russians, who are never too trusting, would withdraw their support."

Both Shannon and Crosby had remained silent during Qaddafi's speech. Neither could believe what they were hearing. He had opened up to an extent Crosby had not believed possible. But what they heard next surprised them even more.

"It would be unwise for me to become involved in the internal affairs of your country. Where does that bring the three of us?" His question was rhetorical.

"Since you have come to me seeking information—help—and I have supplied you with that information, it is time that you help me."

Shannon and Crosby looked at each other. Crosby had let his gun fall to his side.

Qaddafi continued. "By helping me, you can also help yourselves. I will allow both of you to leave my country unharmed

214

if you promise to continue your search for whomever is involved in this plot. They must be stopped."

The call came at exactly the preset time. After one ring the receiver was lifted from its cradle.

"Deathblow." There was anger in the voice.

"They have not been found. There has been no sign of them since the shooting."

Deathblow exploded. "What the hell is going on? I want something done, and I want it done, now. Now. Now. Now. Do you understand?"

"Yes, I. . ."

"Shut up. I am talking. I want them killed. Killed! And if your people can't do the job, I will take care of it myself!"

Looking out the airplane window, Crosby could see the buildings below come into view under the clouds. It occurred to him that Qaddafi had some of the same qualities as Askins. Like Askins, he was trying to do the things he saw as best for his country. The difference was that Qaddafi's power—his view of the world—was based on violence. But Qaddafi had insisted that someone within the U.S. government was behind the assassination plot.

Crosby was depressed—the same kind of depression he had experienced just before leaving the Company. He couldn't let himself slip into that state, there was too much to be done. He began to review the information he knew to be accurate. The first two attempts on Shannon's life, the one in her apartment and the one under the bridge, had been ordered by parties unknown. Qaddafi had had no reason to have her harmed. She had not overheard him discussing the assassination of President Askins or any other American official. Qaddafi had been plotting the assassination of the Ayatollah Khomeini of Iran. He believed that despite an initial reaction of outrage by some countries, secretly, they would be glad the Ayatollah was dead. A new government would be formed, one willing to deal rationally with the outside world. Qaddafi compared it with the Israeli bombing of the nuclear facilities in Iraq. At first, many

215

nations had condemned Israel for its actions, but that was quickly forgotten. No one wanted Iraq to have a nuclear capability.

That information had not helped; Crosby was still no closer to learning who was trying to kill them. It was clear that Shannon had been involved before he had entered the picture. Now she was more deeply involved, and there was no easy way out.

Qaddafi had told him to look inside his own government to find out who was behind the assassinations. Peter Fitzsimmons? he thought. He certainly had the power. He also had the know-how. Fitzsimmons had been in the government at a very high level for a long time. He knew how to manipulate; he had the intelligence; he had the ambition. He had everything he needed—all except one thing. Fitzsimmons was not a leader. He could get things done, but he didn't have it in him to be the top man. Back to square one. Again.

What else did he have? The damaged picture. Was he grasping at straws? But why was the vice president carrying the photo in a locked case?

Then the idea hit him. Had he seen the man before or was his mind playing tricks on him. The killer had come into his life twice that day. Rather than the man—was it the picture he had seen before?

"Are we almost there?" Shannon's voice interrupted his thoughts.

"We're preparing to land," Crosby said softly.

CHAPTER 28

Only a few hours before Shannon Anderson and Allen Crosby landed in Boston, President Askins was making an announcement.

"Placing all personal considerations aside, my good friend, Senator Andrew K. Thomas has agreed to accept the nomination of vice president. Some of you are probably remembering that old cliché 'politics make strange bedfellows.' Well, I want to assure you that any small disagreements we may have had in the past have long since come to an end."

There was a smattering of applause from the crowd, composed mainly of close personal friends and reporters.

Askins continued. "I would be remiss if I failed to address the recent deaths of Vice President Carlson and Secretary Adams. Senator Thomas and I have discussed these unfortunate deaths, and neither of us feel there is need for alarm. Throughout this nation's long history, many men have died while holding public office. We shall move forward with an eye to the future."

As Askins stepped back from the microphones, Peter Fitzsimmons thought how energetic the president sounded. It was almost as if he were campaigning. The old smile was there, the old bounce. After a slow start, his voice had assumed his trademark cadence that, although not impressive to reporters, had a dramatic effect on voters. Fitzsimmons had stood by silently while one of the men he least admired was formally handed the second most prestigious job in the western world. The more he thought about it, the more he wondered why President Askins appeared to be so elated. The two of them had spent several years trying to unseat Thomas. Now, this was a complete turnabout. Maybe the president was getting old, losing his touch. Or maybe he just wanted to unload some of the responsibilities. It had been a rough year. Fitzsimmons shook his head in disbelief as Senator Thomas, smiling broadly, approached the microphones.

"Ma' friends," Thomas began in his most pronounced southern drawl.

The same old bullshit, thought Fitzsimmons.

"I wish to assure you that what the president has just said is deeply shared by me and ma' supporters. I believe ma' confirmation in the Senate will be swift. Ma' colleagues understand the importance of filling such an important vacancy with all deliberate speed."

The cliché was not lost on those among the press who had covered the senator's long career. He had been twenty years behind everyone else in supporting the "deliberate speed" doctrine laid down in *Brown v. Board of Education*. Thomas went on for several minutes, pledging his support to the policies of the present administration, and vowing to do whatever was necessary to help maintain peace throughout the world and prosperity at home. Within hours the photograph of vice presidential nominee Andrew K. Thomas and President Askins, smiling broadly at one another and shaking hands, was on the front page of every major newspaper. In the background, just to the left of the president, stood a grim-faced Peter Fitzsimmons.

The need to get Shannon away from danger was still dominant in Crosby's mind as they made their way through the busy airport. He knew he cared about her much more than he had ever thought himself capable. He was equally certain that she shared those feelings. He knew it was more than the circumstances that had evoked those feelings. People thrown together in life and death situations often experience strong bonding, but the feelings do not always last. When the danger has passed, they often drift apart, never really understanding why they had become involved.

"Where are we going from here?" Shannon asked.

Once again Crosby did not have an answer. A feeling of great weariness fell over him.

"Allen!"

"Were you saying something?"

"Are you all right?"

"Sure." he replied.

They continued walking. A jumble of thoughts raced through his mind. He was back in the thick of things—the pace, the pressure. The Company doctors had said there was a time bomb ticking inside him. What was that supposed to mean? They wanted him to retire—accept a quieter form of employment. He had done that, and he had begun to work on a book. He intended to expose the Company—and the government that supported it—the killing. But the book was unfinished. Shannon had promised to help. Maybe he *would* continue. With her contacts, he might get the book past the CIA censors. They were not tolerant of unauthorized publications. Maybe it could be written as fiction, and after publication, he could reveal it as the truth.

He shook his head without realizing he was doing it. What was he thinking? Why was he thinking about these things? He should be making a plan. The president had given him an assignment. It was essential that he complete it, no matter where it took him. When he was finished, he would retire. For good. Then he would write.

Shannon watched as Crosby automatically walked to a news-stand and purchased a paper. His reaction was immediate. After glancing at it, he looked around him, then rushed to her side.

"Did you see someone?" she inquired, fear creeping into her voice.

"No."

"Allen?"

He was practically pulling her toward the exit.

"I'll tell you in the car." His tone was softer. "We have to hurry."

For the first time in her life Shannon Anderson felt like a

criminal. Running away from trouble went against her grain. She felt dirty.

Outside in the rental car, he turned to her and showed her the newspaper "Look at this."

"Yes, Allen, I see the picture. Senator Thomas and President Askins are shaking hands. And, there's Peter Fitzsimmons in the background. I don't like his looks."

Then she saw the headline—Thomas's acceptance of the nomination. Immediately she thought—a new target for assassination. She sat silently staring at Crosby, waiting for him to explain.

Crosby jerked the rental car into gear and began the winding trip out of the airport parking area. His mind raced over past events. Piece by piece they fell into place. He knew the identity of the man behind the assassinations. The picture Carlson was carrying had been the answer after all. Carlson was on to the man, but he had been cut down before he could get the information to the right people. Mrs. Carlson had told him her husband was working on something he would not discuss. Now he knew what that "something" was. He had to tell Shannon everything he knew before he left her in a safe house.

"About fifteen years ago there were several disclosures regarding assassination attempts on Fidel Castro. Shortly after the election of 1960, John and Robert Kennedy made several attempts to have Castro assassinated. According to many reports, the CIA was heavily involved in the planning and implementation of the "projects." Their record was not good so they went outside for help. A small group within the CIA were given the assignment to get that help from business and terrorist organizations both inside and outside the United States—and members of organized crime. None of the individuals in the group were aware of the others' involvement.

In the mid-1970s one of the members of organized crime admitted his involvement in the plots. He named the former and then current members of the CIA who had been involved. More importantly, he implicated other members of organized crime. One of them was Alberto Calorio. Along with several others, Calorio was the subject of an extensive senate investigation. Before the investigation ended, Calorio was shown on national television as the criminal he really was. In spite of Calorio's obvious guilt, two groups came to his assistance. The first was the Society of Italian Americans. They supplied Calorio with money for his legal fees and conducted extensive lobbying on his behalf. Although they gave no money or, at least, weren't suspected of doing so, the second group was of significantly more importance. . ."

Suddenly the rear window of the rental car exploded, sending shards of glass in all directions. Crosby braked, glancing in the rearview mirror. He saw the car behind them—a nondescript, late model beige sedan, no chrome, no trimmings. Crosby could see a yellow-orange flash from the passenger side of the car behind them. It came in a steady stream. Once again he had been careless. So absorbed in giving Shannon the information, he had forgotten to check for a tail. He hit the gas pedal and they shot forward.

"Get down, Shannon," he screamed, pulling the wheel hard to the right. They were on a two-lane blacktop in a wooded area not far outside Washington—the ideal spot to make their move, Crosby thought.

Crosby swung the car back and forth across the lanes, as the bullets continued to strike against the car. Crosby hunched down; Shannon flattened herself on the seat beside him.

Seeing a break in the trees ahead, he pulled the car wheel to his left—hoping it was a side road. It *was*—or used to be. He swerved hard to the right and headed for it, his lights illuminating the tall grass that covered what might have been a logging trail. The tires screeched and the car rocked as it hit the deep ruts. The steering wheel pulled from side to side trying to shake loose from his hands. But he hung on. At first, the tall grass seemed to swallow the car, reducing his visibility to almost nothing. As fast as he could drive and still maintain control, he guided the car down the road. He switched off the lights, hoping the moon would not disappear behind the clouds.

The silent chase continued. He knew he was keeping well ahead of his pursuers since he caught fewer and fewer glimpses of their headlamps. Five minutes passed—the assassins continued to fall farther behind. Rounding a sharp bend, he stopped, opened the windows, and turned off the ignition.

"Shannon, climb out the window and get into the woods. I don't want the overhead light to go on and give away that we've stopped."

"Wouldn't we be safer in the car?"

"No, inside the car we're targets."

Once in the woods they waited. For a few minutes, they heard nothing. Then, almost simultaneously they heard the hum of an engine and saw the glare of headlights against the trees. The approach was slow. The assassins were taking no chances.

"You stay here," he whispered as he started back to the road.

Shannon grabbed his arm, her voice barely audible. "I'm going with you."

"You'll be safer here," he replied, patting her shoulder and disappearing into the darkness.

"Will *you?*" she asked silently of the night.

In a few moments he was back at the car. He walked behind it a few paces and turned left into the woods. With pistol in hand, he knelt beside a tree and waited. The wait was not long.

The car crept through the tall grass, its lights casting eerie shadows on the foliage. Crosby's muscles began to tense. There was a soft click as he eased his weapon off safety. The hum of the approaching engine grew louder, and within seconds, the lights came into full view.

Coming around the bend, there wasn't sufficient time for the driver to react. The sedan plowed into the rear of the car. Crosby was at the passenger door in an instant. He fired twice. The man's head snapped back. He fired again at the man in the rear seat as he grabbed for the door handle. The bullet caught him in the chest. There was no need for a second shot. Crosby noticed the machine pistol on the back seat. Not that professional, he thought. But the driver had gotten away into the brush. Crosby had left him for last, knowing he could not be holding a weapon as he drove over the rough road. Disgusted with his failure to get all three, Crosby slid back into the tall grass.

The sedan's engine sputtered and then stopped, the car's

overhead light illuminating the grotesque figures sprawled on the blood-stained seats.

Only a few feet from the car, Crosby knelt in the protective grass, listening. He knew there was no immediate danger, but now his enemy had the same protection. And he had Shannon to protect. Would she think the battle was over and come for him? Would she assume he was injured when he did not return immediately? He had to get to her, make sure she stayed under cover. Then he could go after the man.

Crosby backed farther into the tall grass staying low to the ground, his weapon at the ready. He knew, regardless of his caution, the movement of the grass could give away his position. However, his opponent had the same problems. Neither of them could see more than a few feet in any direction.

The duck-walk to the tree line took no more than five seconds. Standing up on his toes, he could see over the grass. He was about twenty feet from where he believed Shannon should be. Crouching low again he made his way toward her.

She was not there. Nausea swept over him. His mind raced wildly, visions of her lying dead in the grass tore at his insides. He had to control himself. There had been no shots. But the killer was a professional. He would not require a weapon. No. There had not been time. The killer would have had to come around both cars and make his way over to this side of the road. Not likely.

Shannon *had* to be nearby, he tried to convince himself. Relief was slow in coming. He decided to go directly back onto the road. That's what she would have done—headed back to the car.

Shannon had not been willing to wait. When she'd heard the sound of the cars colliding followed by the shots, she had been almost paralyzed with fear and concern. She thought—she hoped—the shots were from Allen's gun. The assassins had been firing some type of machine gun. He must have taken them by surprise; she hadn't heard their guns. But she had to make sure he was all right. She started back through the grass.

223

Crosby was near the front of his car when he heard the two short bursts from a machine pistol. The flash had come from the direction of the sedan. He spun to his left and spotted the man standing in the grass at the edge of the road. Crosby watched the assassin pivot, seemingly in slow motion, turning the weapon on him. They fired simultaneously. Crosby felt a stabbing pain in his left shoulder. He knew he had gotten his man but he fired again and again. Then, half-crazed, he leaped to the top of the sedan, his weapon falling from his hand.

There, in the eerie light was her fallen body. The blasts from the machine pistol had caught her along the waist. In an instant—from her eyes—he knew that she was dead. His scream shredded the stillness of the woods.

CHAPTER 29

It seemed a long, long time since he had been home—exactly the way it had felt in the old days with the Company. His mind was tired; his body was tired. The last few days had been like the old days, and nothing he could remember about the old days had been good. "Burnout," the fancy doctors called it. . . When an agent begins to slip over the edge into a fantasy world. Burn-up was more accurate.

Bending over to remove his second Smith & Wesson from the gun cabinet, he winced at the pain in his shoulder. He had gotten rid of the blood-stained shirt. There was nothing left to give him away.

Shannon . . . the thought of her—caring for him, being with him—warmed him for a moment. The man he sought had used Shannon to achieve his goals. It had almost worked. Crosby had almost been fooled. He *had* been misled for days. He, too, had been used. But, as in all previous assignments, the hunter had made a mistake. Deathblow had made a mistake. He had become impatient. He had come out into the open.

The vote for the president's proposed Middle East strategy was scheduled for that day. Anyone who wanted to place nuclear weapons in the volatile Middle East was crazy. Maybe it was time for the meek to inherit the earth. Maybe the world *was* ready for a nuclear freeze, like the one proposed by Senator Kortland.

Crosby was sure there would be guards. Deathblow would know he was coming. Only yesterday, he had thought there was a possibility of a real life, a life away from the guns, away from the intrigue, away from the loneliness that had eaten at him for as long as he could remember.

Shannon's death had been unnecessary. Deathblow had accomplished all he could by using her. Killing her had been cold-blooded murder. It was beyond reason. That was a good description, he thought. Beyond reason. That was exactly how he felt now—how he had felt since yesterday. He had reached "burnout" or "burn-up." He was beyond reason.

As he started up the long row of steps, he noticed the first of the guards. The man was too obvious. Deathblow should send him back to training school, wherever that was. He slowed his pace, and hunched his shoulders, taking the steps slowly. Old men do not climb steps rapidly. About halfway up, he stopped to rest. He wasn't tired, nor was his shoulder wound affecting his movements. The pumping adrenalin was blocking all pain.

No other guards were in view. They would be inside the building, he thought. When he was satisfied he had rested enough—for an old man to catch his breath—he climbed the remainder of the steps. Just inside the glass doors were three guards. They watched everyone who entered, closely.

Climbing the steps to his right was a young woman flanked by two frisky, young boys. One of the children slipped on the top step and fell, crying out in pain. As the mother knelt to comfort him, the other darted away. As the runaway came close, Crosby reached out and grabbed him, careful not to move too quickly. Talking quietly to the child, he walked him toward the still preoccupied woman.

"I see you're having a little trouble, ma'am. So I took the liberty of catching this one before he got away." Crosby held up the boy's hand, showing he was in a firm grip.

"Oh, thank you!" she exclaimed. "They are just being terrors today."

"Are you here to see someone special?" he asked, casually.

"No, we're only here to see the sights."

"Maybe I could show you around. I know this place a little bit."

"Would you do that? That would·be wonderful!"

226

Still holding the child's hand, he walked into the building, closely followed by the mother and second child. Just as he had hoped, the guards took no notice of him.

He directed his group toward Room 218, providing information to his unknowing accomplices about the city. Down the hall outside the door of the man he sought there were no guards. That was what he had expected. Their presence would have raised questions. For that same reason he believed there would be only one guard, at most, inside the office. And that person would not be in uniform.

As they approached the door, Crosby extricated himself from his group by telling them he had an appointment in one of the offices. Looking puzzled, the woman took her children and moved on. Once they had rounded the corner, Crosby straightened. At the same time he removed his disguise. He wanted Deathblow to recognize him. He wanted to see his reaction. Moving quickly, he entered the outer office. After a quick glance around him, he strode directly to the door of the main office.

"You can't go in. . ." he heard the secretary saying. By then he was inside the office. There was instant recognition. To his left, the lone security guard, reached inside his coat. Calmly, Crosby pulled his gun and fired two shots into the man's chest. The impact drove the man against the wall; he slid slowly down to the floor leaving a trail of blood as he fell.

Seated behind his desk, Deathblow did not move. Crosby turned to him, pointing his gun at Deathblow's face—the face of the man who brought about all the chaos and destruction of the past week. This was the man who had destroyed his life.

Without a word, Crosby squeezed the trigger. The bullet entered the middle of the forehead and exited at the base of Senator Thomas's brain.

227

CHAPTER 30

"I hope you can explain what has been going on. . . The newspapers are filled with speculation, and I don't like to read what's going on in *my* country in the damn newspaper," Askins exploded. It had been two days since Allen Crosby had walked into Senator Thomas's office, murdered him, and then turned the gun on himself. Peter Fitzsimmons and Assistant Deputy Director James Denton sat in his office prepared to report.

"Mr. President," Fitzsimmons began, "I brought Jim . . . here . . . along to help explain what we believe happened." Nervously he turned to Denton. "If you don't mind, I'm going to turn this over to Jim."

The president waived his hand signifying Denton to proceed.

"As you know, sir, two days ago Allen Crosby walked into Senator Thomas's office and shot him. Then he apparently killed himself. You must understand . . . since Crosby never reported to anyone, some of what I am going to tell you is purely speculation."

Denton stopped, waiting for a response from Askins.

A harsh "go on" was all he received.

"As you already know, Shannon Anderson was killed. Apparently, she had developed a close relationship with Crosby. Our investigators also discovered this partially destroyed picture on the floor of Crosby's home, not far from his gun case. We believe it was of special significance to him. . ."

"Let me see that," the president interrupted.

Denton carefully handed Askins the picture.

"This is in bad shape. Were you able to identify the men?"

"Only one of them, and the FBI lab was unable to determine where the picture was taken, although they are fairly certain a telescopic lens was used. They did conclude that the picture is no more than six months old."

"What about the other man?" Askins asked impatiently.

"Nothing. But the man we did identify is Alberto Calorio. He's the man whose body was found on the same mountainside where Vice President Carlson's plane crashed. However, the body was found several days after the crash, after the area had been secured and cleaned—after Crosby had been there. We assume that Crosby killed him."

"What does all of this have to do with Senator Thomas's murder?"

"FBI records indicate that Senator Thomas was once the subject of a secret investigation regarding his involvement with members of organized crime—especially, his link to Calorio. Senator Thomas came out in support of him during a senate investigation of Calorio's criminal activities. The investigation of Thomas was inconclusive.

On the floor, next to the picture in Crosby's house, the investigators found a newspaper with the photo of you shaking hands with Senator Thomas. Crosby must have associated the two pictures. Possibly, he was aware of the earlier investigation. We can only speculate, but it looks like Crosby decided that Senator Thomas was involved with the vice president's death, and that he had sent his old friend Calorio to prevent Crosby from discovering that fact. From that Crosby probably reasoned that it was Thomas who had Shannon Anderson killed." Denton hesitated, seeing by the president's expression that he was still puzzled.

"That still doesn't explain the other deaths," Askins said.

"Whoever sent Calorio is responsible for all the deaths. Whether it was on Thomas's orders or some other deranged person with power. It just started with Carlson."

"Are you satisfied, Mr. Denton, that Thomas was the man behind these killings?"

"I think so. Our investigators have uncovered Senator Thomas's psychiatric record. Not pretty. A lot of violence."

"I understand."

229

For the first time since Denton began his report, Fitzsimmons spoke. "I don't see what Thomas had to gain by all this."

All three sat silently for a moment. Finally, the president spoke. "I guess both Thomas and Crosby were just pawns in a much larger chess game."

Fitzsimmons and Denton looked at one another. "I don't understand," Fitzsimmons said.

"Never mind." That will be all for now.

When they were gone, Askins picked up the picture from his desk. He held it for a long time, then reached for the phone. He pressed the code number on his private line.

"This is Deathblow. Complete your assignment." He then made three more separate calls, each time repeating the same words.

On the fifth call he said, "Send a team for James Denton." Askins sat back in his chair, a broad smile on his face.

"What would anyone have to gain?" he said aloud.

EPILOGUE

STATES MOVE IN EMERGENCY REPEAL OF 22nd
AMENDMENT

In an attempt to avert a national emergency, special sessions
have been called in every state to vote for the repeal of the
22nd Amendment.

NATION ASKS PRESIDENT ASKINS TO SERVE 3rd TERM

The fifty states have voted to repeal the 22nd Amendment and
the United States Congress has passed a resolution appealing
to President Askins to accept a 3rd term. . .